too STUPID to LIVE

Anne Tenino

RIPTIDE
PUBLISHING

Riptide Publishing
PO Box 6652
Hillsborough, NJ 08844
http://www.riptidepublishing.com

Too Stupid to Live
Copyright © 2013 by Anne Tenino

Cover Art by L.C. Chase, www.lcchase.com/design.htm
Editors: Tal Valante and Rachel Haimowitz
Layout: L.C. Chase, www.lcchase.com/design.htm

ISBN: 978-1-937551-85-8

First edition
January, 2013

Also available in ebook:
ISBN: 978-1-937551-84-1

too STUPID to LIVE

Anne Tenino

RIPTIDE
PUBLISHING

This book is dedicated to Thorny (and Jazz by proxy). I truly could not have done this without you.

table of **CONTENTS**

table of **CONTENTS**

chapter 1

Ian Cully locked up his house—ex-house—one last time and contemplated throwing away the key.

Nah, quitting his job, selling his home, and moving the hell out of California was probably symbolic enough. Instead he just watched the brass glint in his hand. Then he stared at the deadbolt and the knob.

It isn't too late to go back to the department and drive a desk. That thought triggered a sudden and visceral flash of scraping his back on the asphalt and the sound of his skin sizzling.

Yeah, *fuck it*. He wanted the hell out of California. Wanted to live around family he *liked*. Put some distance between him and his dad.

"That's it?" his cousin Jurgen asked from behind him.

He should probably stop standing on his porch—former porch—staring at the locking hardware. "Uh, yeah."

"C'mon then. I want to get moving before dark." Jurgen's feet scuffed on the wood as he turned, and then Ian felt the boards give as he thudded down the steps.

He stared some more. Jurgen didn't say anything else, even though he was probably waiting by Ian's truck, back crammed full of stuff, ready to take off after the moving van that had left a half hour ago. Leaving the porch had been to give Ian space, although he knew damn well Jurgen wanted to get home to his boyfriend.

Still, Jurgen'd probably wait half the day if Ian needed the time.

Ian turned around, shoving the key in his back pocket, and headed down the stairs. Yeah, it was time to leave. Get rid of the last of the old life, because he was sure the hell ready for a new one.

When he reached his truck, Jurgen didn't move to climb inside. Instead he reached out and gripped Ian's shoulder too hard, pinching a nerve, but Ian didn't let himself flinch.

Jurgen looked him straight in the eye. "You're doing the right thing."

Ian nodded, held there by Jurgen's hand. "I am, yeah."

"Gets you the hell away from the chief."

Ian had to look away. "Yep."

If Jurgen didn't stop the personal sharing shit, Ian might have to rethink the moving near him thing.

Oh, wait. He was supposed to practice expressing his emotions now. He shoved his hands in his pockets and cleared his throat. "Yeah, uh . . . It was stupid, you know? The accident. But I guess it kind of straightened out my priorities." He stepped back from Jurgen, until his hand fell off Ian's shoulder.

Jurgen tipped his chin at Ian and turned toward the passenger door of the truck. That must have been enough bonding time for Jurgen. And thank God, it hadn't even been that hard. He could do this; all of it. No more being a firefighter, no more telling his dad he sometimes dated women, "just to make sure."

Yeah, the previous thirty-odd years hadn't worked out so well, but now he was pretty much free of that old life. Next step was to figure out what the fuck it was he actually *did* want out of the world. How hard could it be?

chapter 2

Sam took a shortcut through a park located smack between the campus bookstore and his place, walking all over leaf-strewn grass he probably shouldn't have, clutching the book he'd hidden under his plaid shirt-jacket. He just needed to get to his apartment before he saw someone he knew.

If he ran into someone he knew, they'd expect him to stop and talk, because that's the kind of guy he was: the smiley, friendly, talky kind. Then, because he didn't have his backpack—*mental note, bring backpack next time*—they'd want to know what he was clutching away so furtively, *guiltily*, under his jacket. And—in spite of aspiring to an MFA in writing—he could never seem to come up with a plausible lie in truly dire situations.

At which point he'd have to make a break for it. Dammit, he was wearing those cool lumberjack boots he'd bought the last time he'd visited Nik in Whitetail Rock, and—newsflash—they sucked for running.

They looked good with plaid shirt-jackets, though.

A shouted "Hey!" interrupted his riotous thoughts.

He knew, he just *knew*, they were shouting at him. And he had a romance novel hidden under his shirt. A romance novel with a lurid cover featuring a bare-chested, kilt-wearing man on horseback, clutching a saloon-girl-cum-fair-maiden to his brawny chest.

"Hey! Get the hell off the field!"

Crap. Sam ran, hunching to protect the book, stumbling in an ungainly sideways sort of run.

He looked back over his shoulder. A whole pack of brawny Highlanders was chasing him. Sure, they had jeans on, and only some of them were bare-chested, but they all had that meaner-than-hell-Scot look in their eyes. It wouldn't have surprised Sam in the least if their knobby-yet-manly knees had been flashing under yards of plaid.

The leader of the clan made Robert the Bruce look like a little nellie boy. He was tall, thickly muscled, and light haired, with scruff Sam could see from ten yards away while running and looking backward over his shoulder. He had one of those brows that bordered on hairy Neanderthal, but somehow looked macho and sexy. His mouth was open, screaming some kind of battle cry, and he was gaining on Sam. Reaching out to grab him.

Sam slowed, considering the merits of letting the sexy Highlander catch him. Then his self-preservation instinct kicked in. He faced forward, clutched the book tighter, and put on some speed.

That was when some projectile clocked him in the back of the head. It nearly sent him into a somersault. His legs couldn't keep up with the forward momentum of his upper body. His knees gave and he pitched forward, throwing out his hands to catch himself.

Which was, of course, when he lost his grip on the book and dropped it. Actually, it was more of a fling than a drop. Sam lay there, cheek on the cold, damp autumnal grass, front getting soaked with dew, stunned and blinking at his book a few feet in front of him. *Verdant*, his brain supplied. *Your romance novel is lying in a verdant field of grass, longing for its reader.* A weird-looking, snub-nosed white football wobbled its way into his field of vision and came to a rocking halt.

Knees dropped onto the grass next to his head, jolting him. Sam strained his eyeballs upward and saw the brawny, shirtless Highlander who'd been leading the pack panting and scowling down at him. His sexy faux-Highlander muscles were straining and his chest was rising and falling rapidly. He had a veritable forest of caramel chest hair.

He made the best living, breathing (panting) romance novel cover Sam had ever seen. Macho and manly and stern and, *oh man*. Sam sighed. Guys like this were never gay. They were always the ones chasing the homos.

At that point it occurred to him to wonder why they'd been chasing him. "What are you doing?" he gurgled. His sluggish brain suddenly started calling out the anxiety attack.

The guy panted a couple of breaths before growling, "Playing smear-the-queer. Waddaya think? We're playing rugby!" He huffed derisively, then turned away. Sam saw him reach for the football, his hand hesitating over the book.

Oh, fuck my life. Sam scrunched his eyes shut. Other feet pounded up around him, and voices asked if he was all right and *What the fuck?* Sam held his breath, waiting for the shaming to begin.

When he felt something shoved roughly under his side, his eyes popped open, and he looked into the smiling, patronizing face of the Highlander. His fingers brushed against Sam's ribcage as he pulled his hand away.

Sam smiled tentatively. The Highlander shook his head in disgust, except he was smiling, just a little. "You all right?" he asked.

"Uh. Yeah." Sam stared dumbly. Was that a chorus of angels he heard? The sounds of the other players faded away as Sam met his Highlander's mossy green eyes. He felt a *something* lock into place inside his chest. *Click.*

Twue wuv.

It appeared to be a one-sided revelation.

His Highlander gazed back at him with some emotion in his eyes. It was . . . confusion. Confusion quickly becoming something more like condescension. He lifted his hand, still on his knees in the grass beside Sam, reaching for him as if in slow motion. Sam realized with horror that the Highlander was going to give him a conciliatory pat on the head and then stand up and walk away. Didn't he feel the *click*, too? How completely unfair that Sam should know instantly that this man was his destiny, but his stupid Highlander had no clue.

Poor, naïve hero. He wouldn't know what hit him when he finally fell in love. Sam almost felt sorry for him. Almost. It was hard to feel sorry for some bastard who was about to pat your head and dismiss you, soul mate or not.

"Ian!" One of his Highlander's clan, um, teammates was suddenly standing there, shaking the Highlander's shoulder.

Ian. His name is Ian. Sam sighed.

The Highlander—Ian—dropped his hand and looked away from Sam. "Yeah?"

"C'mon, man, you gonna play or what?"

Ian looked back at Sam for a second. "Yeah. Just give me a minute." The guys on the team started to wander away while Ian reached again for Sam.

At first Sam thought he was going to get the head pat after all, but Ian held out his hand, palm up. As if he wanted Sam to take it.

Sam stared at the hand a second, then looked back up at Ian. He was an ideal romance novel hero, in Sam's humble (yet well-read) opinion. All those muscles and that curly hair on his chest. Sprinkles of gold above his nipples, thicker on his massive, blocky pectorals. Who knew blocky was so hot? *Guh.* The hair, though. Sublime. Thinner on the sides but growing in toward his center, a line of it defining his sternum, swirling around his navel, arrowing toward his groin. *Happy trails to you . . .*

Ian snorted out a laugh, and Sam jerked his head off the ground. Ian was laughing at him, one side of his mouth curled up.

Oops. Sam might have let the ogling get out of control.

"You need help getting up, or what? C'mon, we wanna play." In a lower voice, he added, "Put your eyes back in your head."

Oh. Sam felt his face get hot as he reached out and took Ian's hand. The way this was going, it would be his only chance to touch his Highlander. Ian pulled him up so fast, he went from prone to standing with no stops in between.

"Jeez, you're strong." *And you, Sam, are a conversational reject.*

Ian just snorted that laugh again and looked at him. Standing, they were about the same height. That was kind of unusual. It made Sam's insides clench.

"You all right, kid?"

Kid? Oh! A pet name. "Um, yeah, think so."

"Let me see your eyes," he said, getting in Sam's face. Sam swallowed and held his breath while Ian scrutinized him carefully for something. Studying his eyes. They *were* his best feature, which wasn't saying much in his opinion. He'd never had someone pay quite this much attention to them, though. "Yeah," Ian muttered. "Same size."

"Uh . . .?"

"Your pupils. That ball hit you pretty hard. You might want to go to urgent care and get your head checked out, but you look all right to me." Ian shrugged, then added, "Not that I'm a professional."

"Oh." *Sparkling small talk, there.* "Um, my name's Sam."

Ian looked smirky, but held out a hand for him to shake. "Ian."

"Yeah, I caught that. Um, you know . . ." The blood started pounding in Sam's ears. Was he really doing this? He pretty much had to; it was the job of any successful romance protagonist. Sam wanted to be a successful romance protagonist, especially in this particular plotline. "Why don't you let me buy you a cup of coffee or something? Kind of a thank you."

Saying thank you with coffee. All the best heroes did it.

Ian eyed Sam, suddenly cautious. "What makes you think I'd be into a date with a guy?"

The click. "Oh, uh . . . Straight guys don't usually realize when I'm, you know, um . . . when I'm checking them out." Sam waved at Ian's naked, sculpted, hairy chest. *Yum.* "Or they get all, you know . . ." Sam bared his teeth and faux-growled instead of continuing.

You are such *a dork.*

"True that." Ian looked away from Sam, crossing his arms over his chest. Oooh, veiny forearms, and biceps like citrus fruits. Sam stared, and Ian finally said in a low voice, "Listen, kid, you're not really my type. Sorry, but . . ." He shrugged.

Sam's stomach bottomed out. He couldn't quite meet Ian's eyes. "Oh, that's not—I mean, I didn't figure I was, just . . . I really wanted to say thank you." Jesus, getting shot down was excruciating. It had never happened to him before. Probably because he'd never asked anyone out before.

It was unlikely he would in the future, either, based on this experience.

"There, you said it. You're welcome. Now go get checked out. And don't forget your book." Ian looked back down on the ground, where the impression of Sam was still fresh in the grass. His romance novel lay about where his heart had been.

Sam felt his face go redder. He bent over and snatched up the book, tucking it into his jacket. "Thanks," he mumbled, not looking at Ian. Shot down and humiliated. Twice.

Ian laughed shortly. It wasn't a mean laugh, exactly. Just a sardonic one. "You're welcome. Go on, Sam." *My name, he said my name.* "And stay off the field from now on, okay?"

Sam watched him walk off. He only meant it to be a glance, but Ian's back was mesmerizing. Yeah, he was sexy, but his skin was a mass of shiny smooth splotches mixed in with swirling scar tissue below his shoulder blades, all the way down, disappearing into his jeans. Three or four different shades of pink and tan. Parallel to his spine just above the small of his back was an incision scar. Dark brown and graphic, maybe five inches long.

Oh! My Highlander's been wounded. A scarred man, looking for the one person who can help his heart heal.

Sam caught himself before he clutched his chest from the angst of it all. He was a fool. A geeky, not-very-attractive fool. A too-tall twink of a fool who didn't get the time of day from hot muscle bears. If he were cute and small and blond (as opposed to towering, underweight, and bland), maybe Ian would want to tie him up and have his way. But Sam wasn't.

He looked down sadly at his book, then covered the heroine's face and most of her cleavage with his thumb and gazed at the Highlander beside her. He seemed so two-dimensional.

Duh.

Just you and me, buddy. You're all the Highlander I'm gonna get.

"Hey, kid!" someone shouted. "Get the hell off the field!"

Dammit.

Ian wasn't into pale, weak guys. Guys with no muscles and too-long, shaggy, wispy hair and blond eyelashes that disappeared unless they were in full sunlight. Long, coltish legs didn't do it for him, either. The fuck *were* coltish legs, anyway? Other than too damn skinny.

Ian liked muscular, barrel-chested, built-like-a-fireplug guys. With dark hair and a five o'clock shadow at 10 a.m.

Most importantly, he liked guys who were shorter than him.

Didn't he?

He shook his head at the memory of the kid making that awkward come-on. Maybe Ian had shot him down kind of hard, but you had to be cruel to be kind. And hell, he didn't have time to try to figure this out, he had too much other stuff to work on.

Tierney calling out to him brought his attention back to the present. He broke into a jog to get back into the game.

Weird how he could still feel the imprint of the kid's hand in his.

chapter 3

Sam didn't go to urgent care; he went to the cafeteria and got coffee. Then he sat down and stared off into various spaces, thinking.

Unrequited love. The bane of the romance novelist. Although it led to a hell of a lot of successful plots.

Actually, it wasn't so much the bane of the romance novelist as the bread and butter.

Not a plot one wanted to undergo in one's own life, though. It never seemed to work out quite the same way it did in books. Sam had a lifetime of experiences that told him that.

He was pretty sure he was supposed to want a guy like himself. An awkward, intellectual not-quite-twink who knew nothing about sports and everything about Proust. A guy who was skinny and washed out and maybe even soft-spoken (they couldn't be alike in every way, after all). The kind of guy who was versatile in bed and didn't have any domination or submission fantasies.

Okay, well, that part wouldn't be much like him. Sam had plenty of kink-laden fantasies.

He'd tried to love a guy like that—a guy someone like him was supposed to love—when he first came out. Bryce had been in the same dorm Sam's freshman year. He was tall and gangly (although not quite as much of either as Sam) and only mildly effeminate (making Bryce the butch one), with hair the same shade of bland as Sam's, that color somewhere between blond and wet sand. Bryce was a philosophy major to Sam's English. They'd been a matched set. Salt and pepper. Well, salt and salt, actually. Sea salt and iodized salt?

After about the third month, Sam realized he'd more or less forgotten Bryce's existence for the past week. So he went down to Bryce's room in a guilt-induced dither and knocked frantically on his door. Bryce took a while to answer, and when he finally did, the room was cloudy with pot smoke and there was a naked, stoned, African-American guy on Bryce's bed. Bryce had a sheet wrapped around his hips, and not another scrap of fabric on.

What a relief.

Later, Bryce admitted he hadn't set out to cheat on Sam. He'd just sort of forgotten he had a boyfriend. And that was before he'd smoked any of the other guy's pot.

Overall, Bryce hadn't been a bad experience, really. Not a good experience, either. Sort of just an experience. When Sam had lost his virginity to him, it was an awkward, slightly painful, but mostly boring ten minutes. Later he returned the favor.

Just the year before last, Sam had tried to love a guy who was the opposite of Bryce. Controlling and imposing. A little like Ian the Highlander, maybe—a little, teeny-tiny, infinitesimal bit.

Marley had dreads and was (gasp) shorter than Sam. He drank a couple six-packs a day, collected unemployment, and generally mooched off the world. He had the necessary domination fantasies, but he didn't particularly care if Sam got off or enjoyed himself.

Not so successful for Sam, in the end.

In the future, Sam planned on loving guys who deserved to be loved by him. Preferably just one guy at a time. One he deserved to be loved by. He stared out the window of the cafeteria. The Highlander would make a nice candidate. Not that his scarred Highlander was interested.

Sigh. Unrequited love. *Hello, old friend.*

Fortunately, before Sam could go mooning off on his personal Fabio (just an expression, because Fabio? *Shudder.* That man's hair looked like straw and his eyes were too close together), his cell rang. He looked down at it, and Nik's cheesy grin glowed up at him.

Sam didn't even think about not answering. He'd hardly seen Nik since last spring when Nik had graduated and moved to Whitetail Rock with Jurgen.

He really needed to talk to his best friend now.

"Hey," he said.

Nik dispensed with greetings when he called Sam. He said it impeded his flow. "You remember when I told you about that Miller Harpe guy from town?"

"The guy with jungle fever?"

"Oh, *that's* nice, Sam, very sensitive. He was just . . . sheltered. He's not the stupid, ignorant redneck I thought he was. Well, he is kind of ignorant, but I'm planning on fixing that. I guess he's still sort of a redneck, too, come to think of it. I'm not sure I can really do much about that, but I can help him with the gay thing."

"He's gay?"

"Keep up, Sam. Yes, he's gay. The fact that he came around while I was in high school trying to get me to pop his cherry was my first clue."

"There's no reason to be a bitch about it."

"Sorry." Nik actually sounded it, too. He really *had* changed since he'd met Jurgen.

"It's okay. You weren't, exactly. So you're calling me because of something to do with this guy, Miller?"

"How astute of you." Clearly, Nik still had a few rough edges Jurgen hadn't managed to smooth. "Yes, I have a plan."

"A plan," Sam repeated slowly.

"Yes."

"Huh."

Nik sighed into the silence. "I'm going to introduce him to suitable gay men. It'll be sort of like a gay Big Brothers program. Shepherding him through the world of queerness until he can survive on his own. Until he can find someone else to shelter him."

For a few seconds, Sam was speechless. "What, like you want to help him catch a husband?" How come Nik didn't feel the need to help *him* catch a husband?

"No! Like I want to help him get a life. A gay life, maybe a little action. You know."

Sam's feathers unruffled. *Ah*. Nik had tried doing that for him. Not such a successful plan, all things considered. "Nik, do you remember when you introduced me to Marl—"

"Anyway," Nik said loudly. Sam had to hold the phone away from his ear for a second. "I'm not getting a lot of support from my *boyfriend*. But I knew you would support me."

He heard Jurgen's voice indistinctly in the background, then Nik practically yelled in his ear, "I am *not* forming up a branch of the Gay Scouts!" Then a slamming door. Then Nik giggling softly. "The big, dumb asshole. He's so cute," he whispered. "Do you think he'd give me a badge for woodcraft?"

"Are you in the closet again?"

"*What*? I've *never* been in the closet."

Sam did his best to keep his voice calm and level. "Did you slam yourself into the hall closet in a huff and are you currently standing there talking on the phone to me? *Again*?"

There was a long pause. Nik cleared his throat. "Yes."

Sam sighed and let it speak for him. Non-verbal communication often got his point across with Nik better than a thousand-word essay would. After he'd judged it effective—he could almost hear Nik squirm—he went on to his next point. "You know, this good deed stuff seems unlike you."

"Being in love has made me a better person," Nik snapped. "Are you in or not?"

Sam screwed up one eye, thinking it over. "I don't know, what are the details of your scheme?"

"Well, my *plan* is to invite Miller to our housewarming party and introduce him to the single gay men on hand." Nik and Jurgen had recently bought a house together after Nik had landed an adjunct position at Cindercone Community College.

Sam nodded slowly. He could probably mitigate more damage by being on scene and pretending to be on board. "Fine. I'll help you. When's our first scout meeting?"

"As soon as we can figure it out. I'll come up this weekend, maybe. Jurgen can go off and have a beer-date with his cousin, and it'll just be us girls."

Sam didn't tell Nik about Ian the Highlander. Instead, he let Nik distract himself—and Sam—with a discussion of plans for the housewarming/introduce-Miller-to-suitable-men party. It was just too embarrassing, and he felt a little too raw. But as his conversation with Nik wound down, the adrenaline crash hit him.

I asked a guy out. And I got shot down in flames.

After saying goodbye to Nik, Sam was forced to put his head between his knees and breathe evenly to keep from fainting. He clasped his hands behind his neck, feeling the bumps on his spine rub against his fingers and trying not to think about how big a freak he must have seemed to Ian the Highlander.

Sam was a dorky, skinny, pale, unmuscled kid who'd tried to hit on a guy so far out of his league that Ian couldn't see Sam due to the curvature of the Earth.

Sam thought about not telling Nik at all, but in the end he bought a bottle of chardonnay and planned on confessing all when Nik came up for the weekend. It was the kind of humiliation that must be shared in person over fermented fruit.

chapter **4**

Driving to Nik and Jurgen's from the city, Ian tried to remember the last party he'd been to. It was the one his oldest brother's wife had thrown for him to welcome him back into the bosom of his family when he'd gotten out of the hospital. He'd been so hopped up on pain meds he barely remembered it, and he could have done without the loving family act in the first place.

Tonight's party would be a different thing altogether. Jurgen had invited him to stay, assuming Ian wouldn't be in any shape to drive an hour and a half home afterward.

He nearly drove off the road when it hit him that he could get laid now.

I could fuck something other than my hand.

Couldn't he?

In his ongoing effort to figure out his life since The Accident that had Changed Everything, he'd committed to not having casual sex. It'd been his idea, and so far it hadn't been that hard. The last seven months had been all about physical therapy, rehab, and "working on" his psyche. The months before that had pretty much been about pain.

But now . . . He had a new job, he was fully functional physically (he crossed himself and sent up a quick thought heavenward in thanks for that), and he *finally* didn't have any physical limitations. Not even any pain. He'd played rugby the last two weeks. He could totally fuck some willing guy. He just needed the willing guy.

Ian firmed his grip on the steering wheel. Tonight would be all about his dick, and he refused to feel bad about it. He was going non-committal, just for this one party.

When Jurgen opened the door for him, Ian stepped in and took stock of the men around him. Hell, he could even afford to be picky. It was a large party, and loud. Reminiscent of keggers from college.

Which was weird, because he hadn't thought Jurgen's boyfriend was the type, but Nik had planned the whole party.

There were a hell of a lot of men on tap. Guys in tight jeans and loose jeans. Cowboy types, cop types, and bear types, with an even mix of the hippie type and the twink type. Ian overlooked the twinks, but stared at the rest of the man buffet.

Jurgen must have read something in his face, because he greeted Ian with, "Nik got lube and condoms for party favors." Then he led the way to the guest room, while Ian grabbed some *party favors* from a convenient candy dish.

"Hey, there's a bag on the bed," he said when he set his own pack down. It was a backpack like his, but that was pretty much where the similarity ended. His was in good condition, solid black, high-denier Cordura, able to take rough travel. The one on the bed was faded dark purple with fraying seams and a broken zipper. It looked so much like a college kid's backpack that Ian half expected it to weigh fifty pounds with books. But it was light when he hefted it, and it was stuffed so full of something soft and shapeless it looked like it would explode if it wasn't handled gently. Probably clothes.

"Must be Sam's," Jurgen said, and the weird note in his voice made Ian raise a brow and look around. Jurgen was frowning at the pack in Ian's hand. "Nik must've told him he could stay, too."

Ian smiled. "Guess you picked out my playmate already?"

Jurgen gave him a level look. "No," he barked. Then he caught himself and ran a hand through his hair, all quarter-inch of it. "Don't mess with Sam."

Ian got the message. Jurgen was the first person in the family who knew about him. Knew about that drunken night when he was nineteen and had stumbled into a bathroom stall in the basement of Cambridge Hall. When he'd stuck his dick through a hole in the wall and had his whole world rocked by the feel of a scratchy chin on his balls and some very masculine grunts coaxing the cum right out of him.

It was some damn college prank gone wrong. Ian had gone in a lukewarm straight guy and come out confused and horny as shit. It took him seven years to admit he liked fucking guys more than women. Liked it a lot more, if he felt like being honest. As in, if he never fucked a woman again? *Eh.* Never fucked a man again? His balls curled up and cried like babies at the very thought.

Jurgen had talked him off the wall lots of times during the last fourteen years. Jurgen had even supported him through his one real attempt at dating a woman even though he'd totally disapproved at the same time. So if he wanted Ian to keep away from some guy, Ian would stay away. There were lots of men here. He could take his pick.

He wasn't likely to get stuck on the guy, anyway. Never had before. He winced at the thought. He was supposed to be working on that.

"Let me move you into the other room. Though there's a few boxes we haven't unpacked in there, still."

Ian shrugged. "Got a bed?"

"Yep."

"Fine with me." He lobbed the pack he was holding back onto the bed and picked up his own. "Lead the way."

A pair of gray-blue eyes met Ian's as he walked into the kitchen to rejoin the party. He recognized them—they were the eyes of the guy who'd interrupted the rugby game a couple weeks ago. Something about that whole scene had stayed with him, so Ian recognized the kid, even though the kid looked away immediately, his gaze skittering off like a mouse.

Sam.

Ian didn't say hello or anything, but it was pretty obvious by the quick glances from under the guy's lashes and the way he flushed when Ian looked at him that Sam recognized him. Twenty bucks said the kid wasn't going to take the initiative and approach him. That was understandable, since Ian had been kind of a jerk to him, shooting him down so fast without giving him a chance. He wouldn't talk to himself either.

Ever since he'd said that Sam wasn't his type, he'd been thinking about it, and really, who was to say what he wanted anymore? Before, his preferences had been all about sex—Ian saw guy, guy was hot, Ian fucked guy, guy left as soon as possible after. He wanted to leave that stuff behind, right? Maybe he needed to, like, cultivate relationships with guys who he didn't want to get naked with on sight.

Maybe guys he wanted to fuck after he thought about it awhile were a step in the right direction. And he'd thought about Sam a few times since that day on the rugby field. He just hadn't expected to actually *see* him again.

If he was truthful, hooking up with Sam sounded kind of interesting.

But he didn't make any moves, because he needed to feel out the situation first. So he just watched the kid occasionally. Right now, Sam was talking to Nik on the other side of the kitchen. Ian grabbed a beer and settled his butt back against the counter, next to Jurgen. Jurgen was in a conversation with some guys he didn't know, and Ian took advantage of his relative social freedom to reconsider Sam.

Sam had long legs. Maybe they weren't bulging with muscle, but they *were* long. Ian might have written the coltish legs thing off too quickly before. Legs like that might feel nice tangled up with his. A guy with Sam's legs could probably hook his ankles behind Ian's neck while Ian fucked him.

What kind of body hair did Sam have? Tough and springy, or was he one of those downy-haired guys? Maybe downy hair would be a nice change of pace.

He looked like he was barely legal. But he was obviously friends with Nik, so chances were he was of age, right?

Ian took another drink while watching him from across the room, over the heads of pretty much everyone. Yeah, they were both that tall. But where Ian was broad and muscular, the kid was skinny. "Lean" was probably a nicer word.

Ian licked a drop of beer from his lower lip, glancing at the kid's face. Sam was watching his tongue. Staring at it. He swallowed, apparently mesmerized by Ian's mouth. Slowly, Ian parted his lips. Sam swallowed again. Ian let his tongue sweep out, catching his lower lip and pulling it in, sinking his teeth into it.

He could actually see Sam's breath speed up, his mouth falling open slightly, his own tongue mimicking Ian's.

He looked up into Ian's eyes and locked gazes with him, then flushed bright red. He turned around so fast he crashed into Nik, spilling wine on him.

Ian watched Sam get even more flustered, apologizing, wiping at Nik's shirt with a hand. Nik rolled his eyes and pushed Sam's hand away. Just before the kid fled the room, he gave Ian one last humiliated glance from under his lashes. When their eyes met again, he turned an even deeper shade of red.

The kid all but ran away. It wasn't an orderly retreat, that was for sure. For a split-second, Ian thought about going after him. But what kind of comfort would he offer? He stayed put and watched Nik follow Sam out.

Okay, so Sam wasn't his usual fare, but if he did make the effort and he got the kid into bed (or against the wall or whatever), how fast could he make him give it up? Would the kid spontaneously combust just from Ian touching him?

Hell. He had to stop thinking about it. He was getting wood. He hadn't even decided for sure to pursue the kid. Sure, he was thinking about it, but . . .

Then Jurgen, who'd been talking to some other guys, leaned over and said, "That's Sam."

"Yeah." Ian was still staring at the door the kid had disappeared through. "I know. I met him."

Then he and Jurgen shared a moment of frozen silence while Ian put two and two together.

"Shit," they said in perfect unison.

"Let me introduce you to Dave," Jurgen continued.

Ian nodded slowly. "Yeah. Do that."

chapter 5

"What in the hell was that about?" Nik asked when he found Sam hiding in his bedroom. He shut the door and walked over to his dresser.

"He was *watching* me," Sam explained.

"Who was watching you?" Nik asked, digging through a drawer.

The Highlander. "That guy. Jurgen's cousin, Ian."

Nik looked up, his mouth forming a perfect "o" of surprise. "That's a good thing, right?" he asked slowly. He pulled a royal blue shirt out of the drawer, not looking at it but at Sam.

"I don't *knoooow.*" That was close to a wail. Sam tried to bring it down a notch. "I don't think I'm his type."

"Type, schmype." Nik flapped a hand at him. "He was *watching* you." Nik started paying attention to unbuttoning his wine-soaked shirt.

Sam swallowed and took a calming breath. "I might have been ogling him. A little. He might have noticed."

"Every guy here is ogling him," Nik said, disgruntled. Understandable: he was used to people ogling his boyfriend. It was a point of pride with him, even if he wouldn't admit it. No matter how much Sam pushed him to. "You're just one of the herd." Nik looked disgustedly at the dirty shirt now in his hand, then threw it toward the bathroom door. Sam watched it sail past a stripper pole he'd just noticed.

Don't ask. "You guys put in a stripper pole?" *D'oh!*

Nik smiled, sighing dreamily. "Yeah." He gazed affectionately at the shiny brass pole, then shook his head and refocused on Sam. "So, what about Ian?"

Another calming breath. "Do you remember when I told you about, um, the guy I asked out?"

"Your future husband?" Nik's eyes got big. So had his voice. He stopped in the middle of pulling on his new shirt.

"Be quiet! I didn't mean that husband thing. I was drunk."

"Yes you did. So, what you aren't saying is . . ." Nik raised a brow, looking delighted. Slowly buttoning his new shirt.

Sam started a sort of horrified nodding. "It was Ian." Nik nodded in unison with him, but in a far less horrified way.

"So maybe, if you watched him back . . ." Nik waggled his brows. It was completely out of character for him.

Sam stared a few seconds before blurting, "He was *checking me out*. I think."

There was that "o" of surprise again. "What did you do?" Nik asked excitedly.

"I bumped into you and spilled wine down your front."

Nik looked at him.

Sam looked at Nik.

"I guess you could have been smoother," Nik finally said, looking far less delighted. He finished buttoning his shirt and planted his hands on his hips. Thinking.

"I guess I could have."

"Okay. Don't worry. I'm going to help you." Nik whirled around and marched out of the room with purpose.

Oh no.

"I'm really not sure this is a situation that can be helped," Sam called after him, already knowing it was pointless.

Nik's idea of helping Sam turned out to be butting in on any conversation Ian had with any gay single guy at the party. Especially Dave Blaylock. Nik still had a few issues with Dave having dated Jurgen, even though he laughed and pretended otherwise whenever Sam brought it up.

Nik got on Dave like a hawk on a mouse. A very small hawk on a very big mouse. A mouse completely unconcerned with any size disparity.

Ian and Dave were sitting on the couch, nursing beers and talking. Sam lurked near a doorway, holding up the wall and looking nonchalant (he doubted), studiously not watching them out of the corner of his eye. He noted with satisfaction that Ian hadn't smiled at Dave once. Or laughed. Sam had made Ian smile *and* laugh when they'd first met.

It didn't really matter that Ian had been smiling and laughing *at* him rather than *with* him, right?

Sam's thoughts were interrupted when Nik insisted on sitting between Dave and Ian. He started chattering, his simpleton smile on his face. Sam watched Nik a minute, and then his eyes drifted back to Ian.

Ian was watching him. Smiling a slight, sort of smug smile.

This is your chance. Smile back.

Sam felt his face flush red, then he looked at the floor and slunk out of the room. God he was suave, wasn't he? He hid in the little hall between the living room and the bedrooms, right off the kitchen. It was deserted for now, but party sounds surrounded him.

"Where's Nik?" Jurgen's voice behind him startled Sam into almost jumping.

He whirled to face Jurgen, instead. "Talking to the guests."

Jurgen narrowed his eyes slightly. "Is he talking to Ian again?"

Was Jurgen jealous? It didn't seem possible, but why else would he care? Sam nodded, trying to figure it out.

"Why is he trying to cock block Ian?" Jurgen's voice was low and compelling.

Sam had sudden sympathy for suspects Jurgen might question. But . . . *cock block*? Really? "I don't know?" It was kind of true. He didn't know why Nik was bothering.

Jurgen crossed his arms over his chest. "Sam, stay away from Ian."

"What?" Like Sam should stay upwind of him, or something more along the lines of "don't let him stick his dick in you"?

"He's not your type. He's a manwhore. He's more likely to fuck you than date you. You deserve better than that."

"Uh . . ." Wait, wasn't Jurgen Ian's cousin? "I do? I mean, I know, but it's kinda weird—"

"He's not 'relationship material.'"

"He's my future husband." *Did I say that out loud?* Sam clapped a belated hand over his mouth.

Jurgen stared at him a minute before dropping his forehead into his palm, growling to himself and massaging his temples. "Ian's *no one's* future husband." Jurgen pulled his head up wearily. "He's got . . . the fuck are those 'issues' again? Nik's always going on about them."

Sam dropped his hand from his mouth. "Commitment issues?" Nik had issues with commitment issues.

Jurgen snapped his fingers. "Commitment issues. He'd use you, Sam. He'll force himself to find some suitable woman and start producing children any year now, and he'll still be fucking guys on the side."

Sam gaped. "Seriously?"

Jurgen rolled his eyes. "Probably not," he admitted, then made a face like he'd licked a toad. "But he *might*. I've seen him try to do it before. And if he does, you don't want to be his convenient fuck on the side."

Reformed rakes make the best husbands. Sam managed to stop himself from blurting that out.

Jurgen gave him a long, silent look. Then he sighed. "Fine." He turned and walked away down the hall.

The rest of the party was semi-torturous. Sam was sure he would have to watch Ian going at it with some guy, somewhere. Ian was a flirt, in spite of not laughing and rarely smiling. Guys threw themselves at him.

Probably Ian was better described as a flirt-magnet. He was also a bastard. Toying with Sam, doing subtly sexy things to make him nuts that no one else seemed to notice. Did a normal guy need to lick that many drops of beer off his lower lip? Did a normal guy wait until each droplet hovered on the point of falling, practically begging for someone else's tongue to suck up said droplet from the bottom of his plump, full lip?

Did normal guys have to scratch their flat, taut bellies, pulling their shirt up with their searching fingers, revealing slivers of skin and clinging hair? When Ian used a pinky fingertip to circle his belly button, not quite dipping in . . . that had to be on purpose, right? Who finger-rimmed their navel at a party *accidentally*?

Only the occasional moments of humor from Nik and Jurgen made the suffering bearable. When Nik wasn't "cock blocking" Ian, he was throwing Miller at every available guy in the place. Sam couldn't imagine where Nik had found half these guys. He recognized a fifth of them, maybe less, and he had a hard time believing Jurgen had that many friends. This had to be every gay man in Marlyle County, and then some.

The only guys Nik didn't throw Miller at were Sam and Ian. "This is worse than my mother introducing me to nice girls at church," Miller complained to Sam at the keg.

A keg! Nik and Jurgen had gotten a keg for this party. Sam shook his head in some shame. "It's appalling," he told Miller, who was pretending to fill his plastic beer cup.

"It sure the hell is," Miller said. Sam had a feeling they were talking about different things. "I can get my own damn gay life," Miller muttered. "Someday. Once I get used to being gay."

"Are you gay?" Sam asked. It seemed appropriate.

"'Pears so," Miller said, as if they were discussing the weather report. Sam had spent enough of last summer on the porch of Nik's parents' store to have some experience discussing farm weather.

"Heard it might rain," Sam returned. The polite reply to any statement about precipitation.

"Heard it might rain men." Miller winked at him. "Really could use some men."

Sam looked around at the sea of men. "We're surrounded by them."

Miller tilted his head in a gesture Sam had only ever seen country folk make. A sort of sideways, single nod. Body language for conceding a point, but . . . "I think I might prefer the ones that fall outta the sky. Less pressure," he said.

Miller was cool. Sam would have talked to him more, but Nik showed up with some guy who had a shaved head and two rings through his lower lip that Miller just had to meet.

Sam was relieved that he didn't just have to meet the guy, too. Not that he had anything against piercings, per se. Though it looked like Miller might, judging by his expression.

Sam looked aside, and there was Jurgen introducing yet another guy to Ian. Jurgen looked serious about not wanting Sam to hook up with his cousin.

Meanwhile, said cousin winked at Sam, then turned to face the newest offering. Ian had his arms crossed over his chest, red plastic beer cup in one hand propped up on the other forearm, showcasing his pecs.

Sam scowled. *Bastard.* Did he think Sam was that easy, that some muscle and a wink would cut it? He snorted and looked away, crossing his own arms over his chest.

Jurgen quirked a knowing brow at Sam.

Sam scowled at Jurgen. *Big, dumb asshole.*

Fuck this. Sam straightened up and walked out.

The place had cleared out by 3 a.m. Not even a single passed-out drunk littered the floor. Sam couldn't believe it. If they were having a kegger, couldn't they at least do it right? Dave had left early, though Sam hadn't even noticed—Miller had told him as much when Sam had found him hiding in the bathroom.

He was so ready for bed. He didn't need any more of this humiliation. No more Ian torturing him for his own amusement. Sam wasn't his type; he'd heard it from the horse's ass himself.

Nik wasn't allowing him to go to bed, however, because—in an effort to be the perfect gay couple or something—Nik and Jurgen had bought a place with a hot tub. Which he insisted Sam get into. Fortunately, Sam had been forewarned this might happen, and he'd come prepared.

Sam put on his swim trunks and walked out into the hall, where he ran right into Nik.

Nik stared at him a second. "What are you *wearing*?"

"What? Are they ugly?" Sam looked down at himself. He looked like himself: too tall and too skinny. He dropped his voice. "Do I look that bad?"

"No, and no. What you look is overdressed."

Sam stared at Nik. Okay, if he was overdressed in a pair of surfer-esque swim trunks, that meant everyone else was wearing . . . "Speedos?" he squeaked.

Nik shook his head and sighed. "Sam, really. What kind of gay men's housewarming party would it be if we went into the hot tub with clothing on? It would be a sham. I would never live that down."

Wait. Nude hot-tubbing? With *Ian*? "Wha . . .? Bu . . ."

"What?"

"I mean, I don't, you know. I'm kinda . . ."

"Are you going to go on about being tired again?"

"No, no." *Damn*! He should have said yes. "I'm just, I'm . . . I mean what if I, you know. I get . . . you know." Judging from Nik's look, he didn't know. He looked truly puzzled, not that sort of simple-but-good-natured puzzled expression he affected when he was messing with people. "Excited," Sam finished.

"Excited."

"Excited."

Nik tilted his head, studying Sam. "I guess the choice is yours. You can be the only guy in the hot tub with shorts on, or you can be like the rest of us and recite baseball stats in your head to keep from getting hard."

"Baseball stats? Like what?"

"No idea. It's just what Jurgen does when he's trying not to pop too early."

"See, I didn't need to know that."

Nik stepped forward to lay a commiserating hand on Sam's upper arm. "I know, Sam. I know. Neither did I."

"Shit. Maybe I'll just be too tired?" Sam asked hopefully. Again.

Nik frowned. "But then there'll only be three guys in the hot tub. I need you in there, or I haven't done my job as a good host. Hosts need an even number of people in the hot tub."

"That's at the table, and you're a modern hostess. You can do this. And what do you mean, 'only three guys'?"

"Host. Modern hosts don't care how many people they have at the table. They care about how many people they have in the hot tub."

"Host. Only three guys?"

Nik blinked at him. "Yeah. Me, Jurgen, and Ian."

Sam squeaked. A tiny squeak, completely involuntary. "Um, what about Miller?"

Nik rolled his eyes until he almost fell over. "Miller and Ian don't really get along, and Miller had some weird *reaction* to me introducing him to all those guys." Nik flapped his hand.

"Like an allergic reaction?"

"I guess. He sure acted like it was giving him hives to be introduced to the finest men I could dig up for him."

"Where did you find all those guys, anyway?"

"I put a personal ad in the paper."

Oh, now that definitely called for the silent treatment. Sam raised his brows and eyed him.

Nik lifted his chin in defiance. "It's good for him. Helps him develop gay social skills."

"*Gay* social skills? How are those different from regular social skills?"

"They aren't. That's the point."

"I'm so lost."

"I don't have time to explain it to you. I have a hot-tubbing to host." In a nicer tone, Nik added, "If you hurry up, you can get in before anyone else and turn on the bubbles. Then no one will be able to see if you get excited."

Sam returned to the guest room posthaste to shuck the shorts.

chapter 6

Sam got naked as fast as he could, wrapped a towel somewhat haphazardly around his hips, and found the hot tub blissfully empty when he got there. *Thank God.*

The water was too damn hot, but he forced himself in and turned on the bubbles. Then he looked down. He almost couldn't see his naked self, except for a pink blob shimmying and shaking in the rapidly moving water. He glanced at his shoulders in the light from the back porch. Yep, they were as white as ever.

Great. That meant that just above his nipples, there would be a demarcation line. Below it, he'd be boiled pink and puffy like a lobster. Above the line he'd look too pale; his natural state. Why couldn't he have skin like Nik's? He was just dark enough that you couldn't see him blush. Even being pale like Jurgen would be better, because he tanned easily. Sam bet he didn't look like a lobster in the hot tub.

Oh. What would Ian look like in the hot tub?

Better not to think about it.

But maybe . . . if he imagined what Ian looked like, he'd be better prepared. Sort of like inoculating himself.

That's a rationalization so you can imagine Ian naked.

Well, yeah . . . but Ian was a bastard and Sam wouldn't touch his dick even if Ian wanted him to. Yet somehow he was still attracted to him. So he needed to do something, right?

But he's a bastard.

Unfortunately, not all of Sam found that unappealing.

Damn.

He closed his eyes. He was going the inoculation route.

This is a very bad idea.

He thought it might take a minute to get a clear visualization, but of course it didn't. There was a naked Ian just waiting for him on the backs of his eyelids. Smirking at him and slowly, smugly stroking his semi-hard dick.

See? Bad idea. Sam opened his eyes.

In real life, a mostly naked Ian was standing there, smirking at him. Sam gasped. Ian added teeth to his grin. Then he reached for the white towel he had wrapped around his waist, like in some kind of porn video. Sam only caught the movement in the bottom of his vision since he couldn't look away from Ian's eyes, but he knew exactly what was going on. Ian's eyes tracked down Sam's neck and across his shoulders.

Don't look down. You don't need any more temptation.

Sam rarely listened to his inner monologue, anyway. *Oh man.* That chest. Just as forested with hair as before, with the blocky pectoral muscles and the dark caramel treasure trail drawing Sam's eyes down. While Sam watched, Ian ran a palm across his belly, riffling the hair there. Tracing across a line of muscle with a finger.

"Like what you see, Sam?"

"Shut up," Sam said. Then, mortified, he looked up into Ian's face.

Smiling, Ian unwrapped the towel and let it fall.

Sam tried not to look. He really, really tried. Sweartagod.

Ian had low-hangers. Hairy balls that dangled so low they skulked at the tip of Ian's dick, which wasn't a small one. Sam nearly squeaked. Then he finally focused on the main event, and he did squeak. Ian was uncut.

Fuck, the heat from the hot tub was making Sam lightheaded or something, because the gazebo was spinning like he was going to faint. He struggled to suck in some oxygen. He couldn't stop staring at Ian, and while he did, Ian started getting hard, his prick bobbing up slightly and his sac tightening. Sam could just see the testicles inside Ian's scrotum, perfect ovals weighting the bottom of the sac, and his mouth watered. Yum. He was even symmetrical.

So Sam had a little bit of a testicle fetish. So he liked to lie on his back and have a guy with big nuts straddling his head, teasing him by dragging them across his lips and skin, pubes tickling him, soft scrotum tightening slowly, until finally the guy told Sam to open his mouth and suck. He loved trying to fit both of those eggs inside his mouth at the same time, trying to feel them in his throat. Laving them with his tongue and tugging gently, sometimes even with his teeth, until the guy was nearly suffocating him, shoving his balls in Sam's mouth, trailing pre-cum on Sam's cheeks and forehead and nose.

"Well, I can see you like *that*." Ian's voice—the real life one, not the fantasy one—jarred Sam.

Camouflaging bubbles, my boiled pink ass. Sam stood up, boner and all, and got the hell out of the hot tub. Without thinking about where he was headed or what he was going to tell Nik (if he ever showed up), he fled.

Ian caught him in the laundry room. Came up silently behind him, sliding an arm around his waist and palming Sam's chest, then pulling him back into his body. His dick poked into Sam's cheek muscle like it was checking him for tenderness.

Sam had ignored it when Ian walked in. He had no clue how Ian had found him in the laundry room, couldn't even explain how he'd ended up there, hands planted on the dryer, trying to get a grip and a full breath. But he'd felt Ian enter the room, and then he'd pretended to not know Ian was there.

God, he was such an idiot. He wanted to tilt his hips back and feel the head of Ian's cock trace down his crack. He wanted Ian to not ask, to simply fuck him. Wanted Ian to bend him forward over the machine and work his cock into him. Wanted to keep pretending that he didn't want it the whole time Ian was inside him. Wanted Ian to just take.

I think it's time for me to accept the current reality. Ian was a bastard and a flirt, and he wanted Sam. Sam could get his rocks off with the hottest guy he'd ever had a chance to be with—probably ever would have the chance to be with—wake up alone in the morning and *then* wait for his Mr. Right.

His second choice was to hang on to the romance-novel ideal, leave the room, and wait forever for his knight in shining armor. 'Cause Ian? Wasn't anyone's knight. Jurgen knew what he was talking about.

"If you aren't interested, kid, you need to tell me." Ian's voice thrummed in the muscles at the nape of Sam's neck.

He didn't say anything. His gut tightened up into an excited ball of energy.

Ian waited a few moments, then slid his hand up, circling Sam's neck. "The way you looked at me, I think you're interested. You've been watching me all night, Sam, haven't you?" Ian's hand slid down, thumb stroking across Sam's nipple. "Tell me."

"Yes." Sam closed his eyes. He might have swayed backward.

"You were watching me out there by the hot tub too. You saw something you liked, didn't you, kid?"

Don't say anything. He doesn't need to know.

Sam nodded when Ian's thumb stroked his nipple again, sending out radiating waves of want.

"What was it, Sam?" Ian murmured in his ear. Sam swallowed. "Want me to guess?" Sam bit his lip. "Hmm. You ever been with a guy who isn't cut, kiddo?"

"No," Sam whispered. His ass cheeks clenched involuntarily. Not exactly what he'd been fantasizing about, but so hot.

"Mmm. You like that? You want it, kid?" Ian pressed himself against Sam, thrusting gently against his ass.

"Yeah." He didn't even know if he was answering Ian's question or simply encouraging him. Either way, he didn't want Ian to stop. Wanted to feel that skin slip against his more.

Ian's other hand drifted down the curve of Sam's butt, stroking him. Ian slid it to the underside of Sam's cheek, fingertips tickling the sensitive skin just where it met his thigh. "You have a nice ass, you know that?"

I do? Sam was so startled he could barely shake his head.

"I want to bury myself in it." Ian's chin scraped Sam's shoulder, the whiskers almost too rough. His lips moved against Sam's ear. "Would you let me fuck you?"

"Yes," Sam gasped. Then he gave in and tilted his hips back, pressing himself against Ian, feeling the hair at Ian's groin rasping against his skin. One of Ian's hands pressed low on his abdomen; his other hand slid back up to Sam's throat.

"Would you let me fuck you right here, bent over the washing machine? Maybe holding your hands behind your back?"

"Oh, God." Sam's breath was coming too fast. He tried to slow it down—hyperventilating and passing out would *suck*. "Dryer. This is a dryer."

"With the door open behind us?"

Sam froze. "The door's open?" He felt Ian smile against the back of his neck. Sam pulled away and turned to see the door ajar. "Where are Nik and Jurgen?"

Now he saw Ian's smug smile, which put another damper on the moment. "I don't think they're going to make it out of their bedroom, judging by the noises I heard."

So typical of Nik to throw him under the bus just because Jurgen wanted to get it on. Of course, if Sam had someone as hot as Jurgen pawing at him, working to convince him to skip the hot-tubbing...

Ian leaned forward until his chest hair just rubbed against Sam's skin, sensitizing it. His jaw scraped across Sam's, and he whispered in Sam's ear, "How about you let me fuck you in your room instead?"

Oh. He *did* have a guy as hot as Jurgen, and Ian was even *working* for it. He wanted Sam enough to put effort into *seducing* him.

It was entirely too much to resist. He let himself reach for Ian, hands on his shoulders but not quite up to meeting his eyes. He met his chin instead. "Okay," he told it.

chapter 7

Ian hadn't expected that getting to know a guy some before fucking him would be so easy. As a matter of fact, it wasn't that different from just agreeing on a time and place and fucking him. It just took a little longer.

Huh. Who'da thought?

He watched Sam walk down the darkened hall ahead of him. The kid was skinny, but he had a cute ass—taut and small, with natural hollows on the sides as if his glutes were always clenched tight. Ian was usually more of a bubble butt kind of guy, but as far as he could tell, with Sam, all bets were off.

His palms and fingers tingled with the need to grip those cheeks and spread them open. The urge to bury himself in that flexing and twisting ass made his balls tighten. Sam stopped in front of his bedroom, and Ian stepped up so close that his dick nudged one of those hollows in Sam's cheeks, making Ian suck in a breath. So close that he could look over Sam's shoulder and watch his trembling hand grip the knob. So close that he couldn't tell if he heard or felt Sam's Adam's apple bob up and down before he white-knuckled the doorknob and turned it, letting the door swing open into the room.

Then Sam simply stood there while Ian watched goose pimples break out on his neck.

"Go in," Ian said.

It made his nuts ache, how fast Sam moved to obey. Was Sam always submissive, or was it just for him? How far could he go?

Not that far without having a conversation about boundaries and safewords, and he wanted to avoid too much talking tonight.

Sam had stopped next to the bed, his back to the door, while Ian watched from the doorway. He stood stock still except for the rapid rise and fall of his shoulders. The only light came from a dim lamp on the nightstand—Ian had made sure to turn on that light when he'd stopped by Sam's room before hitting the hot tub.

He stepped up to Sam's side and traced his vertebrae with one finger, watching his profile. "You like to take orders, Sam?"

Sam nodded and swallowed, gaze fixed on the wall. Ian circled the bony knob just above Sam's crack with his fingertip, then pushed his finger between Sam's cheeks, watching Sam's lips part and his breath come faster. "Good," Ian finally told him, worming his finger a little deeper, looking for puckered skin. "When's the last time someone fucked you, kiddo?"

His finger slid across Sam's asshole, making Sam bite his lips. Sam really had a beautiful mouth. "Wanna fuck your face, too," Ian said, surprised to hear himself speaking.

Sam's eyelids fell closed, and he moaned softly. Ian forced steel into his voice. "Answer the question, Sam."

"Almost two years," Sam whispered.

Ian felt that answer all the way to his balls. He was going to be the first guy in years to fuck this kid. It seemed almost sacrilegious. Something twisted in his chest, but he stomped on it. *He said he wanted it.* "Lie down on the bed, kiddo. On your back."

Sam crawled while Ian watched his every move, knowing Sam could feel his gaze. But when Sam lay flat on his back, he stared straight up at the ceiling. The only things sticking up were his toes and his cock. He was breathing fast again, so Ian laid a calming hand on his chest.

For the first time since the hot tub, Sam turned and met his eyes. He looked scared, but when Ian glanced down, he saw Sam hadn't lost his erection. Fear excited him? Maybe, but for some inexplicable reason, Ian found himself running a knuckle across Sam's nearest cheekbone. "It's okay," he whispered. Sam took his first deep breath since the laundry room, then nodded.

For a second, Ian wished he'd done this differently. Wished he'd had Sam on his knees on the floor, lips wrapped around Ian's cock, eyes looking up into his. He not only had beautiful lips, he had pretty eyes. Something more than that gray-blue color swirled in them.

Ian almost scowled at his own poeticism, but he didn't want to freak Sam out. He turned to the nightstand where he'd stashed the condoms and lube when he'd snuck in earlier. He heard Sam suck in a breath when he got them out and threw them on the bed. Ian looked at him and smiled. Sam swallowed.

Then Ian climbed on the bed and straddled Sam's head. He started to put on a condom, but Sam grabbed his hand. "I'd rather not."

Ian stared down at him. Did the kid do shit like this regularly and not use a condom?

"I mean—" Sam swallowed "—we should, but if you told me you were, you know, *clean*, I'd believe you . . ."

You shouldn't agree.

But Sam's lips were slick from his tongue, and they looked like they could mold themselves around anything. Ian dropped the condom. He grasped his cock and traced Sam's mouth with the tip. Sam opened up, but didn't try to lick or suck him in, just panted warm wet air on him, waiting for Ian to push forward.

Ian let the anticipation build, then eased into Sam's mouth. The stroke of Sam's tongue around his foreskin made him groan, and he leaned forward, planting his hands on the wall.

Sam's mouth felt like magic wrapped around his cock, sucking and licking him, sometimes humming or moaning, while Sam's hand snuck up to fondle Ian's balls. He worked Ian's foreskin, gently probing at first, getting more aggressive as Ian pushed in slowly, breath speeding up, occasional gasps escaping him. Sam responded with his tongue or lips to every move of Ian's hips and every barely conscious noise.

Fuck. Sam's mouth was just so . . . perfect. Ian tried to think of a better word, distracting himself because he seriously needed distraction. It was—*oh, hell*—wet. Wet mouth. Tight and hot and then sloppy, tongue circling his glans softly enough that Ian could breathe for a moment, then sucking so hard he thought he would lose his mind.

It had been a year since anyone had done this for him. Much longer since anyone had sucked him this well. That was Ian's only excuse for losing control when Sam's gray-blue eyes met his, and he found himself thrusting hard into Sam's throat. Sam just opened right up for Ian as if he'd expected it, wrapping around Ian with his lips and tongue and cheeks and even his fucking tonsils. Fondling his nuts, sending shooting sensations into his gut and making his cock throb and feel like all the blood in his body was pooled right there, waiting for its turn in Sam's mouth.

He came, and Sam moaned around him, sucking him dry, stroking his taint and rolling Ian's balls between his fingers. Ian convulsed in Sam's mouth, ass tightening up and cum rushing through him from his sensitized balls while Sam rubbed his fingertip across Ian's hole. Encouraging him to just let it all out.

Ian did, until he was arched forward and clawing drywall, his back muscles strained, his cheek pressed hard against the wall, sliding in his own sweat.

He nearly collapsed onto Sam's head, but managed to push himself to the side, closing his eyes and gasping, head bent uncomfortably against the headboard.

What the hell was that?

It was an amazing blowjob, that's what it was. He wouldn't have pegged Sam as being a champion cocksucker, but that would teach him not to judge a book by its cover.

Slowly, the blood receded from Ian's ears, and he became aware of some other rhythmic noise: a hand working a cock. Ian cracked his eyes to see Sam jerking himself off. "Stop that."

Sam stopped instantly, even though he must have been close, hips lifting off the bed. Ian's voice hadn't even been hard or commanding. "I don't get to come?" Sam asked.

Ian straightened himself out on the bed so his neck wasn't at such a painful angle. He looked into Sam's face. "C'mere. On your knees, straddling my shoulders."

Sam blinked at him. "Why?"

Why? "It's up to you. You can come in your hand, or in my mouth." It was the least the kid deserved after a performance like his.

Sam clambered up his body so fast it was downright flattering. Ian grinned at him. "Thought so."

chapter 8

an was licking at Sam's glans, which Sam found heart-stoppingly amazing. It'd been more than three years since anyone had sucked him off.

It was Ian's other hand, though, sliding along behind his balls, *shudder*, that found his secret—his guiche piercing. Ian pulled his mouth off, making Sam jerk when cold air hit his wet skin. He looked down to see Ian leering at him.

"What's this?" Ian ran a finger across the bar buried under Sam's skin.

"You know what it is," Sam said. His heart pounded in his ears, going faster than it had been with Ian's tongue sliding around his dick. No one had ever touched his guiche except him and the girl who'd pierced him. And now Ian's finger dragged across his skin from bead to bead along the barbell, pressing lightly. It felt better than Sam would have thought, having someone else play with the piercing.

Ian smiled bigger. "Turn around, Sam. I want to see it."

Sam hesitated. Ian just looked at him, waiting for him to comply. Not smiling anymore, but not angry. Sam didn't know if he cou—

Ian tugged gently on one bead of the guiche, and Sam arched his back and pushed up onto his knees. It felt like having an unreachable itch scratched, only a thousand times better.

He turned around, his muscles shaky and not really supporting him, his legs straining to hold his ass right above Ian's face.

"Nice," Ian said, like he'd found a new plaything. Sam felt his voice resonating in the guiche. Then Ian licked him, tongue sliding across the skin-covered bar, under the ends, between the beads and Sam's skin.

Oh God. Oh fuck. Sam dug his fingers into the bed. Ian blew on the skin he'd wetted. "Oh God," Sam whispered, his head falling forward. Then Ian's thumbs were pulling his ass cheeks apart, and Ian's wet finger was sliding from the guiche to Sam's asshole. Sam sucked in a breath and straightened up, tensing with anticipation.

Sam had always been tight, and Ian had a fantastically thick finger, and he used a light touch to tease Sam before finally pushing steadily inside, making Sam clench even tighter for a second before loosening.

"You're snug." Ian's voice sounded admiring. Even excited. "You'll feel so good on my cock."

Sam whimpered and shoved himself back onto Ian's finger. Oh God, Ian's knuckle was stretching him wider. The spit wasn't enough, but Sam wasn't about to complain. It ached and pulled a little, which was perfect.

Then Sam felt something amazing—hot breath on his asshole and Ian's tongue licking around it. Sam locked his elbows to keep from face-planting. Ian licked him, sparking up Sam's nerves and lubing his own finger when he started to stroke. He worked in a second finger, grunting in a pleased-caveman way when Sam squeezed both with his ass muscles. Ian slid in and out more and rubbed less, but it was still achingly good. Sam needed that friction so much he was rocking his hips, breathing out small noises. He just needed to feel full. "Yeah."

"That's good?"

"Oh, fuck."

Ian laughed, blasting air across Sam's ass. "Must be a yes."

When Ian's fingers slid across his prostate, Sam groaned and jerked, his elbows shaking and his back bowing, knees slipping on the sheets.

"Make yourself come," Ian said, his jaw scraping whiskers against Sam's ass cheeks, making Sam shiver.

Sam held on tight to his dick, moving as fast as he could make it, while Ian finger-fucked him harder, winding up the nerves. But it was Ian's tug on his nuts that made Sam howl and come. He was certain he shot off fireworks, releasing all that painfully built-up pleasure.

He fell forward onto Ian's legs, drained. Ian eased his fingers out of Sam's ass after a minute. Or an hour; Sam couldn't be sure.

"That's good," he mumbled.

Ian laughed.

Sam made a face into Ian's knee and rolled over onto his back. He felt so relaxed he could have passed out right there. He found a blanket to wipe himself off and cover up with, making a lazy mental note to throw it in the washer before he left Nik and Jurgen's.

"You going to come up here?"

Sam shrugged in answer and groped around for a pillow. When he found one, he stuffed it under his head and rolled onto his side, Ian's knee brushing his spine.

"Guess not," Ian muttered. The bed squeaked and bounced while Ian turned himself around and cleaned himself with something; Sam's sock, for all he knew. Then Ian sighed contentedly and settled in behind him, body heat just touching his.

"Warm," Sam mumbled into the sheet.

"Huh?" Ian asked, but Sam ignored him. Too much effort to answer.

Ian didn't seem to care. He patted Sam's hip. "You're better than I would have guessed."

Bastard. But really, what did you expect?

Pretty much what he got: a superlative orgasm. "You, too," he said. The sudden, stunned silence from Ian's side of the bed made him smile. "You never got around to fucking me," he added right before he fell asleep.

chapter 9

In his previous sex life, Ian would have left after that first time, especially when the kid just passed out on him like that. But this was his new sex life, where he should probably hang out after, so instead he fell asleep too. He woke up when it was barely light out, and the first thing he saw was Sam's pale, tight ass peeking out from under the sheet in front of him.

He liked that ass—fully intended to fuck that ass, putting his hands all over it and waking Sam up by caressing it. But for some reason, when things got to the point where he should have been easing himself inside Sam, he lubed up and pushed his dick between Sam's thighs instead, bumping into Sam's balls with each thrust between his legs.

The noises Sam made were real, not porn-star fake. He whimpered and caught his breath over and over because he couldn't help it, not because they were hooking up and he had a part to play. And where did that come from? Because Ian'd never thought that about the guys he'd been with before, but right now he was certain Sam was the only genuinely grateful fuck he'd ever had.

Even though they weren't actually fucking.

It didn't matter because it was hot, and before Ian knew it the noises Sam made had become groans from his gut, rattling around in his throat, and Ian realized he wanted to kiss Sam. Just lay his lips right where Sam's neck met his shoulder, on that stringy trapezius.

Or force Sam's head back and take his mouth.

He wasn't about to do that. He kissed guys, sure, but not guys who might read more into it than just sex, and even if this was more than *simply* sex, it wasn't the beginning of a relationship. That would be cruel, to let Sam think there might be more to this. Ian couldn't kiss him. It didn't matter that Sam sounded hoarse from moaning so much so deeply, or that Ian could feel those moans strumming in his dick. Ian couldn't kiss him again.

But if Sam didn't stop it, he wouldn't be able to *not* kiss him. Trying to muffle the noise, he covered Sam's mouth with his hand.

He was rewarded with a startled cry that leaked out around his fingers and stuck in his ears, making the urge to kiss Sam that much stronger.

And fuck, he could *taste* Sam. Breathe in his heat and sweat and the scent of his hair and Jesus Christ he *couldn't* do this.

So he bit the kid instead.

Sam came in his hand, pushing his ass back and stroking Ian with downy, smooth skin over wiry muscles.

To his shock, Ian came too—just popped. Really, really fucking hard, pushing Sam over onto his stomach and grinding into him, fingers digging into his pelvis.

For a while, Ian couldn't move. Maybe thirty seconds of panting against Sam's neck, teeth still on his skin. It was when he started grazing them along the muscle that ran behind Sam's ear to his clavicle that Ian forced himself off the kid. He shoved himself away, so they weren't touching anywhere, and listened to Sam's breathing slowly change from post-coital panting to sleep.

Then Ian lay there, thinking so fast it was like thinking nothing, but less relaxing. He'd come hard enough that he should be out cold for hours, but between that crazy-strong orgasm and Sam just passing out after? Ian couldn't sleep.

Maybe he'd eaten something funny.

Sam was clearly having no issues sleeping. He hadn't eaten the same things, probably. Ian rolled onto his side. He meant to roll away from Sam, but his body somehow got the wrong message and he rolled to face Sam instead. The kid was stomach-down, hugging the sheets like a lover, head turned away from Ian.

Aw, fuck. Ian forced himself onto his back again, and watched the room grow lighter as the sun came up. East-facing window. He'd never fall asleep here with an east-facing window.

Hell, he might as well get up and leave. His work here was done, he knew the kid well enough, right? It'd be at least an hour until he could get it up again. He was thirty-three; he just couldn't fuck forever the way he'd used to.

He should leave before anyone in the house woke up.

Fuck. Jurgen.

There was no way he could explain why he'd ignored Jurgen's request to leave Sam alone. And he had an inkling that Jurgen wouldn't quite see the "getting to know him first" thing the same way Ian had.

Why had he done that? He'd never just ignored a request from Jurgen like that. It was totally out of character. Things had just . . . gotten out of hand. Sam had been in that hot tub, looking nervous and, well, cute, and then he'd reacted so perfectly when Ian dropped his towel. As if he could've come just by looking at him.

Ian turned his head, looking one more time at Sam. He snuffled, rubbing his nose in his sleep, then sighed and rolled over.

Hell.

Okay, he probably needed to think about this. Come up with an explanation for Jurgen. Staying here, waiting for Jurgen to get up and plan out an ambush, was probably a bad idea, though. Best course of action was to get out of bed before anyone was up, get out of here, and head back to the city until he came up with a reasonable explanation.

That was why he needed to leave. To think.

He refused to listen to the little voice inside spouting off opinions about running away and bad decisions.

Of course, Jurgen was in the kitchen reading the paper and drinking coffee. When Ian walked in, pack over his shoulder and carrying his shoes, Jurgen pointed at an empty cup waiting for him on the counter next to the coffee pot.

Ian winced, accepted the inevitability of having a conversation with his cousin, and filled his mug. He probably deserved whatever was about to happen.

"So," Jurgen said once Ian sat down next to him.

"So," Ian returned. He sipped his coffee. Jurgen smiled. Ian cleared his throat. "Sorry. I mean, what can I say?"

Jurgen shrugged. "Nothing." He turned back to his paper. "Have a good time last night?"

Aw, fuck. "Yeah," Ian said. "Thanks for inviting me." He sipped again.

"Sounded like you had a good time."

Ian closed his eyes and pinched the bridge of his nose. "Just say it."

"You fucked Sam."

"Sort of." Not that Jurgen would care about the gray areas.

"I told you to leave Sam alone."

"Yes." He met Jurgen's eyes. Jurgen didn't just look angry, he looked *disappointed*. "I'm sorry," he said again.

Jurgen threw down the paper and stood up. "Don't apologize to me." Ian thought he wanted more coffee, but Jurgen headed toward the hallway instead. "You should probably get the hell out of here. You start that new job on Monday," he added before he hit the door.

Aw, fuck. They'd never talked about Sherri—Ian's single failure at a relationship in the past, the one that had pissed Jurgen off so totally—but for the first time Ian felt like he wanted to try. He had a good relationship with his cousin most of the time, except when it came to this.

"Listen, I get that you're still pissed about Sherri." Jurgen stopped in the doorway, so Ian kept talking. "But it was seven years ago. I was a fucked-up kid. I wasn't trying to use her, I really thought . . ."

"Thought you could be straight?"

"I thought it might be a mistake. Maybe I *was* straight. I liked her, I even loved her, but not—you know—like that."

Jurgen sighed and turned around, folding his arms across his chest. "You haven't been serious about anyone since then."

"You've never been serious about anyone until Nik."

Jurgen stared at him a long time. "So what are you trying to say?"

He wished he knew. "Just, maybe I'm trying to figure some shit out."

"This is how you figure shit out? Take advantage of a guy like Sam and sneak out before he wakes up?"

"It's not like he didn't want it. He wanted to be with me too."

"So did Sherri."

Hell. Ian closed his eyes and listened to Jurgen walk out. Seemed like a good idea, so he left too.

chapter 10

Having a job, going to school full time, and being a Graduate Teaching Fellow was a pain in the ass. Sam spent half of his fifteen-minute break at Fatty's trying to think up things that would suck worse.

Having an incurable disease and no health care. That would suck much worse. Meh. Wasn't working. He didn't care how much some hypothetical life would suck, because his real life sucked right now.

Okay, time to think of the positives.

He was going to have a big, fat, juicy (yet cooked to "well done" to avoid any nasty intestinal bugs) cheeseburger for dinner, and it wasn't going to cost him a thing. The internal happy meter barely wiggled. That thought had held more power six months ago, when he'd started working at Fatty's. Having a cheeseburger for dinner twice a week for six months—even a Fatty Burger—had somewhat dimmed the simple joy of meat, cheese, Fat Sauce, and no bill.

How about he finally had his own place because of this job? If the happy meter were a penis, it would have blinked with interest, but mostly just lain there like a fat, disinterested slug.

I had the best sex of my life eleven days ago.

Ding ding ding! The happy meter had a stiffy. Sam sighed, smiling.

"Break's over," Tineke said, bursting through the kitchen door and making Sam jump. She had an annoying habit of being very *present* wherever she went. Right now, she began messing with lemons or something, meddling with Juan Miguel's plating while he scowled. She didn't seem to care.

"You have a big group just seated in the center," she said to Sam. "I had to push three tables together." She stopped harassing Juan Miguel and looked at him. "Are you thinking about that guy again?"

Sam sighed happily. "Yep."

Juan Miguel snatched his plate away from her while she was distracted. "Stop it," he grumped, fixing whatever she'd "fixed." Juan started muttering to himself in Spanish.

Tineke bounced and clapped her hands. "Tell me about him again. Pleeease?"

Sam rolled his eyes and stood up from the rickety chair he'd been occupying. He managed to stifle his grin. "Later. I have to go back to work now."

Tineke pouted, but she was professional enough not to argue. Barely. She was head of the waitstaff, so she couldn't really get away with making him sit back down and talk. "Okay. But maybe we can overlap our dinner breaks a little?"

Sam laughed.

"I checked your other tables and got menus for the new group, but I bet they're ready to order drinks now," Tineke said, turning back to Juan Miguel and reaching for the plate. He slapped her hand away as Sam walked out of the kitchen, checking the pocket of his apron for his order pad. He kind of liked the white apron thing. It was the only nod to a uniform at Fatty's. Other than jeans, but that was more habit than requirement.

The group in the center was big, but the lighting at Fatty's was so low it was hard to make them all out. Fatty's was all about the mood, the booze, and the burgers. At least that's what Sheff, the owner, said. As far as Sam understood, for Sheff, "ambiance" meant "almost too dark to see your food." Since Fatty's didn't have many windows, it was pretty much always dark, not to mention loud. The acoustics matched the ambiance.

Sam ambled over to the new table. From what he could tell, there were about twelve customers, and everyone in the group wore a suit. They sat a bit stiffly, as if they didn't know each other that well, but they were comfortable enough to chat. The people at the table were mostly men, but a woman sat on the corner closest to him. Something in her body language screamed that she was in charge.

Regardless, he'd learned it was smart to make the women happy; they always seemed to be in control of the tip. Sam smiled his extra-friendly smile as he walked up to her. "Hi! How are all of you doing tonight?"

"We're just fine," the woman answered, smiling back at him. Murmurs around the group agreed with her, and someone coughed.

"I can take your drink orders now and give you all a little longer with the menu, if you need." Sam made a show of looking around the table, even to the shadowy figures at the dim far end, but he focused mostly on the woman in charge.

She didn't even bother to ask anyone. "We'll order drinks and appetizers now—three orders of the truffle-oil fries—and we'll be ready to order dinner when you get back with the drinks."

Oh, she was so in charge. Sam started playing the guessing game as he worked his way around the table, taking orders. What business were they in? A conservative one, judging by the clothes, but not a lucrative business. Not sales—the suits didn't have that flashy edge, and no one was ordering fruity drinks. Salespeople were tropical drinks people.

Not stockbrokers or bankers; they ordered brand-name alcohol with special instructions, like, "I'll have a Sapphire tonic with two limes, a lemon, and a cherry on one of those little plastic swords—a red sword, please." These people were a little more down to earth.

They couldn't be lawyers, either. The suits weren't quite expensive enough, and no one had ordered a $25 glass of wine yet. Lawyers always had at least one wine snob in the group, even at a place like Fatty's.

Fatty's *did* take its booze very seriously.

Sam turned to his ninth customer, down at the shadowy end of the table.

"Hi, Sam," Ian said. He looked entirely too calm, as if he'd had fair warning he was about to see a previous hookup, unlike some people.

"Ian!" Sam gulped. Ian smiled tightly at him, while Sam just stared.

"Friend of yours, Ian?" a woman asked.

"Sam, this is Andrea, one of my coworkers." Sam managed to flick the woman next to Ian a smile, then his eyes went back to Ian. "Sam's my cousin's—" *cough* "—partner's friend. We met a couple weeks ago at a party."

"Eleven days," Sam said.

D'oh! Heat flooded his face. That had to be an attractive look. And telling.

The woman—Andrea—looked at him assessingly.

"Nik's party was eleven days ago," Sam explained to her. *Lame.*

She smiled like the cat with the creamy man and asked Ian, "Is Nik your cousin?"

Ian hesitated just long enough that Sam knew he wasn't comfortable. "No, my cousin's name is Jurgen."

Her surprise was very subtle. Sam wasn't entirely sure he saw it, but he didn't imagine her pausing slightly too long. "That's a very German name."

"Jurgen's father was from Germany."

"Can I take your drink orders?" Sam interrupted, because he really needed to get this over with. Oh, and because it was his job. Yeah. He forced a polite smile.

Ian looked back at him, his face blank. "I'll have a beer, whatever featured microbrew you have on tap."

Andrea ordered a white wine, and Sam moved on around the table on autopilot. Thank God he had the little pad to write orders on, because he didn't remember the rest of the faces he saw, and certainly couldn't recall their individual drinks. He'd have to ask when he came back. He usually prided himself on not having to, but pride had run screaming off about three orders before he finished the group.

Sam dropped the orders off at the bar, nodding woodenly when Sheff grumbled about how many drinks he had to mix. He threw the order for fries on the pass-through, then slammed through the kitchen door. Where the hell was his coat?

Tineke looked up from her magazine, eyes widening. "Sam?"

Sam ignored her and ran back to the employee coatroom to dig out his phone. He nearly dropped it, and thank God Nik was on speed dial because Sam's fingers were fumbley.

"What does Ian do?" Sam asked as soon as Nik answered.

"What? What do you mean?"

"His *job*. What does he *do*?"

"He's some kind of administrator for the State Health Division. I told you this."

"No you didn't!" Sam lowered his voice. "You told me Jurgen's *cousin* worked for the Health Division."

"Yeees," Nik said. "And Ian is Jurgen's cousin, now, isn't he?"

"Yes, but I didn't know that when you told me, did I?"

There was a momentary silence. "Good point," Nik finally said.

"I thought Ian was a firefighter." Sam knew he sounded accusatory, but he couldn't seem to rein it in.

"You heard that, but you didn't hear the thing about the Health Division?"

"He *looks* like a firefighter."

"Well, he was a firefighter, but then he was injured, so now he's an *administrator*."

"How can he be an administrator? No one ordered drinks requiring salt on the rim."

"What are you *talking* about? He's some kind of interagency emergency coordinator. Apparently they don't make enough for salted drinks. Are you at Fatty's?"

"Shit." Sam ran a hand down his face, then beat his forehead against the wall. "Is he out? At work?" he hissed.

He heard Nik asking Jurgen, then, "No, he's passing. Is he at Fatty's *right now*?"

"Shit." Sam hung up and looked into Tineke's excited, horrified face. "Oh my God," he groaned, this time running both hands through his hair.

"Do you want me to take the table, Sam?" He had to give her credit, she dealt with the important stuff first. Before pumping him for information. "Which one is he?"

"No. That's just being cowardly. I may be a giant dork, but I'm not a coward." Sam straightened up. "He's the one in the dark suit, red tie, next to the cougar."

"They all have dark suits and red ties," Tineke said.

"They don't all have cougars." Sam pushed past her to head back out.

Tineke trotted after him. "The woman at the end?"

"No, the other one."

"She's not a cougar! She can't be much over thirty."

"Shit," Sam muttered and walked faster.

"I'm arranging our dinner breaks together," Tineke called after him. "We can commiserate. And you aren't a giant dork."

"I have three younger sisters," Sam said over his shoulder. "I know what 'commiserate' means."

She just smiled.

By the time Sam got back to the dining room, the first of the drink orders was ready to go. And great, Ian's was on the tray. That would be the one order he did know.

Okay, he could do this. Sam steeled himself and picked up the heavy tray, balancing it on his shoulder.

As he was coming up behind Ian's end of the table—approaching Ian from the back; he needed all the advantage he could get—he heard the guy next to Ian say, "Looks like the waiter has a crush on you, Ian."

Sam stopped dead. Could the humiliation get any worse?

It could. It did when Ian chuckled in reply. He clearly forced it out, but he *chuckled*. It was a vaguely familiar sound that, for a split second, drew Sam back into the laundry room of his mind.

Andrea leaned forward, looking past Ian to the guy who'd made the comment. Sam cringed, waiting for whatever she was about to say.

"Tierney, that was uncalled for," she said. The guy spluttered.

Sam blinked. Oh. That was . . . not mean.

As Andrea sat back, she glanced over her shoulder and saw Sam. She must have made a noise, because Ian turned, too, and then the other guy, Tierney. They stared at him with different degrees of embarrassment. For just a millisecond, Ian closed his eyes. Then he stood up. "I'll help you with that," he said, taking a step toward Sam.

"No." Sam was surprised to hear how hard his voice sounded. He cleared his throat, looking Ian in the eye, and kept his voice low so only Ian would hear. "I don't need your help."

Ian looked away. "Sorry." He hesitated a second before sitting back down.

Sorry for what? The one-night stand, or laughing at what that asshole said, or for assuming I'm too weak to lift my own damn tray of drinks?

Did it fucking matter?

Suddenly Tineke was there with the second tray of drinks, looking at him in concern but smiling for the customers, most of whom didn't even know anything was wrong. It was too loud in Fatty's for normal voices to carry far.

With Tineke's help, Sam made it through distributing drinks, and even taking orders—she took the shadowy end of the table, which Sam refused to look at. She even whispered something into Juan Miguel's ear in the kitchen, resulting in his growling and casting hateful glances toward the dining room.

Ian and that dick sitting next to him both got screwed up orders, and Juan Miguel's normally attractive plating was sloppy.

The whole staff rallied around Sam, even Sheff, and Sam hadn't known the man had a clue how to rally. In the end, the group containing Ian left without Sam having to speak with him again, or even meet his eyes.

Afterward, Tineke arranged most of their dinner break together. Sam didn't know how she did it, but Sheff actually helped the other waitstaff when the bar wasn't busy.

"Okay," Tineke interrupted after listening for ten minutes to Sam whining about what had happened, how humiliated he was, and how he was now getting *pissed off*, dammit. "Which pisses you off the most: him saying sorry for the sex, the chuckle, or him offering to take the drinks tray?"

She always asked the hard questions. Sam slumped back in his chair, crossed his arms over his chest, and glared.

She laughed. "Dude, I've got a ten-year-old son. Do your worst. I can take it."

There was only one reasonable response to that. Sam stuck out his tongue at her.

Sam made it through the rest of the night. By the time he helped Tineke shut the place down at eleven thirty, he felt tired, dispirited, and sick. Not *really* sick, just the sort of sick he got when something icky happened in his life and he had to deal with it. Because what else was he going to do? He was a too-tall, too-skinny, not-very-attractive, very-obviously-gay dork. He had shit to deal with on occasion. So he dealt.

It was moments like this Sam wished he was a drinker. Or a runner. Maybe both. Not at the same time, though.

Tineke followed him out the back door, still talking at him. "C'mon, you don't want to ride the bus home after a night like that. Let me give you a ride."

"Don't you need to get home to your kids?"

"My husband's there. They're fine."

Sam stopped in the circle of the parking lot light at the employee entrance. He turned and squeezed Tineke's shoulder. "Really, I just need to be alone."

She wouldn't believe him. Girls never believed anyone wanted to lick their wounds alone; females wanted to pet and coddle and share things. It drove Sam nuts. If he needed coddling and petting, he wanted a hot guy doing it.

But Tineke cocked her head and looked at him carefully. "You really would rather be alone, wouldn't you? Okay, hon, but I expect you to feel better by your shift Saturday. All right?"

Sam was so surprised and relieved, he hugged her. She looked dazed when he let her go, and he felt sort of proud of himself for befuddling her. *Bet her ten-year-old can't do that.*

Sam walked down to the bus stop at the dark end of Fatty's parking lot and checked his watch. Five minutes until the bus arrived. If it was actually on time. He was just debating whether to sit on the bench in the shelter when Ian's voice nearly made him jump out of his skin.

"Sam."

He whirled around to see Ian step out of the shadows under a tree. He could just make out a pickup behind him. "*Shit*! What is *with* you? Can't you lurk in well-lit areas so I know you're there? My God."

Ian stepped closer to the light. "Let me give you a ride home." He was still wearing the suit, but he'd taken off his tie. Sam really hated how good he looked in those clothes, especially with the two top shirt buttons undone. Regardless, a tiny part of him patted itself on the back. *I hooked up with him.*

"No, I'm taking the bus. Go away, Ian."

Ian looked at him silently for a long second. "Please." Somehow, the way he said it, Sam got the feeling it wasn't a word he often dusted off and put into use.

He hesitated. "No."

"Sam."

"Stop saying my name like that! Sheesh, you think that's going to work? It's not. Why do you even want to give me a ride home? We hooked up once because I was convenient, you know it and *I* know it and I'm okay with that, so you can stop feeling guilty. Go away."

"That's not why I feel guilty," Ian said, as if guys felt guilty all the time for how they treated Sam. Well, they did, but they usually weren't such persistent apologizers.

Sam felt righteously annoyed, and surely when he opened his mouth, his brain would provide a scathing retort. "Do you have to sound so *reasonable*? You were a bastard."

Miserable fail.

"I'm sorry. Let me give you a ride home, and I'll show you how sorry I am."

Sam's stomach muscles clenched without his express permission. "Why does that sound like a line?"

"It's not, I swear." Ian hesitated, and Sam could see a smile in the corners of his lips. "Unless you want it to be."

Sam opened his mouth to deny it.

Another miserable fail. "What are you sorry for?" he asked instead, after far too long a pause.

Ian hung his head a second, then looked back up. "For laughing at Tierney's lame comment. That was . . . I'm sorry."

Sam almost shrugged, but he sighed instead. At least Ian wasn't sorry for hooking up. "Okay."

"Okay, you'll let me drive you home?"

"Okay, you're sorry. It's fine. I wish you hadn't done it, but, whatever."

"Let me drive you home?"

The man was a talking parrot with a limited vocabulary. And so fucking sexy in that suit. *Maybe if you let him take you home, you can play businessman and delivery boy.* Sam rolled his eyes at himself. Ian's smile grew.

Sam huffed out an annoyed breath—not that he had any clue who he was annoyed with. "Okay. Drive me home already."

chapter 11

The worst thing about having laughed, even weakly, at Tierney's stupid comment was that Ian had promised himself he wouldn't put up with the man's homophobic crap anymore. After they'd left the restaurant—riding in Tierney's stupid, phallic BMW 7-series back to Ian's work, where they'd left his truck—Tierney had asked, "So what, dude, you fuck that kid? Throw the gay boy a little bone? C'mon, man, you can tell ol' Tierney if you sometimes get a jones for cock."

"Lay off Sam," Ian had growled. Tierney had laughed at him and punched him in the shoulder, but he'd dropped it. Tierney always had that vicious edge in his voice when he joked about Ian's sexual orientation—something he brought up a lot. It was only a matter of time before Tierney saw the obvious, had his little tantrum, and then refused to be buddies with Ian anymore.

Why the fuck were they friends again? Maybe he should have let Tierney fall by the wayside in the last year, just like his job and his occasional half-assed attempts to find women attractive.

But this was his new life, right? Driving a guy he was into home, hoping to, uh, further the relationship. Sometime tonight, Ian had decided he didn't need to figure out why Sam did it for him. It obviously wasn't going away. He'd spent the last eleven days thinking about the kid at random times, sometimes very inopportune ones. Seeing him tonight had convinced Ian the attraction wasn't some weird figment of his imagination.

Sam wasn't really a kid, anyway. More like an adult. And yeah, he wasn't the kind of guy Ian was normally into, but maybe after the accident his tastes had changed. Sometimes people became allergic to stuff as adults. Maybe his hormones had gotten re-keyed or something. Who cared? *Forget about that stuff and focus on Sam.*

"Nik said you used to be a firefighter," Sam said suddenly.

Hell. "Yeah."

Sam waited a few seconds before going on. "But you aren't anymore."

"Nope."

Sam sighed loud enough to fill the truck's cab. "So why is that?"

Ian gripped the steering wheel harder. "Had an accident at work."

Silence. They came to a stop at a red light, only the slight growl of the engine audible. Ian closed his eyes a second, steeling himself. "I had to have surgery on my back, and it took about a year to get back to normal. Sort of normal. I could have had an admin position at the department, but it seemed like a good time to move on."

"Oh," Sam all but whispered, then added in a louder voice, "So, you moved here?"

The light turned green, so Ian started moving, saying casually, "I like Jurgen." *More than the rest of my damn family.*

They drove the rest of the way in near silence, broken only by Sam giving Ian directions while he thought about the best way to talk himself into Sam's place, then talk Sam out of his clothes. The important ones, at least.

Yeah, he was a bastard, thinking about ways to seduce Sam again, but he was nearly certain Sam wanted it too. Ian didn't do dubious consent, but he wasn't feeling dubious tonight, in his dark truck, the air humming with Sam's nerves. The kid kept clearing his throat and readjusting his legs. Ian caught him readjusting his package once.

Yeah, Sam wanted him.

When they pulled into the lot at Sam's apartment complex, Ian still hadn't come up with the best way into the kid's pants.

He could hear the nerves shaking in Sam's voice as he handed Ian the opening he needed. "I thought you were going to show me how sorry you were."

Ian parked in a visitor spot. "You have a roommate?" he asked as he killed the engine and took the keys out of the ignition.

Sam cleared his throat again and poked at a hole in the denim covering his knee. "No."

"I'll come up to your place and show you there."

"That sounds like another line," Sam muttered. Ian got out of the cab and walked around to Sam's side, then watched him through the window as he kept worrying the hole in his jeans. What did the kid's internal dialogue sound like?

Sam's internal dialogue went on forever. He sat there so long that Ian became concerned Sam would talk himself out of this. When he did eventually get out of the pickup, he stood there a few more seconds, looking at Ian. His hand trembled slightly where it rested on the door.

"Okay," Sam said quietly. He sounded hypnotized. That was it: Ian was a snake and had charmed him—the snake analogy fit him tonight. Wait, wasn't it the snake who was charmed by the handler? But he probably shouldn't think like that, or he'd be the one who'd back out.

When Sam finally moved, he kept looking back over his shoulder, so much so that he ran into the handrail of his stairs. Ian grabbed his arm to steady him. "Be careful, kid."

Sam yanked his arm out of Ian's hold. "It's your fault, following me like that. Distracting me."

Good. "Don't let yourself get distracted by me, kiddo," he said.

Sam turned and started upstairs, conspicuously looking forward. He was almost to the top before he said, "Don't tell me what to do. I don't take orders."

Ian took the last three steps in one. He walked up right behind Sam, forcing his body into the alcove of Sam's front door. Pressing his front all along Sam's back, arms bracketing him, palms on the door. "Oh, yes you do, kiddo," Ian said into his ear. "From me you do."

chapter 12

Well, he'd set that up nicely, hadn't he? Gave Ian the perfect opening to go all dominant alpha hero on him. If Sam didn't know better, he'd think his subconscious mind had planned this, but that didn't seem possible. He'd never seen evidence of any part of his mind displaying this kind of intelligence in the past. Of course, his subconscious had never had Ian for motivation before.

He closed his eyes as Ian pressed in closer and spoke again in that threatening, thrilling tone. "You like to fight it, don't you? You try to pretend you aren't submissive, but you like it, kiddo." He started rocking his hips slowly, pushing against Sam's ass.

Oh, God, he's already hard. Sam's forehead thudded softly against the door. He couldn't stop himself from pushing back against Ian. Except . . . something was a little off. Sam struggled to turn around in Ian's hold.

"I don't do that anymore," he said into Ian's face. "I don't take orders." When Ian looked at him with raised eyebrows, Sam amended, "Unless I feel like it."

Ian looked at him from under his lashes. It was a strangely flirty look that threw Sam off-balance. Well, further off-balance. "Do you feel like it tonight?" Ian pulled one hand off the door, sliding it down Sam's arm, then his hip, across his jeans to cup Sam's groin. He even moved in a slightly menacing, completely exciting way. Slowly. Controlled and planned. *Foreplay aforethought.* It made Sam's heart race, and the back of his head hit the door.

Ian's hand found his erection pushing against his fly through the denim. His fingers traced the shape of him while Sam watched in the porch light. "Wanna come inside?" he croaked.

They didn't make it past the entry. Ian shut the front door behind him with a soft *click* and pushed Sam against the wall, forcefully enough that it made his knees weak. Ian stared at him, hand splayed on Sam's chest, so close but not kissing him—Sam could read the indecision in his face, and then the moment when he decided not to. *That* firmed his knees up again.

So it was like that. *Of course it's like that, idiot. It's always been like that.* Sam nearly shook his head at his romantic self. Ian wasn't some gothic, tortured, romantic lead; he was just some horny guy in real life.

Besides, in tortured, gothic romances it took the hero *way* longer than this to give in to his heart's desires and kiss the heroine. Therefore, Ian couldn't be that type of character; Sam's proof was in the way Ian's thumb started slowly stroking his chest, smoothing and pulling the fabric of his shirt across his sensitive skin. He was totally giving in to his urges, just not the ones involving his lips.

But say Ian *was* a TGH (Tortured, Gothic Hero). The timeline for Main Character One to accept the love of Main Character Two was really long in those old-school romances, so Ian not kissing him was putting them right on track. Sam (as Main Character Two, of course—he preferred that to "heroine") couldn't expect the salve of his love and tenderness to heal the wounded heart of Ian (Main Character One) for at least two hundred pages. So it was *possible*, right?

Okay, genius, if he's the tortured hero, what does that make you?

That was a tough question, one he was having difficulty working out the answer to with Ian gently kneading his chest, staring into his eyes, his rapid breaths falling on Sam's mouth as he leaned closer. Sam could see each whisker on Ian's face, and not only watch but *feel* Ian's lips part. He tilted his head a tiny bit, preparing for the kiss he might get after all, telling Ian he *wanted* it.

Then Ian's face veered slightly to the side, his cheek rasping across Sam's like an iceberg grazing a cruise ship.

"I want you to suck my cock," Ian whispered in Sam's ear before biting his lobe. And that's when it hit Sam. If Ian was a TGH, that made Sam . . .

Too Stupid to Live.

Sam closed his eyes in resignation. He was TSTL. Stupid enough to investigate the locked fourth story of the manor house, where the human screams originated; stupid enough to run out onto the moors at night to find the howling wolves. Stupid enough to want to suck Ian's cock again. And the whole time, he'd be thinking he could somehow further the plot via his stupidity.

They stood there in some kind of sexual stasis while Sam thought it over. The problem was he loved sucking cock. *Loved* it. Could almost come from it alone. He wanted to know more about what it felt like to suck a guy with foreskin, but even more, he wanted the chance to get Ian's bull nuts into his mouth. If he could do that . . . roll Ian's balls across his tongue and fist his dick, stroke him until Ian came in his hair . . . Sam hit his knees, still shivering from the image.

He'd opened Ian's slacks and was mouthing him through his briefs before Ian could finish sucking in a surprised breath. He pulled Ian's pants down just past his hips, then his plain white underwear. He had to get those out of the way; just tucking them behind Ian's scrotum—*guh*—wouldn't give him the kind of access he'd want later. He wrapped his fingers around Ian's cock, watching the skin slide back on his shaft and then cover the glans again. Then he felt Ian's hand grip his hair. Shit, should he have asked before touching?

Sam stopped and looked up at Ian.

"You can explore." Ian's voice sounded strained. "Feels good."

Something was missing. Sam slowly stroked Ian's cock again, watching his face. Glassy eyes; check. Parted, wet lips; check. Breath coming faster; check. *Hmmm.* "Where's your tie?"

"What?" Ian asked. "My what?" His slitted eyes widened.

"That tie you had on earlier. The red one. Put it on, please?"

"You want to suck me while I'm wearing a tie?" Ian looked befuddled. Sam lowered his head to avoid smiling in Ian's face, and watched his own hand smoothly stroke down and up Ian's cock, the blunt tip appearing and disappearing, slightly wet and glistening. It was so tempting, but . . . Sam looked back up. Ian had stopped breathing.

Sam made himself meet Ian's eyes. "Yeah," he whispered. "Please wear the tie?"

Ian started fumbling in his suit pockets, then his coat pockets, finally pulling it out of the parka. "This tie?" He ran his hands along it. Sam could hear them smooth across the fabric.

"That tie. Please?" If Ian wrapped that around Sam's dick, would he be able to feel the difference? Know when Ian had his hand on silk or on skin?

Ian brought the tie around the back of his neck, almost dropping it. "You have a fantasy about being on your knees in front of a guy with a tie on, don't you kiddo?" He was trying to knot it, throwing one end around the other in a way Sam knew wasn't going to work.

Sam swallowed and tilted his head back a little more, continuing the slow stroking rhythm. "I do now."

Ian's fingers looked like they were doing more harm than good to the tie. Sam ducked his head quickly, hiding another smile. He had a feeling Ian wasn't in this position very often—the one of being unsteady and possibly flustered. Sam let go of his dick, stood up, and reached for the tie. "Let me tie it."

"I know how to tie a tie," Ian said in a breathy but sharp voice.

"I figured, since you manage to dress yourself in the mornings. Just let me do it. It's part of the fantasy." That last bit was supposed to be a way for Ian to save face, but Sam realized it was true. The only thing he'd like better than knotting Ian's tie and kneeling to suck his cock would be to have Ian wrap the tie around his wrists and bind them together.

Sam looked up from the red fabric. Had Ian heard that noise he'd made? He was still watching Sam's hands.

He concentrated on the knot again, but his fingers now shook. He might, kinda sorta, want Ian to tie him up *someday*, but not tonight. He didn't know Ian. Couldn't actually trust him. Maybe if they saw each other a few times . . .

He dropped back to his knees, gripped Ian's dick again, and let himself taste—slowly, in small doses, licking every part of his head. When he slid his tongue under Ian's foreskin, Ian gasped and gripped his hair tighter. He had no idea what that hand was doing to fuel Sam's fantasies, like the one of Ian grabbing his hair while fucking Sam's mouth . . .

Sam sucked Ian in by millimeters, looking up to see his eyes were closed and his teeth were clenched. *I put that look on his face.* Sam took all the little victories he could. He knew he wasn't the best cocksucker in the world; Marley had told him so enough times. He just really, really liked to do it. Liked the flavor and the noise and, yes, liked being on his knees.

If this was just sex between them? Ian could damn well suffer through a mediocre blowjob, because that's what Sam wanted to do.

He focused on learning all about foreskin. He discovered he could slide it back, and it would turn itself inside out and cover Ian's cock in sensitive, almost raw-looking skin. Sam formed his mouth into an "o" and slid his spit-slicked lips up and down the pink, all the way to where it ended at a rougher patch. Ian grunted, yanking on Sam's hair, which sent messages like "action imminent, prepare the troops" straight to his nuts. He moaned, looking up, and Ian's slitted eyes met his for an instant.

Some circuit completed itself when they locked gazes. A current traveled through Sam and flowed into Ian's body, but then Ian closed his eyes and it ended.

Sam's own aching dick clamored for attention, but he let the tension build. Ignored his complaining knees and closed his eyes and sunk himself into the feel and sound of bringing Ian off. He sucked cock mostly by sound. The sound of his tongue sliding over skin, the sucking noises, but most importantly the sounds Ian made. Little involuntary noises, the feels-so-good *mmmmm*'s and vocal exhalations. Soft *uh*'s and surprised grunts when Sam got creative. Moans stifled in the back of his throat. Sam felt each little sound like a drop of water hitting his body.

When the feel of Ian's fingers gripping his hair ached as much as Sam's dick, and Ian's hips were rocking fast, Sam grasped him with a hand and used his tongue to follow a vein down Ian's shaft until Ian's balls were bumping his chin.

Fuck, it smelled so good right there, like concentrated skin and that sweat smell and musk unique to Ian. Ian's scent was so thick in this one perfect spot that Sam could taste him in the air. It made his muscles weak and invigorated him at the same time.

Straining his eyes, he could just see the shaking tip of his tongue reaching for Ian's balls. His first *real* taste of Ian was almost sweet. Sam brought the flavor into his mouth and savored it. Was it his imagination that men in their thirties tasted differently? Aged like fine wine.

"Sam?" Ian asked, still breathing heavily.

Sam was beyond caring what Ian wanted. He jacked his hand up, slipping foreskin over the head of Ian's cock to keep him busy while Sam gave into temptation and ate Ian's balls. Sucked them in and rolled them around, dragged the broad flat of his tongue across soft skin and hair. Worked his way behind them to taste the flavor right there, because that's where the gold was.

And thank God for wide mouths, because he could fit both of Ian's nuts in at the same time. Barely, but he'd gladly look like a chipmunk to suck on them like this. He felt Ian's hand close over his on Ian's dick, forcing Sam to stroke him faster, foreskin slipping back and forth. Sam could see Ian's red tie at the edge of his vision, knuckles flying past, and Ian's thighs tensing and trembling.

He gorged on testicles until he was gasping, drool running down his chin, the sound of skin on skin loud in his ears. Ian yanked on his hair, but didn't really care what the message might be.

Sam almost gagged from stuffing too much of Ian into his mouth and down his throat, but then he found that secret, concentrated taste he was looking for: the caviar of ball fetishists. Licking him there was a full-on mouthgasm. Sam moaned and kneaded his own dick roughly, happy to find his hand already on it.

"Fuck," Ian groaned, and then he was coming. His scrotum pulled up, fighting Sam for possession of his nuts. His hand yanked on Sam's hair and then he shot cum into it, and with Ian's flavor on Sam's tongue, it was too much to resist. Sam came in his jeans, moaning and fighting to keep his prize in his mouth right until the last second.

When he finally pulled off and collapsed on the floor, Ian fell against the wall, gasping for breath. Sam shut his eyes and did the same where he lay.

That was so worth debasing myself for. If he was going to let some guy use him, at least he got what he'd wanted out of it.

Except for the rapidly cooling wet patch on his jeans. He could have done without that.

chapter **13**

Ian watched Sam sprawled on the floor, sucking in air, face wet and red, his light, wispy hair sticking to his forehead. His lips looked like someone had injected them with saline, a sight so hot Ian's balls tingled. And *fuck*—his balls. He'd never felt anything quite like that.

Looked like his kiddo had a taste for testicles. Ian slid down the wall, not bothering to pull up his pants, and—to his surprise—flopped on the floor on his side, facing Sam. "Jesus Christ you're good at that," he said, still panting. He watched Sam's eyes fly open to stare at the ceiling.

"I am?"

"Hasn't anyone ever told you before?"

"No. I mean, Marley told me I was okay at it—"

Sam flushed at Ian's snort. "Sam, I've had my dick sucked by a lot of guys, and you're in the top three." Ian winced as soon as he heard himself say the words. Not the most complimentary way to put it.

But Sam flushed even deeper and turned his head away, like he was trying to hide his embarrassed smile. "Thank you," he said in the softest, shyest voice imaginable, turning his head back to meet Ian's eyes.

Ian wanted to touch Sam's face, but his hand felt paralyzed. The fuck was that? He held still—held his breath, even—as Sam lost the pleased smile and his eyebrows pulled together, putting a little line between them.

Ian was still staring at it when Sam said, "Is that why you hooked up with me again?"

Hell. He had the feeling he was swimming in shark-infested waters. He didn't know what to say, so he was just going to have to lay it on the line, like he would with any guy. "I couldn't stop thinking about you."

Not what he'd meant to say.

Sam still had that wrinkle between his brows. If Ian was going to say something revealing, the least Sam could do was lose the worry line. Instead he looked annoyed. When he suddenly pulled his T-shirt up to wipe off his face, it was with jerky movements. Ian looked at his soft, concave stomach.

So not his type.

"I'm not your type, Ian."

"What? Says who?"

"You," Sam said. "The day we met."

Aw, fuck it. Ian reached out for Sam, resting a hand on his dished-in abdomen. "Maybe my type has changed."

"Why, 'cause your type can't generally suck dick like I can?" He sounded sarcastic, but Ian could see the small smile Sam still fought. He liked being good at that.

"'Cause I got to know you, and I like you."

"You barely know me."

"I didn't say I know you well. Just a little. A guy can change his mind, can't he? Or can only women do that?"

"Oh my God," Sam muttered. "He's a misogynist, too."

"That's not misogyny, it's sarcasm."

Sam lost the brow wrinkle. Now Ian kind of missed it. "Nik said you're some kind of public administrator."

"I'm the Interagency Disaster Relief Coordination Director for the State Health Division." Ian thought back to make sure he'd recited all the words that made up his stupid title.

"Oh," Sam said. They stared at each other. "I'm still not your type."

Hell, they were back to this? "Why don't you tell me why not."

"I'm too skinny," Sam said.

"No you aren't. You're fine. You don't look anorexic or anything."

"There's a big difference between not being anorexic and being hot. I'm in between those two points and you know it. You like muscle on your guys. Tell me you thought I was attractive when you first saw me."

Ian opened his mouth, and barely stopped himself from saying, "I didn't." But he was left with his mouth hanging open, looking suspicious. Like maybe he'd been about to say, "I didn't."

Sam looked away. Farther away. He'd been looking at Ian's chin before, but now he was staring over his shoulder. "Exactly. I'm not attractive. You know how many guys I've ever asked out? One. You, when we first met. You shot me down." The entryway filled with silence, except for the sound of Ian shifting his legs uncomfortably. Jesus, was he fidgeting?

Sam went on with the torture. "You think any guy like you has ever come on to me before? A guy who could have anyone? Of course not, *because* you can have anyone, so why would you want a guy who's gangly and too skinny? Except my mouth. That's too big."

Finally. "It's not too big. Every time I look at your mouth I get turned on."

Now Sam focused on him, twisting his sexy-puffy lips. "What, all three times you've seen me?"

Hell. "Okay, fine." Fuck it, he wasn't going to lie. "The first time, no. I mean, I kind of thought you looked like that guy on that show where those kids sing, but it didn't do anything for me. Not until after you sucked me off. Now that I know what you can do with your mouth, yeah, it makes me hot."

"What show where the kids sing?"

"They're in high school. They sing. They get slushies in the face."

"*Glee*? You think I look like Trouty Mouth on *Glee*?" Sam asked, like maybe that was an okay thing.

"Uh, yeah. Your mouth looks like his." Especially when he had puffy, pink dick lips.

Sam scrunched his brow. "So you're saying tonight it got you hot. Was that before or after you laughed at your friend's comment about the gay waiter?"

Fuck, he could *not* be blushing. Ian didn't do that. He tried to force the heat out of his cheeks with the power of his mind.

Sam pointed a finger in his face. "You know what got to me most about that? That he knew I was gay just by looking at me. Not because I'm one of those cute little blond gay boys who're six inches under average height and have sexy asses. No, I'm an overgrown bland gay boy who can't hide it. When you're one of those cute little twink guys, at least you have fag hags and the other stereotypical benefits of being gay, like clothes hanging well on you. But *noooo*, I'm the dorky type of gay guy. I'm swishy, but I'm too tall and gawky to pull it off."

Wait, why did it sound like Sam blamed him for this? "What the hell? What do you want me to say, Sam? I barely know you."

Sam's face blanched, and he pushed up from the floor and sat against the wall, bringing his knees up in front of him. Ian closed his eyes, feeling weird. Guilty. But what the fuck did he have to feel guilty about?

"You're right," Sam said. "You barely know me. I think this hookup is over, and you need to go."

Ian hadn't expected to get away this easily. He'd thought it over earlier and figured if he went home with Sam tonight he'd be here for the duration. What a relief.

Shouldn't I feel more relieved?

"Bye, Ian," Sam prodded.

He sighed, rolled over onto his back and put himself away, then pushed up. Sam was staring at the floor in front of him. Ian couldn't help but touch his head for just a moment. "Bye, Sam." When he pulled his hand away, there was cum on it.

Nice. He probably deserved that.

Sam didn't look at him as Ian let himself out.

chapter 14

The phone rang way too early the next morning. Sam cracked an eyelid and made himself focus on the clock. 11:23 ante meridiem. Therefore, too early, at least on the mornings after he worked at Fatty's and then whored himself in his entryway. But because Sam was unfailingly nice, he answered the dumb phone.

"'Lo?"

"Can you talk?" Nik hissed in his ear.

Huh? "Mom says I started right after my first birthday. I pretty much have it down pat by now."

Nik continued in a hushed voice, "Shut up. Ian didn't stay?"

Sam sat up. "How did you know about Ian?"

"I *knew* something happened last night! Tell."

Great. Sam flopped back on his pillow. "No. Mind your own business."

"Come on. I tell you about me and Jurgen," Nik whined.

"No, you actually don't." He ran a hand through his hair, wincing when it got stuck on something and pulled on his scalp. Oh yeah. He'd been so depressed last night he'd gone to bed without washing the cum out. *Yuck.*

"That's because it's . . . different." Nik's voice was weird. Soft. He usually spoke in sharp tones.

"How's that?" Sam asked, honestly curious. He threw back the blankets and pulled himself out of bed, heading for the shower.

There was a silence—another unusual feature when talking with Nik. Sam stopped moving and held his breath. "He's special. To me," Nik finally said, sounding like he was confessing a sin.

"Oh, Nik," Sam breathed. "That's sweet." See? That's what Sam wanted: someone special. Not Ian.

"Shut up," Nik said. "So, is that why you won't tell me about Ian? Because it's special?"

"Ha. It was demeaning." Okay, that might have been a bit harsh. "It was just a hookup," he amended. "Nothing important." Nothing romantic. Just really, really hot.

"So you can tell me."

Sam huffed out a breath. "He gave me a ride home, I blew him in the entryway, he left. He didn't even kiss me."

"No kiss?" Nik sounded disappointed. He may be annoying, but he really was a good friend. "That's *not* special. And you don't really have an entryway. You just have a linoleum square."

But Nik was mostly just annoying. "*That's* my entryway," Sam reminded him.

"Why won't you get a bigger place with a roommate again?"

"I'm tired of having a roommate. I like living by myself. Besides, if I had a roommate, I couldn't give blowjobs in my entryway."

They began the familiar argument. Nik never passed up the opportunity to urge Sam to move, though why he cared was a mystery. Finally, they argued themselves to a standstill. Before hanging up, Sam asked Nik not to tell Jurgen about Ian.

"I don't have to tell him, he's been listening to my side of the conversation."

Sam pinched the bridge of his nose. "Okay, can you just ask him not to say anything to Ian?"

"I'll try," Nik said. Sam was not reassured. It didn't matter anyway, because he was never going to see Ian again.

chapter 15

On Thursday morning, Ian went to work and found himself staring at his desk for fifteen minutes before Andrea knocked on his door and walked in, carrying a mug. He grabbed a pen and a notepad, trying to seem like he'd actually been doing something.

Andy carefully set the coffee-filled mug on his desk and readjusted a couple of paper clips, his stapler, and a pen. She straightened up, inspecting her redecoration attempts and smoothing her skirt.

Ian wasn't the best with body language, but he got the feeling she was nervous.

"How's your coffee?" she said.

That was for *him?* In spite of being her boss, she'd never brought him coffee before. Huh. "I haven't tried it yet." *Obviously.* "Thank you for bringing me some."

Andy clasped her hands and straightened her shoulders. "Ian, um, I have something to talk to you about."

"Okay, have a seat."

She sat in the chair across from him.

They looked at each other across the desk.

"Is this about work?" he asked.

Andy nodded quickly. "Um, sort of. It's work-related." She took a deep breath. "Are you attracted to men?"

Ian's brain skidded to a halt. He stared across his desk at her.

She slowly turned red. "I really don't care, I was just curious," she said. "It was none of my business, I shouldn't have asked." She was saying the right things, but something in her face made him think that it did kind of matter somehow.

Ian ran a hand across his jaw. *Okay* . . . "So, you don't need to talk about work."

She ducked her head. "Sort of. I mean . . . No. I was just . . . I'm sorry."

"Does it matter to you if I'm gay?"

She jerked upright. "No!" This time he believed her—she looked at him like he had completely missed some point. *What the fuck?*

Andy closed her eyes after a second and leaned forward to massage her forehead with her hand. "Listen," she said. "It's none of my business, it's just that Tierney's a known homophobe, and I know he's a college buddy of yours. I thought, if you were gay and didn't know about him . . ." She shrugged stiffly.

Ian coughed. "I'm well aware Tierney's a 'phobe."

Andy nodded slowly, looking down at the surface of his desk. Ian stared at her, thinking hard. He hadn't expected this to happen quite this soon. He had a planned answer for these kinds of situations, but now that he was facing it . . .

Wuss.

Fine. He unstuck his tongue from the roof of his mouth and took a breath. "Yeah. I'm gay."

Andy's eyes widened. "You seem so *straight*."

Oh, for fuck's sake. The first time he'd ever come out to anyone outside his family, and that's the reply he got?

"Oh, God," Andy moaned, covering her face with her hand. "I'm so sorry, that was the lamest thing to say. Just tell me to shut up."

"Shut up."

"Thank you," she said from between her fingers.

"You're welcome."

Another uncomfortable pause, then they both spoke at once.

"Since you and Tierney are working on that project—"

"Listen, I've never told anyone I work with—"

They shut up in unison.

Ian held up a hand and tried again. "Tierney doesn't know, okay? You're officially the only person I've ever worked with who knows, and I'm trusting you to keep quiet until I tell people—"

Andy overrode his hand. "Oh my God, Ian! I would never *out* you. What kind of person do you think I am?"

"The kind of person who asks her boss if he's gay?"

She bit her lip. "Oh, crap. I guess I did do that. I won't tell anyone, you can trust me. And at least we don't have anyone else in this suite to worry about overhearing us yet."

Ian jumped right on that subject as a viable escape from the current one. "Yeah, we need some help around here. Are we ready to start interviewing?" They needed to hire two coordinators to assist them and a secretary for the brand new Interagency Disaster Relief Coordination Department that Ian headed in the Health Division.

"Yeah, um, that's another thing I wanted to talk to you about. My little brother has some secretarial experience, and—"

"Are you serious?" Ian groaned.

"He's gay?" she offered.

"So I'm supposed to hire him because he's *family*? Andy, c'mon." They quickly fell into the sort of banter Ian had already become used to with her. *Thank God.* He finally agreed to interview her brother, and she agreed to do some of his paperwork in exchange.

Before Andy left, he told her, "I trust you."

She smiled, then asked, "Did you apologize to your friend for laughing at Tierney's comment?"

If Ian hadn't been so surprised Andy had the balls to ask, he would have refused to answer. But he only cleared his throat and said, "Yeah."

Andy was a wily thing.

On Friday morning during his appointment with his therapist, Janet, Ian spent the first half of the hour staring at her spider plant and talking about all the things he'd been avoiding during his previous sessions. The spider plant was the most colorful thing in the room. She had a pale yellow couch, cream walls, white shades over the windows— streaming white light into the room. Even her desk was white.

He'd only been her client a month, so he didn't have a lot of material for avoidance, and the spider plant wasn't much of an assist. If he were still in California with his former therapist, he'd have been able to fill the whole hour with problems he'd dodged. Besides, Ned had a really colorful oriental rug.

Finally, it was either talk about his mother's death or talk about the other thing he'd been trying to avoid. He gave up on the plant and turned to Janet, trying to decide. She looked back at him with her customary calm.

Hell. He slumped in his seat. "I met someone."

Janet raised an eyebrow, somehow still looking benign. It was a ruse. "A man?"

"Yes." Ian paused to clear the frog out of his throat. "He's a lot younger than me."

She smiled. "Is he of legal age?"

"Of course!"

"Then does it matter how much younger he is?"

"Don't know," he muttered.

"Do you want to talk about him?"

Ian crossed his arms over his chest. "No."

She shrugged. "Okay, what do you want to talk about?"

"He's almost ten years younger than me. That's not so bad, right?"

"Lots of men your age feel pride when they attract someone in their early twenties."

Ian straightened up, struck by the thought.

Janet broke the silence again. "So, you're seeing someone?"

"No, I met someone."

"Well, it must be significant for you to mention it."

"Yeah, well . . . I had sex with him."

Janet raised both eyebrows but didn't say anything.

Ian sighed. "I know I wasn't supposed to hop into bed with anyone until . . ."

Janet waited a few seconds for him to go on before she said, "You're the one who decided it was better for your development to not have casual sex. I don't disagree with your choice, and neither did Ned, but that doesn't make it a bad thing, or equate to failure. If he means something to you . . ." That damn eyebrow went up again, and she tilted her head. He knew that trick—she was trying to make direct eye contact.

Ian looked out the window. "I don't know if I *feel* anything. I'm supposed to be making—" he cleared his throat and *didn't* squirm "—emotional connections with, um, people."

"So this was a purely sexual connection?"

"No." He rubbed his palm on his thigh. God this was uncomfortable. He paid this woman to listen to all kinds of shit he didn't want to talk about, and this was the worst so far. "Not *purely* sexual." Mostly, maybe.

"I didn't think so. I don't think you would have mentioned him to me if it was."

Damn her damned doctorate in psychology. Ian sighed. "I guess not."

"You want to see this man again?"

"Yes." That surprised the hell out of him—more so than hearing himself say it wasn't just a sexual connection. "I do."

"Have you asked him how he feels?"

Ian lifted his head, horrified. "Am I supposed to?"

"Generally yes, that's the way these things work. I'd recommend not just informing him he's going to see you because you like him." Janet failed to smother a laugh.

"Thanks," he muttered.

"No problem. That'll be one hundred fifty dollars."

Ian went back to staring at her. "My insurance pays for—"

"That was a joke, Ian," she gently interrupted.

"Are therapists allowed to crack jokes?"

"This one is, unless you'd prefer she didn't."

Ian rubbed his thigh more, thinking. "No. I guess I kind of like it."

On Saturday night, Ian stood at Sam's door, waiting for him to arrive home from work. He couldn't explain away why he was doing something so supremely dorky, so he had another approach in mind. And here came Sam now, climbing the stairs. Waiting here for him was phase one of Ian's master plan.

Sam reached the top—after plodding up like only the truly exhausted working stiff could—and stopped. He frowned at Ian, as if he wasn't quite sure what he was.

Ian smiled.

Sam blinked. Blink. Blink, blink.

"Can I come in?" Ian asked after a few more blinks.

Sam heaved a sigh. "I guess," he said, finally digging his keys out of his pocket. Ian stood behind him, not too close, while he worked the lock. Once Sam had the apartment door open, Ian followed him in, and immediately moved to phase two of the plan.

He grabbed Sam's arm, turned him around, and backed him up against a wall, looking into his eyes the entire time he leaned toward him, right until Sam got too blurry to see. He wanted Sam to know he knew what he was doing.

A guy like him didn't purposely kiss a guy like Sam without it meaning something. A guy like him didn't *date* a guy like Sam without talking about it first. This kiss would make sure Sam knew what was coming.

Sort of. It made sense to him.

When he kissed Sam, nothing made sense anymore.

In spite of advancing slowly, staring into Sam's eyes the whole time, the kid wasn't ready for the kiss. Ian could tell by the way his jaw hung slack for those first few seconds. Then his chin tilted up as he stretched for more. He tilted his head and opened wider, rubbing his tongue against Ian's like an affectionate cat that wanted to be petted.

Theoretically, Ian owned this kiss, but in reality he didn't own shit. Sam was soft and malleable in his mouth and under his lips, and he responded to tiny cues from Ian, until Ian just needed *more*. More of Sam, and more of his acquiescence. He let go of Sam's tongue and bit his lip instead, making him moan back in his throat and push his hips off the wall and into Ian's. When Sam moaned like that—so low Ian felt the vibrations—Ian realized who was really in control here.

It's only for this one kiss.

When he finally did end the kiss, pulling slowly away and letting go of Sam, he couldn't catch his breath. He stood there panting into Sam's face, unable to make himself move more than an inch or two. He needed to keep that mouth nearby. It was some kind of national treasure only Ian knew about. He watched his thumb tracing Sam's reddened lower lip. Had he bitten it too hard? He had to fight back the urge to test Sam's limits for teeth.

Would he like to be bitten other places? He'd liked it when Ian had bitten his shoulder. Suddenly, Ian wanted to bite Sam's sharp, bony hip so badly he nearly dropped to his knees. He reached for Sam's zipper with the hand not occupied with Sam's lips.

"Why did you kiss me?"

Oh, yeah, talking. Ian redirected his hand to Sam's hip, resting it there. He let his fingers have some license, splaying them on Sam's butt cheek and hooking his thumb over his iliac crest. *Right there. I wanna bite him right there.*

"Ian?" Sam's voice was losing its breathless quality.

He cleared his throat. "I wanted to kiss you."

"Why?"

"I want to see you."

"You're looking at me."

"No, I mean I want to *see* you."

Sam's mouth fell open. Then snapped shut. Then fell open again. "*See* me?"

"Yeah." Ian looked into his grayish eyes. Sam had lots of reasons to tell Ian to fuck off, and only one—great sex—to say okay. Ian had an inkling it might take him longer than an hour or two to shrug it off if Sam said no.

"Why?"

"I like you."

"You barely know me."

"I like what I know."

"I'm still not attractive."

"Yes you are. You're cute." Ian winced when he said it. *Hell*. What guy wanted to be called cute?

Sam, apparently. His cheeks slowly pinked, and his eyes got round. "I'm cute?"

Ian cleared his throat again. "Yeah. Cute."

Sam laid his hand on Ian's chest. "Okay."

Relief flowed through him from Sam's touch. Ian kissed him one more time, quickly. He had plans; he didn't want to stay here making out and grinding Sam into the wall all night. Well, he did, but he wanted something else even more. "Come home with me?"

Sam's Adam's apple bobbed as he swallowed. "Okay," he said, and Ian couldn't help but smile at him.

"You need to get some stuff together?" Sam nodded. "You eat anything tonight?" Sam's eyes got big all over again, and he bit his lip before nodding. Ian watched his teeth gnaw on his flesh.

"You better get moving, then." He forced himself back before he replaced those teeth with his own. Slowly, Sam pushed himself off the wall, stepping from the square of linoleum to the carpet.

chapter 16

Cute.

The word floated in Sam's brain while he was throwing things together to go to Ian's. Picking his way through the piles of clothes, books, and whatever that populated his floor. And his furniture. No wonder Ian wanted to go to his place.

Cute.

Ian thought he was *cute*. No one had ever called him anything like cute before. Not even Nik, who often told him to stop worrying, he was attractive to a certain type of guy. Sam had always assumed Nik meant the kind of guy who wasn't attractive to much of anyone, like Marley.

He snuck another glance at Ian, standing near the door with his thumbs hooked in the pockets of his jeans, his black leather jacket spilling over his forearms, watching him. Sam stumbled over something on the floor. He looked down, embarrassed at being a klutz in front of Ian, even if it was kind of Ian's fault for making him nervous.

Oh. He'd tripped over the single bare patch of floor in his entire apartment.

Sam sighed and wished Ian would stop watching him. There was that tiny little place inside of him that was terrified Ian would see how gawky and unattractive he really was, and say, "You know what? I changed my mind."

Okay, well, it was actually a biggish part inside of him.

"I think I'll wait outside." Sam jumped and whirled to face Ian when he spoke. He looked like he was trying to stifle a smile.

"Okay," Sam croaked.

After Ian walked out, Sam slumped in relief—until it occurred to him that Ian might be making his getaway. He tiptoe-ran over and put his ear to the door, sucking in a breath when he heard Ian's footsteps trail off toward the stairs. *Dammit, he decided I'm a dork, he is leav—*

Sam's inner monologue shut up when he heard Ian's feet stop, then start up again, but this time heading back toward Sam's door. *He changed his mind!*

Ian's footsteps reached the door, then paused. Sam heard a sort of foot-drag sound, then Ian started walking away again. Slowly. *Shit! He changed his mind. Again!*

Sam listened to Ian make the circuit three or four more times before he realized Ian was pacing. Impatiently? Had *he* made Ian impatient? Sam leapt away from the door and started shoving random items into his backpack again.

He was in the bathroom, grabbing whatever, thinking about how Ian had actually wanted to *feed* him before taking him home and fucking him, when he realized he needed to take a shower. He froze mid-reach, staring at himself in the mirror.

He knew what was going to happen when they got to Ian's house, and he definitely needed to wash first.

Okay. Ian would probably let him take a shower there, right? He wasn't inviting Sam over to *sleep* with him. He wanted to *stay awake* with him. And he'd want Sam to be, you know, *clean* before they got all dirty. So Ian would let him take a shower.

Or maybe he should ask. He groaned at himself in the mirror. Oh, God, no. That was dorky, wasn't it?

Sam argued himself into a mental dither. Finally, he took himself firmly in hand, grabbed his toothbrush, and determined he'd simply ask if he could take a shower when they got to Ian's place.

When he whipped the front door open, Ian was standing right outside it. Sam watched his shoulders drop—if he didn't know better, he'd think Ian's shoulders had been trying to climb to his ears.

"I was starting to think you'd changed your mind," Ian said, smiling a small, tight smile. Sam stared at him. Seriously? Why would he ever change his mind?

"Ready to go?" Ian asked in a stronger voice.

"Totally." Sam nodded and threw his backpack over his shoulder.

chapter 17

Ian looked at Sam in his living room and thought about what he needed to say, now that they'd made it this far.

Yes, he wanted to see Sam. But he had some rules . . . maybe he should call them guidelines. He had some guidelines he needed to put into place before anything else happened, especially after that kiss. He didn't really want to do this now, but they needed to have the conversation he'd been avoiding since the first time they hooked up.

He also needed to make sure Sam understood that this might not lead to anything. Thinking you maybe might kinda want more than sex wasn't good enough. What if it turned out he didn't? He couldn't mislead Sam. Jurgen would never forgive him.

Ian took a breath. "So, if we're going to start—" he cleared his throat "—seeing each other regularly, maybe we need a few, um, parameters." Parameters—that was the perfect word.

Sam stopped looking around and turned to Ian, silent for a long second. "Parameters?" he asked.

"Yeah, so there are no misunderstandings about how serious this is going to get."

Sam fiddled with the strap of the pack hanging in his hand, frowning. "You're going to put a limit on how serious *this* will be? What's *this*, exactly?"

Okay, yeah, excellent place to start. "This is you and me, hooking up a few times a week because we have hot sex. And I like you, you know, platonically."

This time there were many, many seconds of silence while Sam studied him with slightly narrowed eyes. "Sooo . . . by 'seeing' me, you meant you'll see me naked in bed a couple times a week, but you won't be seen *with* me. In public. Were you going to get me a Batphone or something, so you can call me up and tell me when to meet you in the Batcave? What about Batgirl, is she invited? Because I don't really want to perform for her or, you know, *involve* her."

Ian laughed, but it fell flat on the floor. He choked it off. "Well, yeah, it's about sex—"

Sam pointed a finger at him. "I'm not going to be someone's secret gay hookup." He pulled his hand back and slapped himself in the forehead. "I should have known when I found out you were passing as straight to just stay the hell—"

"I'm not passing as straight." He was so surprised he took a step toward Sam. "I used to when I worked for the fire department, but I'm not denying I'm gay anymore. Is that what Jurgen told you?" Dammit, Jurgen would do anything to fuck this up for him, wouldn't he? *Asshole.*

Sam looked at him from under his hand. "Nik told me," he mumbled.

Ian clenched his teeth and counted to ten in his head. Fine. He'd never told Nik and Jurgen otherwise. Not to mention getting mad at Nik wouldn't get him what he wanted. "I'm not going to hide you away," he said evenly.

"Okay," Sam said. He didn't sound convinced. He gripped his too-long hair, pulling on it.

Dammit. Ian took another step forward. "I'm honest about it with people if they ask. I'm not sending announcements out, but I'm not lying anymore." One of his hands wanted to reach for the kid, but he didn't let it.

"'Kay," Sam said, nodding slightly. "So . . . did anyone ask you after that night at Fatty's?" He lowered his hand to his side, looking up at Ian from under his brows.

Hell. "Yeah. Two people."

"And you told them?"

Ian took an unobtrusive deep breath. "I told one, but the other guy . . . he wasn't really asking. The guy who made that remark about you, Tierney—he was just trying to give me shit. I'll tell him eventually." Ian had the sense he was losing Sam, here. "I told my assistant Andrea when she asked, though."

Sam chewed on his lip. "So . . . Andrea works with you, and so does Tierney?"

"Sort of. He's the government affairs officer of the local ambulance company, and the liaison to my department from the State Ambulance

Association. I went to college with him, and he helped me get this job."

Sam ran a hand through his shaggy hair. "And you didn't want to fuck that up?"

"He's a 'phobe, but me telling him isn't going to change our working relationship. I mean, I'll have to deal with him no matter what. I'm going to say something to him, but I've known the guy fifteen years *without* outing myself. Doing it now will be . . . difficult."

Sam sighed. "Maybe you should tell me about your 'parameters.'"

Another step forward, trying not to spook Sam, but getting close enough to make his physical presence felt. "I'm doing this for you, setting parameters. You don't want to get into this not knowing where you stand, or thinking it could be more serious than it is. I'm a casual guy." A casual, emotionally connected guy.

Sam blew out a breath and dropped Ian's gaze. "I sort of knew that already." He added something too low for Ian to catch. This wasn't looking good. He needed to get Sam to focus on the benefits of being with him.

"Look at me," Ian barked. Sam did immediately. "See?" he continued in a softer voice. "You respond to being told what to do, don't you? You like it, even."

Sam swallowed, Adam's apple bobbing up and down his throat. "Sometimes."

"With me."

Sam nodded jerkily.

"You ever have sex like you do with me, Sam? That good?"

Sam's nostrils flared. "No."

"It's fucking hot for me too. You know I have a hell of a lot more experience than you." Ian had to tread carefully—more carefully—here. "It could be even better. Maybe the best sex I've ever had."

Hell. So much for treading carefully. But Sam didn't look mad or upset, and for whatever reason that irked Ian. Sam should be pissed it wasn't the best sex Ian had ever had, shouldn't he? Instead, Sam cocked his head curiously and asked, "How?"

Ian shook off his annoyance. He had Sam just where he wanted him, right? Right. He took a step closer, within intimate touching distance. He meant to grip the back of Sam's neck, but instead he tucked a chunk of sort-of-too-long sandy hair behind Sam's ear, *then* rested his hand on the back of Sam's neck. "I want you to trust me."

Sam sucked in a quick breath. "Why?"

"You have fantasies. You need to trust someone before you can get into them, right?" Sam nodded hesitantly after a moment. "Maybe you want someone else to take away your choices. Just during sex," Ian added quickly when Sam opened his mouth. "Tie you up." Tension invaded Sam's neck under his palm. Ian leaned forward, speaking into Sam's ear. "Tell you when you can come. Feed you his nuts until you choke on them." Sam gasped, and Ian watched his cheeks flush. "If you trust me, I can make those fantasies real."

Sam wouldn't quite look at him. "You can't tie me up until I'm ready," he said quickly.

Ian's surprise and curiosity flared up, but he only squeezed Sam's nape gently. "Of course not." They sure the hell were going to be talking about that later.

Sam slowly raised his eyes to Ian's, parting his lips to lick them. "Maybe," he whispered. Ian smiled at him, circling Sam's wrist with his free hand and pulling him forward. Before he could press his mouth against Sam's and slide his tongue into it, Sam asked, "But what about your parameters?"

Parameters? Oh, those. "How about just that one, for now."

"What one?" Damn he was stubborn.

"About this being just sex." Ian didn't give Sam a chance to answer; he pulled him forward with the hand on the back of his neck and kissed him.

chapter 18

Sam let Ian kiss him, because it was a novelty still and because Ian owed him. When Ian ended it, Sam was breathless. That's what stopped him from shoving Ian back, telling him what he thought about his "parameter," then demanding to be taken home. Ian had almost had him with that awesome sex thing, and the trust thing. Then he had to ruin it by reminding Sam of his stupid "parameter." How the hell was he supposed to trust someone who started a relationship by saying it wasn't one and never would be? He deserved better than just sex. He needed to tell Ian that and get out of here.

Just as soon as he caught his breath.

He let his forehead rest against Ian's while he waited for his willpower to kick in. Unfortunately, his libido was lobbying for congress with Ian. *We can have true love later, can't we? Someone else will come along.* His libido was thinking about the here and now, and how it would feed all his secret fantasies. *You already trust Ian some,* it argued. *Why not get what we can from someone we know can deliver?*

Because I'm worth more *than just sex,* his willpower whined.

But when it came right down to it, Sam was just as horny as the next guy. It was hard to turn down someone who promised to hand you all your sex fantasies on a platter. He could go with the (very sexy, extremely appealing) frog for now, and wait for his prince to come later, right? Frogs could be fun.

Then Ian, the evil genius, stomped all over the remnants of Sam's will. "You know what I can't stop thinking about? When we first got together at the party, you were walking down the hall naked in front of me. I can still see it if I close my eyes. You have the sweetest little ass." Ian paused, moving to Sam's ear and kissing it. "I want to bury myself in you," he whispered against Sam's neck. "I want to watch you taking me inside you while you ride me."

Oh, he was *such* a bastard. Did he know compliments were Sam's mortal weakness?

Fortitude. He was going to open his mouth and tell Ian he could just occupy himself with the memory for the foreseeable future.

"I don't know how many times I've jerked off thinking about that. At least a dozen."

Sam nearly choked. Was Ian saying he'd . . . *fantasized* about him? Ian was the only man on the planet—the only *person*—who'd ever, *ever* done that. Sam couldn't breathe right. *Don't hyperventilate . . .*

Ian's hand had somehow made its way from Sam's wrist to his lower back, his fingers running along just inside Sam's waistband, stroking the sensitive skin there, making breathing even harder for him. Ian pulled him closer until Sam could feel his hard dick through their jeans, all the while forcing his hand down the back of Sam's pants and working his fingers under Sam's briefs. Crowding his way in until he was cupping Sam's ass, fingers tickling the curve above his thigh, then sliding in between his cheeks to find Sam's guiche piercing and play with it. Sam made a sobbing sort of gasp, gripping the sides of Ian's head, not sure when he'd grabbed him at all. "I owe you, Sam," Ian whispered. "I promised you I'd fuck you."

Sam exhaled slowly, trying to get his lungs under control. "I need to take a shower."

What was one more night of slutdom, in the grand scheme of things?

Sam was hallucinating; had to be. He'd been wandering so long in a sexual desert that he'd stumbled into some kind of lust-fueled mirage, because it *could not* feel this amazing to have Ian kissing him, flattening him on the bed with his naked body. Sex didn't feel this amazing except in romance novels. Or—hopefully—with his One True Love.

Ian was not his One True Love. *Remember that.*

Maybe Ian was his One True Fuck. Sam groaned. Ian chuckled into his mouth, still kissing him. All Sam could do was alternately grip Ian's head or his shoulders, arching up into him and craning his neck, trying to keep their mouths together when Ian pulled away.

"Roll over," Ian whispered.

Sam let his head fall back, staring stupidly at Ian. What? Why did he want—oh. He bit his lip and a shiver curled its way down his spine. He rolled onto his stomach.

Ian's hand stroked his shoulders and his back, palms flat against Sam's skin. He pulled himself closer, then draped himself half over Sam, planting one hand on the bed in front of his face and whispering into his ear. "You need a safeword."

Sam's whole body went rigid. He did? He'd never had one with Marley.

Like that's some kind of recommendation.

"I don't expect you'll need it tonight, but you should pick one." Sam watched the muscles in Ian's hand and forearm straining as he held himself up. The muscles flexed when Sam remained silent, then he felt the heat from Ian's cock and its soft skin on his lower back. He gasped.

That gasp broke the dam—he could speak again. "Like what?"

"Whatever you'd like." Ian slowly started moving again, pushing up until his dick was stroking the muscles along Sam's spine.

Sam's eyes drifted shut, completely seduced by that feeling. Like being tickled with sex. "Grapefruit," he mumbled thoughtlessly.

Ian finally lowered himself on the other side of Sam, chuckling. "Why does everyone pick food?"

Sam's eyes flew open. Everyone who? How many people had Ian been with that had needed a safeword? Then Ian kissed the back of his neck and down his spine, and Sam decided he didn't need to know.

Ian was a slow lover. Sam felt every caress, got the most sensation possible out of it, leaving him pretty sure this was the Death by Chocolate version of sex. Ian acted amused by his moans and groans and gasps, but Sam couldn't be bothered to give a damn. By the time Ian snapped open the lube, Sam no longer cared that this was just sex, or that Ian might have been with hundreds of other guys. He didn't think anymore about how his body looked or whether Ian was really turned on or faking it (but seriously, how could anyone fake something that hard?).

When Ian pushed inside Sam with his lubed finger, Sam thrust himself back onto it, but Ian whispered for him to hold still. He managed it, but when Ian slowly and carefully worked in a second finger, Sam couldn't stop his moaning, or the rocking of his hips, and Ian—predictably—chuckled.

Ian's fingers made him twist and finally break down. "Ian, please." Sam groaned as Ian eased out, then back in, going farther. "Please. Wanna be full."

"Full of my fingers?"

"Want you to fuck me," Sam whined. He clutched the sheets, half on his stomach, one leg hiked up nearly to his chin. Would Ian notice if he snuck his hand down to his dick? He moaned louder as the head of his cock made contact with the sheet. *High thread count, combed cotton.* Sam thrust against the bed.

Ian loomed over him, and then the fucker crooned, "Kiddo, are you being bad and humping the sheets?" while his fingers twisted and stroked inside Sam.

"Gaaawd."

Ian laughed again. "No, just Ian, but you can call me whatever you need."

"That's an overused—" he broke off to gasp "—joke."

Ian pulled his fingers out. He was gentle, but he left Sam suddenly bereft and motionless in horror.

Then he heard the condom wrapper. "OhthankGod," he breathed.

"Thank Ian."

"Thank you, Ian."

"Oh, you'll thank me, Sam."

Oh, please. Let it be worth thanking this egomaniac for.

Suddenly Ian moved away. Sam looked over his shoulder to see him sitting against the headboard. Ian patted one thigh. "Straddle me, facing the foot of the bed."

Part of Sam cringed, but his cock leaked out pre-cum as he got on his knees over Ian, feeling Ian's hands trail across his guiche, then his hole, finally resting on his hips. "You're gonna ride me, Sam."

God, he fucking hoped so.

Ian's fingers dug into his hips, guiding him down until he could feel the head of Ian's cock pressing against him, pushing in.

Whimper.

"Anyone ever tell you how tight you are?"

As tight as your voice? "It's been mentioned," Sam panted.

Ian laughed again, and Sam vibrated with the sound. Then it was all about getting lost in a haze of sensation, working himself onto Ian's cock, stroking the hotspots inside with the perfect made-for-it tool until Sam was sitting fully on Ian's groin, against his skin and wiry hair. Ian's hand circled his throat like a collar and leash.

Sam reached down and found Ian's balls, fondling and rubbing them against his own. They were tight, but still long enough to play with—so much bigger than his ever got. Ian *hmmm*ed and gripped Sam's hip harder.

Sam didn't know how Ian could stay still like that. He himself was having difficulty with it, his muscles throbbing from Ian's cock inside him. He tried rocking forward.

"Stop." Ian's hands tightened, one on his hip and the other still at his throat. Sam took in a shuddering breath, quivering with the effort of holding still.

"Lean back on your hands."

Oh, God, that just changed all the angles. Sam's elbows shook against Ian's ribs as he planted his hands on pillows on either side of Ian's waist. He could feel Ian's breath in his hair, coming fast. "That's good, kiddo. Now fuck yourself on my dick."

He wished he had words to describe the feeling when he lifted his hips and Ian's head moved inside him. He described it instead with a soft grunt that formed in the back of his throat every time he pushed himself down. But that glide and drag when he lifted his hips almost felt better. No, shoving himself down, filling himself, that felt best. Or maybe it was feeling the pressure ease, but then he just ached to be stretched again.

Ian's fingers around his throat were so hot, capturing him, but not controlling their rhythm. He got lost in riding Ian, didn't even remember his dick until Ian's hand wrapped around it, making Sam's tempo stutter. Ian started a slow, twisting stroke. "You're making a lot of noise," he panted in Sam's ear.

"Sorry."

Ian slipped his hand up from Sam's neck and covered his mouth.

Sam was pretty sure he thrashed then, and he knew he was yelling against Ian's palm, feeling Ian's cock thrusting hard, forcing the intrusion while his hand corkscrewed on Sam's dick.

Sam let go. Came all over Ian's hand and his own stomach, elbows giving out, muscles beyond his control, exploding from ass to dick with sensations shooting down his legs. The room went gray, his whole world pooling somewhere in his balls and spilling out.

He collapsed, draped all over Ian, dimly aware Ian had come. He groaned and let his head roll on Ian's shoulder, twitching occasionally, until Ian forced a hand between their bodies and gripped the base of his dick and, presumably, the condom. Then Sam made himself flip over, off of Ian and onto his stomach on the bed. He twitched on the sheets while his cum soaked into the zillion-thread-count, Egyptian long-staple cotton. "Laundry," he mumbled.

"'Zat all you can say?"

"Uh-huh." Sam tried to nod, but it was a no-go.

"Guess I'll consider it a compliment that I fucked you senseless."

Sam giggled. Then he dropped right into sleep.

Ian chased him all over the bed during the first half of the night. Sam hadn't slept more than an hour before Ian was shoving him off the edge. His heart sank at the thought that Ian didn't want him there, but when he tried to get up to move to the couch, Ian grabbed him and hung on.

"Ian?"

Ian snored in response. He was asleep? Seriously? Sam managed to crank his head around far enough to see. If Ian was faking sleep, he deserved props for the drooling.

After the third time Sam woke up to find Ian squeezing the life out of him, he couldn't avoid the conclusion that Ian was a sleep cuddler. Crazy. He didn't *look* like a sleep cuddler; he looked like two weeks was his idea of long-term commitment.

The snuggling wasn't bad—very nice actually. The problem was the way Ian kept Sam balanced right on the edge of the mattress, in constant danger of going over. The fourth time Sam woke up—when Ian's hold loosened and he went tumbling off the bed—he crawled around to the other side and got in, scooting up behind Ian and wrapping an arm around him.

He managed to sleep the rest of the night after that.

chapter 19

When Ian woke up in the morning, Sam wasn't there. It surprised the hell out of him and left him feeling strangely flat. He looked at the pillow Sam had used—on the opposite side from where he'd fallen asleep, but it had a head indent and a straight dirty-blond hair on the white case—and tried to figure out what this meant.

He had no problem understanding why Sam wasn't there. He was trying to determine why he felt flat inside. Because he'd achieved some of that elusive "emotional connectedness"? If he had, it was overrated.

He heard a sound and rolled onto his back to see Sam standing in the doorway and looking at him. Ian was ridiculously relieved.

"Morning," Sam said. He didn't look nervous, exactly; he looked out of place and confused, like a startled fawn.

Maybe he looked more like a newborn calf. It was cute. All big, blinking eyes, long nose, and spindly limbs. Ian stared until Sam turned away, cheeks pinking up. He cleared his throat. "Morning. How long have you been up?"

"An hour. I needed to get some writing in." Sam seemed mildly out of it still. He wandered into the room, stopping when he met Ian's eyes in the mirror on the closet door.

"You're in school, right?" Ian propped his head on his hand, truly, surprisingly curious.

"Yeah," Sam said. "I'm getting my Master of Fine Arts in writing." His face in the mirror looked resigned. He *sounded* resigned.

"Isn't that what Nik has?"

"Yeah."

"You don't sound very happy about it."

Sam grimaced in the mirror. Ian thought he would have to prod him—*and just why am I asking him about this*?—but Sam said, "I sometimes think I'd rather get a doctorate in literature."

That right there should have been a conversation killer. Ian didn't know literature from graffiti, and he'd never found his life lacking because of it. "So get that instead. As far as I can tell, a degree in writing doesn't make you highly employable."

Sam snorted softly. "Neither does a doctorate in literature."

"Life's too short to get the degree someone else wants you to get, only to hit your thirties and realize you don't care what they think anymore. Do what you want. You gotta be able to get a decent job with a doctorate." *Hell*. Like that wasn't a revealing thing to say.

Sam turned around to look at him directly. "Is that what you did?'

"Yeah."

They stared at each other silently while Ian steeled himself for questions.

"Want some coffee? I found it and made some."

Ian opened his mouth, but nothing came out for a second. Then, "Uh, sure."

Sam brought him coffee with a splash of milk. How did he know that's how Ian liked it? Most people assumed he was a black coffee kind of guy. He usually took it black in public because somehow needing that splash of milk seemed like a weakness.

Sam sat on the bed next to him, took a sip of his own coffee, set it down, and asked nervously, "Can I look at your back?"

Ian rolled onto his side silently, more to avoid looking at Sam than as an answer.

A few seconds passed before he felt Sam's fingertips on his skin. In his mind, he followed their progress tracing his healed wounds. The swirly burned patch below his left shoulder, then the rough patch closer to his spine. Sam worked his way down, and it didn't feel awful. When he traced the surgical scar along Ian's lower back, Ian blurted, "I thought you'd left."

Sam's hand stilled. "Huh?"

"When I woke up and you weren't here in bed."

"Should I have left?" Sam asked uncertainly, hand hovering just over the scar.

"No." Ian added an indifferent shrug.

Sam's hand settled on him again, and Ian let his eyes drift shut while Sam's fingertips mapped his injuries. It was sort of lulling.

"Do you ever talk about what happened?"

"No," Ian said reflexively. "I was in an accident at work."

"You already told me that." The mild exasperation in his voice made Ian smile. He liked Sam with attitude. Sam stretched out on the bed behind him and continued touching him, retracing areas he'd already visited. It almost felt like a caress.

"It's a dumb story. The fire was dumb; I was dumb. It's embarrassing." Ian sighed. In for a penny or whatever . . . "I got hit by a car on fire."

"*What?*"

Exactly the response he'd expected. Ian laughed shortly, but Sam's hand never stopped moving on his back, which must have been why he went on. "I was the Battalion Chief on duty that night. Morning, rather; I guess it was a little after two. Anyway, they tapped out a car fire behind a strip mall. Engine nine went, and they reported a fully involved Volkswagen bus. I figured someone stole a van and torched it when they were done with their joyride. Normal shit."

"But it wasn't." Sam's hand rubbed circles on his lower back, as if the skin there was the same as any other skin. "What does 'tapped out' mean?"

"It's slang for broadcasting tones." That probably wasn't much clearer. "Every time emergency vehicles are sent to a scene, tones precede the information given by the dispatcher to open the radios at the correct station. Like an audio key for the station."

"Oh. 'Kay." Ian suspected Sam didn't really understand. "So . . . 'fully involved' means it was engulfed in flames?"

"Yeah. They didn't report the year of the van. As I pulled up, they put the hose on it, and it just exploded."

Sam didn't say anything, tracing the ribs in Ian's back now.

"The bus was late sixties, and the engine was on fire. Those engines are made of magnesium, which burns in water—it burns anything with oxygen in it. Magnesium will just break the chemical bond and feed the fire with the oxygen atoms."

"Oh," Sam said softly. "Chemistry."

Ian snorted. "Yeah, chemistry. The guys weren't awake or something, I don't know. So I jumped out of the command unit without putting on my turnouts—my protective gear. The captain started yelling at the kid on the nozzle, but it took a few seconds before we yanked him off. So then we were standing there, laughing at him, and the stupid thing was still on fire. Geller smothered it with a fire extinguisher, and all of a sudden the vehicle started rolling."

Sam's fingers stopped. "It could still roll?"

"Yeah. Came right for us. I guess we ran, I don't remember, but it hit me in the back. It was out, but still hot. Geller said after I was down, the wheel rolled right over my ass and kept going until it hit the green strip. Blunt force trauma with a red-hot '68 Volkswagen does some damage. I was lying in this pass-through behind a grocery store and there was gravel in my cheek, and I could see lights streaming across wet pavement. That's what I remember. Didn't even hurt. You know when you get third-degree burns, it sometimes doesn't hurt because all the nerves are cauterized? All the lesser burns around it hurt, and when you start healing it hurts like hell, but at first I couldn't feel much of anything."

Ian craned his neck to watch Sam over his shoulder. And oh fuck, he'd said a lot. It was all over Sam's face. Ian didn't want to see that expression, because it meant he felt something for Ian. Pity and horror and—he started to get up, but Sam grabbed him, skinny bicep squeezing tight around his chest. Ian's heart pounded under Sam's palm, and Sam's arm felt like another band of steel—an external one to match the internal one that he'd swear was wrapped around his ribs right now.

"Sam, I gotta . . ." he croaked. The kid let him go, slowly.

Ian didn't get up. It was the weirdest thing. He simply lay there and soaked in Sam's body heat.

It was soothing.

After a while, Sam's fingers traced his scars again, hesitantly at first. They didn't talk, and Ian ignored his coffee, but the room stopped closing in on him.

He wouldn't think about why it was all right to tell that story to Sam.

Sam dropped a kiss on his shoulder. Ian sighed, closed his eyes, and felt Sam's light touch on his back, making him shiver. Or possibly making his skin crawl, he wasn't sure. Not an unpleasant sort of crawling—some stimulating mix of exhilaration and apprehension.

Sam slid his arm back around Ian and pulled himself closer. It was almost like cuddling, but what the hell. If it made Sam happy to almost-cuddle him like that, fine. He *had* seemed pretty freaked out by Ian's story. The kid probably needed some reassurance. He could deal with it if it made Sam feel better.

He could feel how much Sam liked the cuddling in the ridge of his hardening erection. Sam wriggled his hips until he was teasing Ian's crack with it, and Sam was breathing light and fast.

"You wanna fuck me, Sam?"

Sam froze. "You'd let me?" he squeaked.

Would he? "Yeah, sure, why not? I already kissed you."

Sam giggled, and it was too cute not to smile about.

"I don't want to right now," Sam said eventually, still rubbing up against Ian. Was that Ian's cue to roll over and start something? He didn't. He felt warm and lazy now—post-adrenaline lassitude. Now that they weren't talking about the accident and the kid's shivery-crawly fingers had stopped.

His touch had felt kind of like a massage: a little uncomfortable while it lasted, but afterward a guy could relax more. Ian pushed back lazily into Sam's hips, and Sam gusted breath against the nape of his neck.

"Ian," Sam whispered, tracing circles on Ian's chest, between his pecs, playing with the hair. He waited to see what else Sam would do.

Sam circled his nipple with those shivery-crawly fingertips, and this time Ian was less conflicted about whether it felt good or not. He pushed his hips back into Sam again, reflexively this time.

Sam hesitated. "You want me to stop?"

"No."

Sam worked his hand down Ian's body in small circles, sliding under the blankets at his waist, making Ian start when cool air slipped in with him. But then his fingers were tracing Ian's belly button, and there was enough heat to go around.

It took next to forever for Sam to follow the trail of hair down to his dick. Ian had expected it, but he still gasped when Sam's fingers circled the base of his prick. Sam's touch changed from light to firm as he stroked Ian.

For a kid who'd never seen a foreskin before, Sam was a fast learner. He laid his talented fingertips on the skin covering Ian's head and worked it, sliding over and back, occasionally squeezing, wiggling his dick between Ian's cheeks, panting against the back of Ian's neck like he was the one getting a handjob.

It was uncomfortably exciting. Ian wasn't used to being the passive one, but Sam's hand was too tight and moved too perfectly to stop, so Ian managed to ignore his discomfort.

More like he rode the naughtiness of not being in control like a rollercoaster. He reached back and gripped Sam's hip tight, pulling him into his ass, telling Sam with his body not to stop. It was a hell of a ride, and coming in Sam's hand felt like going through three upside-down death spirals in a row, especially with Sam's cum dripping off his lower back and Sam's mouth all over Ian's neck.

Ian rolled onto his back, letting the sheets soak up the wet stuff, and gave up the pretense Sam was the only cuddler here by pulling the kid onto his chest. He rested, feeling Sam's breath on his skin slow from panting to sleep.

Crazy how the kid fell asleep seconds after coming. How did he jerk off in the shower?

Whatever. Ian let Sam's weight sink into him, drifting off himself within minutes.

chapter 20

hen Sam woke up in Ian's bed the second time, the air tasted different. *That makes no sense.* Regardless, Sam lay still, savoring the change. Something had happened between him and Ian that wasn't purely sexual. Very carefully—because it seemed fragile and translucent—he put whatever it was aside in his mind, resolving not to think about it right now.

Ian wasn't in bed with him. Occasional noises filtered into the bedroom from somewhere close by. Maybe the bathroom Sam had found on his explorations earlier, while Ian had slept. He rolled over to see the bathroom door shut, but the bedroom door was open, and he could see the arm of Ian's couch and a slice of the mission-style coffee table.

Sam had padded carefully around after the first time he woke up, looking at Ian's house. Not in the medicine cabinet or anything, just . . . around. He'd found colorful rugs on hardwood floors and nice furniture. Two leather chairs in the living room flanked a muted sage, velvet-upholstered couch.

Ian was very neat. The dishes were done and the counters were clear. Someone had cleaned the floors recently, and there was no coating of dust on the end tables. Sam felt very out of place. Even the sheets on the guest bed (guest bed!) were high thread count and crisply white, covered by a damask comforter.

Most shocking of all, there was no television. Or at least he'd thought so, until he'd carefully opened what looked like an armoire in the living room—if Sam had an armoire, at a minimum the hinges would squeak—and found a small set.

It had all felt a little bit like visiting an alien landscape, not because Sam's place was so different (which it was), but because Ian didn't seem like the kind of guy who cared about stuff like this. Truthfully, Sam had expected an array of vibrating recliners sporting built-in cup holders facing a big-screen TV and a fridge full of nothing but beer. He thought Ian would be the type of guy who bought pans at the dollar store and threw them away when they got too dirty to use. It worked for him, after all.

Instead, it was the type of place Sam would like to become accustomed to. He could live here; would *love* to be surrounded by the comfortable but attractive tidiness of it all. He'd live that way now if he could, he just seemed to lack any decorative skill or even an iota of talent for organization. Or cleanliness. Yet another stereotypical benefit of being gay Sam seemed to have been shorted on.

A toilet flushed, water ran, and Sam quickly rolled over. He felt the door to the bathroom open with a rush of air across his arm. He did his best to fake sleep—something he'd always sucked at—and listened to Ian creep into the room, across the wood and rugs.

Ian leaned over him in bed, nearly jolting Sam into opening his eyes. He didn't, though. Should he pretend to wake up now?

"Sam?" Ian whispered.

"Mmm?" Half-consciousness seemed like a good compromise.

"I have to go. Someone's picking me up for a rugby game."

Sam opened his eyes and turned to look into Ian's face a few inches above his. He'd shaved, and Sam wanted to rub his cheek against Ian's smooth jaw, but he didn't. After a few seconds, he remembered to blink sleepily, like he'd just awakened. *Oops.*

Ian smiled at him. "You don't have to get up." He gripped Sam's chin between his fingers and leaned down to kiss him quickly, and again, as if once wasn't quite enough. "I'm leaving you a key so you can lock the door behind you when you go."

Ian wanted him to leave?

Okay, sheesh, that was stupid. Even if he . . . well, he wanted to stay, but he shouldn't because he had a lot to do and—

Wait. Ian was giving him a key? Sam's mouth went dry. What did that mean?

"You probably have a lot to do today, huh?" Ian sat back on the bed, letting go of Sam's chin and propping himself up on one arm.

"Yeah." Sam nodded vigorously. "I have homework and a class to prepare for and you know. Housework and stuff."

Ian looked like he had to stifle a smile. Sam had a feeling he wasn't buying the housework excuse. "You teach?" he asked.

Sam nodded some more. "Yeah. I teach freshman and sophomore undergrads how *not* to write."

Ian scrunched his brow. "How do you teach someone not to do something?"

"Mostly by telling them the way they did it is wrong."

"So positive reinforcement isn't a teaching method you use a lot?"

"It's not from lack of trying," Sam said.

Ian opened his mouth, but a knock on the front door cut him off. "Hell, there's my ride." He didn't move. "Stay in bed awhile, the key is on the table next to the front door."

"How will I get it back to you?" Sam held his breath.

"Next time you come over," Ian said. The doorbell rang. "'Kay, kiddo, gotta go. Um, I took your number off your cell and programmed mine into it," he added, standing up and grabbing something off his dresser.

Sneaky of him, but *so* thrilling. "'Kay." Sam smiled happily, since Ian wasn't looking. Then Ian turned and caught him smiling. *Damn it.*

Ian smiled back. "Maybe we can, uh, hook up next weekend?" Sam nodded, trying to tamp down his eagerness. "Okay, I'll call you during the week," Ian said, walking backward out of the room. A muffled voice was shouting his name through the front door. "Can you strip the sheets off the bed before you go?"

"Yeah. Bye." Sam gave up trying not to smile. Ian winked at him and walked out. Sam heard a complaining voice when Ian opened the front door, then Ian's answer—short and curt, the way he usually sounded.

chapter 21

"Why do we always take your car?" Ian asked on the way to Tierney's parking spot. He knew asking wasn't going to change shit, but he thought he would spread some of his annoyance around. He wasn't annoyed at taking Tierney's damn car again so much as annoyed at Tierney, period. For breathing. For knocking on his damn door when Ian had a warm, naked guy in his bed.

Warm, naked Sam. Ian nearly tripped over his own feet.

Tierney saved him from any potential moments of introspection, thank fuck. "Dude, my car's hawt," he answered with a leer for his "baby," stroking the hood as they reached his stupid car. "Chicks dig it."

"Oh my God," Ian groaned, walking around to the passenger side. "You're just . . . such a fucking stereotype." It was times like this he remembered why Tierney had insisted—unsuccessfully—on being called "T-bone" in college. He hadn't been as fond of his other nickname: "T-boner."

"What?" Tierney stared at him over the roof, brow furrowed. "What crawled up your ass and died this morning?"

That surprised a laugh out of Ian. "Nothing. Open the fucking car and let's go."

Tierney hit the unlock button and jerked his door open, looking annoyed and confused. *I just need to chill out.* It wasn't Tierney's fault Ian would rather be crawling up someone else's ass right now. And it wasn't like Ian hadn't always known Tierney was a shallow prick.

After they got in, Ian could see Tierney's hand trembling as he forced the key into the ignition and started the car. Had he pissed T off that much? He sighed. "Sorry, man. I didn't sleep much last night." Completely true, and it had been totally worth it.

"There was a time when you were just as big a horndog as you think I am, asshole." Tierney slammed the gearshift into reverse. He planted a hand on the back of Ian's seat, turning to see where he was going, but he stopped to scowl at Ian.

"Yeah, well I thought I had something to prove," Ian muttered. He was skirting dangerous territory, but that conversation would be unavoidable sooner or later.

For a second he wanted to make Tierney face it head-on, tell him he liked guys and was totally, completely fucking gay, no two ways about it (anymore). But he lost the impulse when Tierney laughed, telling him, "Everyone has something to prove in college."

"And you didn't prove it *enough*?" Ian shot back, and instantly regretted it.

"What the fuck, dude? What is your fucking *problem*?" Tierney stomped on the gas pedal, squealing backward out of the parking space and jerking to a stop.

"Nothing."

They were silent for the rest of the way to the park where they played, and Ian spent the ride thinking about his fucking problem.

Nothing went right after that conversation with Tierney. Ian's team lost the rugby game, and during the ritual after-game beers, all the guys talked about chicks. Ian just didn't care enough to fake it anymore. Then when he finally got back to his place, Sam was gone.

Which was what he'd wanted, right?

Right.

On Monday morning, he woke up convinced his skin had shrunk. Or maybe his muscles and bones had grown. It just felt *off*, like things inside had shifted around and he needed some sort of dermal alteration, and possibly a couple of extra ribs.

He probably needed to adjust to these changes before calling Sam.

When Ian got to the office and Andrea asked how his weekend had been, he growled something at her. She lifted her eyebrows and went to make coffee. "You can get your own," she said as she walked off.

"What the hell kind of assistant are you if you won't even get me coffee?"

"I'm your assistant *director*. If you want someone to get you coffee, hire my little brother."

Ian's glare bounced right off the back of her head.

They spent the rest of the week interviewing people for the three positions they had to fill, and Ian was forced to be polite. Weirdly, he was starting to feel more polite. His skin settled into its new shape, and now he wasn't calling Sam because he needed to . . . well, he wasn't sure what, but something.

On Thursday, Dalton came in for his interview. Andy skipped that one, since she was his sister, so it was just Ian and a cute twink with big eyes and a sweet, elfin face. *That's the kind of guy Sam should be with, not me.* Ian wanted to reach across the desk and throttle him.

Not that Sam was *with* him, of course.

Ian spent a half hour interviewing Dalton, but his mind was on Sam the whole time. It was distracting and maddening and completely fucking unprofessional and probably the worst interview Dalton had ever suffered through. Ian was just lucky he had a list of prepared questions.

After the first ten minutes, he found himself looking at the frown line between Dalton's brows more than anything else. Sam had a little line like that sometimes. Ian devoted a lot of effort to remembering just exactly when that wrinkle appeared on Sam's forehead—when he was doing something specific, Ian thought. He didn't have that furrow all the time. It wasn't the same as the wrinkle he had when he came.

"You seem very busy," Dalton said suddenly, interrupting himself mid-answer to one of Ian's questions. Whatever question that might have been. "I know you're just interviewing me because Andy twisted your arm somehow, so maybe I should go." He leaned over to pick up his messenger bag from the chair next to him, his mouth a perfect, upside down "U."

Ian coughed uncomfortably. "I guess I'm busy . . . but I'm supposed to be busy interviewing people."

Dalton shrugged. "You're preoccupied," he said simply, buckling buckles and zipping zippers. His bag was a nice one, leather and vaguely military-esque. Very fashionable. Ian had a flash image of him walking down the street with it bouncing along on his back.

But that wasn't quite right, was it? He really looked at Dalton for the first time. He had an edge of experience, a hardness around his eyes.

"How old are you, Dalton?" Had he already asked this?

Dalton's lips pursed, which probably meant Dalton had already told him. "I'll be twenty-seven in March," he said. "I worked full-time while going to school and finally earned my bachelor's from State University in June."

"The guy I'm seeing is a grad student there." Ian nearly slapped his hand over his mouth. The *fuck* had he said that for? Dalton's head bobbed up, and he looked as surprised as Ian felt.

"Oh. Um, is that why you're sort of . . ." Dalton made a circling motion with his index finger near his temple. Ian's eyes bugged out. *Crazy?* "Inattentive?" Dalton finished.

"Um . . ."

"Maybe I should get you some coffee?" Dalton offered.

"I guess . . ."

Dalton bounced up out of his seat. "Okay," he said.

Ian watched him walk out, then looked down at the résumé in front of him. Dalton Lehnart had worked in the Dean of Admission's office for five of his six college years. He typed seventy words per minute. Was that fast? It *seemed* fast.

"Here you go," Dalton sang, traipsing back into the room. He set a mug in front of Ian. The right mug, no less—Ian's favorite solid red, cylindrical one.

The coffee was the color Ian liked it, too, lightened with just enough milk. "Did you use the two-percent in the fridge?" he asked, wrapping his palm around the cup.

"Yes, I did."

Ian sipped. It was perfect. He looked up and studied Dalton, still standing beside his desk with his hands clasped. "Did you ask Andy how to make my coffee?"

Dalton looked at him quizzically. "Of course I did. How else would I know how to make it?"

"When can you start?"

chapter **22**

On Sunday, when Sam got home, he did all his homework, prepared for his classes, and then actually stooped to cleaning in order to avoid thinking about Ian and that morning. Cleaning sounded very distracting. And it *was* very distracting, at first, but before Sam realized it, he'd fallen into a pattern of work and his brain was free to roam again.

Bad brain. Bad. Because all roads led back to Ian, and if he thought about Ian, he would begin to analyze what had happened, and *that* would result in him searching for parallels to a romance novel plot. It was his single worst vice. Probably.

Don't think about it.

The thing was, whatever had happened between him and Ian was certainly fraught with internal conflict, because all romances—okay, romance *novels*—had some kind of conflict, and if it wasn't external it had to be internal. Since Ian wasn't saving Sam from international drug-smuggling terrorists, and he wasn't the captain of an enemy starship that had captured Sam in battle (*ungh*, revenge sex), their plotline—his and Ian's—had to center on internal conflict.

AKA *emotional* conflict.

Obviously, if an outside observer had to guess which of them had the more serious emotional conflict, they'd pick Ian. Sam wasn't the one who didn't even know what constituted a relationship. By default, that made Ian the screwed-up one, right?

Focus on something other than Ian. Like cleaning the toilet.

Maybe he should call Nik and see who he favored for the more serious emotional conflict. But what if he accidentally let slip what had happened this morning? He couldn't just *tell* Nik the story of Ian's injury. Ian had acted as if sharing that was unusual for him. Sam definitely didn't want to tell Nik about how it had felt to make Ian come in his hand—like Sam had comforted him, and they'd created a connection beyond sex. That was private.

Sam suddenly felt lightheaded. What happened this morning had been *special*. The big, important special, maybe even a little like what

Nik had with Jurgen. He tried to put his head between his knees, but the toilet bowl was there already.

Oh, look at that. The porcelain was sparkling white, and he didn't even remember cleaning it.

When he went to mop the kitchen floor, his thoughts gained control again, and he recalled the weird scene when Ian had to leave. He'd given Sam a *key*. Sam let himself marvel over that for a bit, but the suspicious little thought he'd been walling out finally wormed its way into his head.

Maybe Ian had wanted him to stay in bed because he was afraid his friend would see him.

Ian said he was telling people if they asked, but was he trying to keep people from asking? Sam wandering around his apartment early on a Sunday afternoon would look suspicious. It wasn't as if he could pass for straight, like, ever.

When looked at in that light, the formerly bright, shiny key to Ian's apartment seemed tarnished.

You're thinking about it.

Yeah, but just for a minute.

Sam knew damn well that if he were a good little romance novel hero, he would dismiss the possibility of love. For him to actually *get* love, he needed to wander into it all unknowing, like a lamb stumbling innocently to the slaughter.

Wait, that analogy wasn't quite right. Um . . . the birthday boy walking blindly into his surprise party. That worked.

Point was, for this to be a romance novel plot, Sam should naïvely assume that Ian had meant it when he said he didn't want anything more than sex.

It just seemed like Ian wanted more.

This is nothing like any plot I can recall.

Maybe that's because it's real life and not a romance novel.

Sam sighed. Here he was, back to thinking about things he shouldn't be. And he'd mopped himself into a corner.

On Monday, Sam took his courage (and other pertinent body parts) into his hands and did something he'd been planning on since he'd been pierced.

He bought a captive bead ring—ten gauge (gulp), five-eighths inch in diameter.

The word *captive* made him a bit shivery, and possibly sympathetic to women in gothic novels who were prone to swooning. He began to see the appeal.

Having the girl who'd pierced him in the first place change his jewelry from bar to ring was less fun. She was the first, last, and only girl—other than his mother, presumably, but like he wanted to think about *that*—who had ever handled Sam's manly bits. He'd had some idea he could do it himself, but she looked at him askance when he asked her if he'd need any special equipment for changing his body jewelry.

"It'd be better if I did it for you," she told him.

"Have I told you I'm gay? I'm not really into—"

"I'm not trying to get a free grope," Piercing Girl said, tucking her hands in her back pockets. "I just know from experience that it's safest for the client if the piercer does it. What kind of phone do you have?"

"Wha . . .? Phone?"

"Your cell phone," she elaborated, still patient, and possibly concerned about his native intelligence. "What is it?"

Sam gaped at her a second. "It's an iPhone," he finally told her.

Her brows lifted slightly, as if she found that amusing. He began to feel like a stereotype. "When you bought it, did you have them put the screen protector on or did you do it yourself?"

His face got hot. "I had to take it back and have the salesgirl do it. Those things are . . . yeah." Sales Girl had been bossy, too.

Piercing Girl seemed to feel a single raised brow was all the answer he needed.

"How hard can it be?" Sam asked, annoyed by her attitude *and* the attitude of the girl who'd sold him the damn phone.

"Okay," Piercing Girl said, turning to dig through some shiny tool things in a box. "You'll need at least one pair of pliers, but I recommend you get both the ring-opening and the ring-closing pliers.

These—" she turned back to show him some instrument of torture "—are the ring-opening pliers."

Sam could feel the blood draining from his head. "Never mind," he croaked. "You can do it." *Ian had better be worth this.*

Not that he was doing it for Ian.

She was kind enough to hide her smirk by turning away to drop the pliers back in the box. "Okay, get naked below the waist, then lie on the table with your feet in the stirrups."

He had the strangest feeling she enjoyed saying that.

He spent most of Monday and Tuesday dealing with the new realities of having a heavier and now ring-shaped thing living behind his balls. Realities like relearning how to sit, and trying not to adjust himself too frequently in public. Not to mention the concentration required to keep himself calm every time he walked and the weight between his legs swung, just behind his nuts . . .

Oh God.

In class on Tuesday morning, the girl who always sat next to him—Eva of the multiple facial piercings—caught Sam trying to reposition the damn ring through his jeans. He'd sort of lost all pretense of subtlety in the previous twenty-four hours.

She looked impressed. "It's good to see you butching it up a little," she whispered.

"Thanks, Eva," he whispered back. The professor wasn't even there, but classroom habits died hard. "Adjusting myself in public is butch?"

"Totally."

Ian hadn't called him by Tuesday evening. Nothing to worry about—he couldn't appear eager, after all. Sam knew they had *some* kind of connection. Ian would call him eventually. He went to sleep confident things would be fine.

Worry had set in by the time he woke up Wednesday. He went to the library and sort of managed to concentrate on his short story, but by evening he was sure that the strange sense of intimacy they'd achieved on Sunday morning had been too much for Ian. He never should have mentioned Ian's injury, or asked him what happened. He should have pretended to believe Ian's taciturn bastard act.

But being incurably curious and dopey, Sam had just had to pry a little. He'd thought he could see some of the paint peeling from Ian's facade, so he'd picked at it until he could look underneath. When would he ever learn? Guys like Ian didn't do sharing time. This wasn't a romance novel, it was real life, and Sam had ruined everything. No more scorching hot, parametered sex for him.

Which was just fine, right? Because he needed to find out that Ian wasn't the right guy for him and move on. Sam was a husband hunter, pure and simple. He didn't have time to stop and smell the roses (*snerk*) with guys who were only stellar in bed and had nothing else to offer.

Okay, good, he'd settled that. Now he could stop staring at the phone.

He finally stopped staring at the phone Wednesday afternoon when he had to go work his shift at Fatty's. Tineke eyed him suspiciously, but seemed to know better than to do more than circle him and wait. Married straight women could sense gay boy heartache like a shark could scent blood in the water.

By the time he had to teach his Thursday evening class, Sam had worn a cell phone outline into the back right pocket of his favorite jeans—the ones he wore for comfort when things weren't going well. Sometimes, when life really sucked, he slept in them—just because undressing was too much work, not because they gave him an increased sense of security or anything.

That's what his vintage Snoopy "Later Skater" T-shirt was for.

He barely made it through his class outline with the group of mostly uninterested freshman and sophomores. He let them go early.

At 3 a.m. Friday morning, he lay in bed wearing his comfort jeans with the newly redecorated pocket, his Snoopy security shirt, and his Batman Underoos, staring at his cell phone in the dim and lonely glow of the digital clock on his nightstand.

I'm truly, inarguably pathetic.

It might be time to call in the shock troops. But Nik would be in bed asleep already.

In bed, beside his boyfriend. His gorgeous, manly, in-love-with-him boyfriend. Probably wrapped in his possessive arms.

Sam sighed. *At least Jurgen doesn't have much chest hair.* Nik couldn't have *everything* Sam ever wanted, after all.

chapter 23

On Friday morning, Ian found himself hard-pressed to say *anything* to his therapist. Janet's pleasant expression wore thin on the edges as he stalled. "Is this the use you want to be making of your time with me?" she asked him after a particularly long silence.

Ian slumped. "Not really."

"Is there something you don't want to talk about?"

"Yes," he muttered, crossing his arms on his chest.

"I'm not going to make you talk about it, but we might want to talk about *something*." Her knuckles were going white where she clasped her hands in her lap.

That was satisfying. He smirked, just the corners of his mouth. "I don't want to talk about anything."

"That's your choice, Ian."

"I saw that guy again."

Janet raised an interested eyebrow, but said nothing.

"I told him I just wanted sex."

"Ah."

"What does that mean?" Ian snapped.

"It means, 'I see.'" He studied her suspiciously. Was she biting the inside of her cheek to keep from smiling? He wouldn't put it above her. "I'm not judging you."

Strangely, he believed her. His shoulders relaxed. "I'm not supposed to do that anymore," he said. "Just hook up with guys."

Janet looked completely serious for once. "You said you didn't want to anymore, yes. Is this helping you to develop a personal connection to someone?"

"No." Damn, he sounded like a sulky teenager.

"Have you thought about giving up on this man and looking—"

"I want *him*," Ian interrupted. *Hell.* He closed his eyes and let his head fall back against the chair. "Okay . . . I got in the car with my buddy from college, Tierney. He's got this fucking car, you know what I mean?" How could she possibly know what he meant? "It's all about him being a chick magnet. He's fostering the image of himself as a player."

"And he's not?" Janet asked. She would let him go on in this nonsensical direction only so long, he knew from experience.

Ian opened his eyes. "I don't know if he is anymore. He used to be, you know? It's why we were friends in the first place, because I was just like him. But I had something to prove." He lifted his head slightly, to see if she got it.

"You wanted to prove you weren't gay?"

Ian didn't know if that was all there had been to it, but for now he shrugged. "I guess. So, I was watching Tierney pull this shit on Sunday, looking like a fucking idiot. He just looked *old*, you know?"

Janet opened her mouth, then paused. "No, I don't know what you mean."

Ian sat up and planted his elbows on his knees. "He looked like a lonely, thirty-something jackass trying to prove he's still young and hot and all he needs out of life is sex."

Janet nodded, although Ian had no clue if she got what he said. *He* didn't get it. "I used to be that guy, and I'm looking at him and wondering if I'm still that guy. I mean, what the fuck do I know about personal relationships? My mom died when I was barely a teenager, and after that, my dad was a neglectful asshole, and I've just told the guy I was supposed to be *connecting* with that all I want is more sex."

"Is that really all you want?"

"No!" Ian shot out of his chair and turned to the window. "But I don't know if I know how to do anything else." Shit, he'd said that out loud. He could feel the blood drain from his head.

Janet was silent until he got his breathing under control and turned to her, barely able to meet her eyes.

"Ian, what you were before doesn't have to define what you are now, or what you will be in the future."

He fisted one hand on his hip. "What the fuck does that *mean*?"

Janet watched him calmly. "It means you aren't that guy now, but you have to continue to choose not to be him again."

Ian dropped back into his chair and sighed. "Hell," he muttered.

"That'll be one hundred fifty dollars, please."

"Ha. Ha." But then he ruined his mad-on by laughing.

chapter 24

Friday night.

Date night, or so he'd always heard. Sam had a date with a glass of wine and the phone. He took a sip of the first and eyed the second, working up to calling Nik. Not that Nik would be anything less than sympathetic, but Sam couldn't help feeling like a failed, pathetic fool. And then there was the issue of Jurgen overhearing everything and thinking, "I told him so."

It sucked that Jurgen didn't have a GPS friend-spying app on his phone. Sam had stalked—that is, *monitored*—Nik's whereabouts all day with that app to determine where he was and when might be a good time to call him. He checked his phone one more time. Nik was at home. Chances were Jurgen was there too, but . . . yeah. He chugged the rest of his wine and reached for the phone.

The doorbell rang.

Sam's fingers froze in midair. Who would ring his doorbell? No one rang his doorbell, his friends all knocked. He scoffed at his irrational hope that it was Ian and dropped his hand to think. It was Friday night, so the only people likely to ring his doorbell were . . . *Proselytizers.*

Hmm, hide or answer, pretending to be a mentally unstable Satan worshipper? Both options had their charms. The doorbell rang again, and Sam found himself walking toward his entryway, trying to screw his face into an off-balance expression.

But when he opened the door, no religious zealots awaited him there. Just Ian.

"Hey," he said when Sam didn't say anything.

"Hey," Sam said steadily in spite of his galloping heart.

Ian ran a hand through his hair. "Um, do you want to . . ." He trailed off, shifting his weight from one foot to the other, staring at Sam's hand on the knob.

"You never called me."

"I was hoping you wouldn't notice that," Ian mumbled. He cleared his throat. "Sam, would you go out to dinner with me tonight? Please?" he added when Sam just stared.

"I guess . . . I have my own parameter."

Ian finally looked up at him, eyes widening.

"When you say you'll call me, you actually will."

Ian nodded quickly. "Okay."

"Let me change and we can go."

chapter 25

Sam obviously felt confused, and probably nervous. That seemed all right to Ian, because he himself definitely was feeling confused and maybe a little bit . . . agitated. He didn't really know what to do here. How much emotional connection was too much? How much of this stuff indicated more feeling than he really had for Sam?

By the way, how do *you feel about Sam?*

He nearly groaned. Now was so not the time to try to figure that out, not while they were waiting for his name to be called at this restaurant Andy had recommended. She'd said her brother Dalton's "more upscale" dates took him here. Ian could totally see some forty-year-old guy taking Andy's twenty-something brother to wine and dine here, thinking he'd get a superlative blowjob for his trouble and all the dough he dropped at dinner.

Not that Ian actually thought that way about Dalton, but this place had that vibe.

Jesus, why had he thought this was a good idea? So he sort of needed to make up for not calling when he'd actually meant to and really did want to see Sam again. But this place? White tablecloths and reservations and freaking candlelit tables? What did Sam think it meant? Ian's chest started to tighten up.

He shifted in his chair, trying to get more comfortable in the over-lit waiting area. Out of the corner of his eye, he saw Sam picking at his fingernails. He put his hand over Sam's to get him to stop. Sam flinched when he touched him, his head hitting the back of his chair. A snort of laughter escaped Ian before he could smother it, and when he looked at Sam he could see his cheeks going from too pale to too pink.

"Are you nervous?" Ian asked. Thank fuck he wasn't the only one.

Sam shook his head *no*, still looking at his hands. Then he slowly started nodding *yes*.

"Why?"

Sam glanced at him, then looked away. "No one's ever taken me on a date like this."

"No one's ever taken you on a date?" His voice rose, and Sam's cheeks flushed darker.

"Of course I've been on dates," he hissed. "Just not to a place with white tablecloths and candlelight, that's all. And we're wearing *jeans*."

"Hell, most of the guys here are wearing jeans. The only people dressed up are the waiters." And the chicken hawks. Ian had intended to bluff his way through this, but if Sam could be honest, so could he. "I've never taken a date to a place like this." He'd barely had *any* dates, with guys at least.

The look on Sam's face was worth every honest syllable. "You haven't?" he asked. "I'm it?"

Oh Jesus, now Ian felt himself blushing. He cleared his throat but met Sam's eyes. "Yeah. You're it." Sam ducked his head again, looking still pink and maybe embarrassed, but for a different reason, Ian hoped.

Or wait, did he? *Hell.*

They were seated before Sam spoke again. "So, you've never been here before?"

Ian studied his menu, seeing nothing. "Nope."

Unfortunately, Sam continued his line of questioning. Ian tried not to squirm. "How did you find it?"

Ian sighed and put down his menu. "I asked Andy—my assistant, remember?" Sam nodded. "I asked her if there was a place in town where I could take you and not be, um, conspicuous."

"Conspicuous," Sam repeated flatly.

Hell, had he fucked up somehow? "Yeah. Stick out, you know."

"I know what it means." He didn't snap it out, so maybe Ian hadn't screwed up. "How would your assistant know where two guys might want to go on a date?"

Ian picked up his menu again, but couldn't really concentrate on it yet. "Her little brother's gay. She said some of his dates have taken him here."

When he peeked over the top of his menu, he could see Sam's mouth forming a silent "oh" while he looked around curiously. Ian smiled to himself and finally managed to read his menu.

"They have coquilles Saint Jacques," he said, surprised.

"Scallops? You like scallops?" Sam looked at him strangely.

"Yeah."

Sam kept staring at him. "You know, you aren't really what you seemed at first," he finally said. "I thought you'd be this working-class guy who drinks beer and watches ESPN2 hoping women's gymnastics is on. But you're into guys and you can say coquilles Saint Jacques with a quasi-French accent."

Ian smirked. "I like beer and gymnastics, but I'm hoping the men's team is competing."

Sam cocked his head. "To be the director of a department at a state agency, don't you need to have a degree? I know you said something about college . . ."

Ian gave him a look. "Seriously? You think most guys who're firefighters never went to school, don't you? Firefighting's competitive—most people have at least a two-year degree in Fire Science." He looked back at his menu. "I got a bachelor's in chemistry before I became a paramedic." When he glanced up from under his brows, Sam had that silent "oh" on his lips again.

Hell. "And I finished up my master's in public administration while I was recovering from the accident," he said.

Sam's eyebrows flew up, though he didn't look surprised exactly—he looked smug. Ian felt Sam's foot nudge his calf under the table. "You got yourself some book learnin', huh?"

Ian laughed loudly enough that people nearby looked at him, but what the hell? Sam was cute.

After telling Ian he'd decided on the cedar-plank salmon, Sam leaned over the table to whisper, "Did you notice the kinds of guys that are in here?"

He looked around. There was the odd male-female pairing, but mostly he saw guys. Usually two to a table, mostly on dates as far as he could see. "Gay guys?" he whispered back.

Sam kicked him lightly in the shin, scowling playfully. "I mean what type of gay guys."

Ian looked again. He couldn't suppress the smirk. Definitely a few older guys with very young dates. "Looks like chicken is the house specialty."

Sam nearly snorted out the water he was drinking. He kicked Ian again while laughing. "Does that mean I'm your boy?"

Yes. "No." Ian smirked. "I should have asked Dalton where to take you myself," he continued, "but he won't start work until next week. I have a feeling his take on this place would be different than Andy's."

"He's working for you?"

Ian nodded. "Just hired him yesterday. He's a nice kid. More your type than I am." He folded his menu and let his eyes wander around the room.

"What do you mean?" Sam asked. Fortunately, their waiter showed up to take their orders before Ian had to answer. After that, Ian got him to talk about what he read. It was supposed to be a simple, polite question, because he wasn't really into reading—Ian read when he had to, and otherwise didn't—but Sam was full of surprises.

"You read romance novels?"

Sam lifted his chin and took a turn looking around the room. "Yes," he answered firmly. "I do."

"So . . . gay romance novels?" *Were* there gay romance novels?

Sam fiddled with the wine he'd ordered, twirling the glass in slow circles on the tablecloth. "Yes, and het ones."

"Het like heterosexual?" Ian was trying not to smile. He'd been getting used to thinking of Sam as cute, but this was a whole new level of cuteness.

"Yeah, like heterosexual."

Their salads came, so Ian let Sam have a breather, but he had no intention of letting him off the hook.

"So, reading romance novels, this helps you with your writing?" Ian asked as soon as the waiter had ground their pepper and otherwise made himself necessary, then left.

Sam sighed and put his fork down, biting his lip. "No. I just like to read them. If anything, they *keep* me from writing."

"So that's not what you want to write?"

Sam shrugged one shoulder and took a sip of wine. Ian had a drink of some beer, thinking. "I know you're getting something out of it," he finally said. "You like them, but you also . . . study them, right?"

Sam gaped at him. "How'd you know that?"

Ian smiled instead of answering. He didn't know how he knew, he just did.

Sam took a deep breath. "Well . . ." He paused, inspecting Ian, probably to see if he really cared.

Shockingly, Ian did. He tried to look interested and encouraging, but since he'd never tried either of those expressions before, he had no clue if it worked. Something did, though.

"It's like, in romance novels, you always have two plots. There's the relationship plotline, and then there's a second story arc, you know?" Sam looked at him.

Ian nodded, just as if he did actually know. Hell, this showing interest thing was easy.

"Pretty much, you always know what's going to happen in the relationship plotline. But the oth—"

"Wait, if you know what's going to happen, why read it?'

Sam shrugged. "To find out *how* it happens."

"I don't get it." Ian picked up his beer again and took a drink. "Who cares how it happens? It happens; that's it. Knowing ruins the ending." Sam looked downright affronted. Ian had to hide his smile by taking another sip.

"Oh, that's so sad," Sam said, shaking his head. Ian waited for him to say *what* was so sad, but he sighed and looked down at his salad, carefully selecting his next bite.

"Fine, I'll ask. What's so sad?"

Sam looked at him with wide eyes. "You're one of those people who don't enjoy life, aren't you? You just work toward the next goal you set for yourself, never thinking about how you get there, only satisfied by reaching it. And when you don't reach it, you feel a sense of failure, right? Oh Ian, that explains so much about you."

What? He could only stare.

Sam burst out laughing, and it took Ian a few seconds to put it all together. Sam was *giving him shit*. That was just . . . beyond cute. It was *darling*.

"Oh my God," he muttered, dropping his head in his palm. *Darling*. This was way out of hand. Next thing he knew, he'd be calling Sam "kitten" or something. It was enough to put him off his salad. But he found himself smiling by the time Sam sputtered to a grinning stop.

They argued about whether knowing the ending of the story ruined it or not right through dessert. Sam tried to relate it to rugby, but since he didn't know anything about the sport—and Ian refused to help him—he ended up saying only, "You don't just play the game to win, right? You also play to *play*."

Which made total sense, but Ian refused to admit it. He couldn't kill his grin though, even as he argued right up until Sam gave in, throwing a piece of bread at Ian and then blushing furiously, looking around to see if anyone had seen.

It was so cute, Ian laughed. Fuck it, Sam *was* darling. That didn't mean anyone had to know Ian thought that. As long as he never slipped and used the name—or any other similar term of endearment—he'd be golden.

"Okay, kiddo, you ready to get out of here?"

Sam smiled up at him. "Thank you." Then he stood, giving Ian a few necessary seconds to recover from the wattage of the kid's gratitude.

Weird how, on a real date, all he really needed to get out of it was making Sam happy.

chapter 26

Dinner had been so easy—well, eventually—and this silence was anything but. Sam didn't like it. He was supposed to feel comfortable with quiet between them, but he had to clamp his teeth together to keep from babbling nervously while Ian parked the truck in a guest spot at Sam's apartment building.

And actually, the night hadn't been comfortable so much as exciting and fun and *omigod* Ian was turning off the engine. Sam froze like a scared rabbit, staring out the windshield with all his might.

"Do you want to come over to my place tonight?" Ian asked, and Sam nearly jumped. Well, he might have a little. Hopefully Ian wouldn't notice, but it would be hard not to since there were parking lot lights everywhere and the whole cab of Ian's pickup was bathed in that sort of orangey color of the kind of lights that they put in parking lots—

"Sam?"

Deep breath. What was *wrong* with him? He'd had sex with this guy. Why was this so different?

Duh. Because it was a date, not a hookup. "That wasn't just sex." He forced himself to turn his head and look at Ian across the cab. "That was, like, dinner and conversation and a date."

Ian looked at the steering wheel, following its curve with a fingertip. "Yeah."

"Why?"

"I might, um, have feelings for you."

Ker-thump went Sam's heart. "Like, friendship?"

Ian twisted his fists around the steering wheel. "Well, yeah, and maybe more stuff . . . I mean, it's more than sex, yeah," he said in a low voice.

Oh my God, how sweet was this shy, nervous guy where that uncaring bastard used to be? It was enough to give Sam courage. "When did you decide that?"

Ian muttered what sounded like a string of curses, then cleared his throat and spoke up, still barely loud enough for Sam to hear. "I kinda thought that since I came to your place last Saturday."

Well, that was just . . . irritating. "What was with your parameter, then?"

Ian huffed a big breath, still gripping the steering wheel like he was choking it. "I just . . . I didn't want to hurt you if I was wrong and it wasn't more than sex, or maybe not enough more, I don't know. Hell."

What a completely adorable idiot. Couldn't he see what was going on here? Obviously not. "What if *I* hurt *you*?"

Ian jerked his head around to look at him, eyes wide.

Sam barely kept himself from smirking. *Take* that *little dose of reality.*

chapter **27**

Sam had agreed to come home with him. Ian was happy about that, yeah, but also completely freaked out. Something had changed in the cab of his pickup, and he had an idea it might be the balance of power, which he really didn't want to think about.

Just go with the flow. It's a learning experience. You're learning about emotional connectedness.

That night he learned a lot about Sam. He learned that a blowjob made Sam's toes curl and his hips lift off the bed. When he reached for a condom, Sam breathlessly said, "Wait."

"Wha'?" Ian had thought all systems were go. He was sure as hell getting a green light from Sam's body.

Sam rolled onto his side and pushed on Ian's chest until he fell onto his back on the bed, while Ian mostly tried to hide that his chest was heaving. Sam looked at him seriously

Holy fuck, were they going to *talk*? Now? Ian just managed not to groan.

Sam took a deep breath. "Can we do it standing up?"

"Huh?"

"I've never been with anyone tall enough," Sam said, not quite looking at Ian. He lay on his side, one hand pillowing his head, nervously running fingers up and down Ian's arm.

The thought of Sam up against the wall, his pale skin and long, bony back and that tight little ass tensed up and waiting for him—that was pretty damned appealing. Ian cleared his throat. "You want to try it?" he asked.

"Yeah," Sam whispered, running his hand up to Ian's shoulder and stroking the muscle there. Finally he raised his gaze, too, meeting Ian's.

He couldn't help but kiss Sam. Not because his blood was pounding inside him—and it was—but because Sam was just . . . Sam. "Go stand next to the closet, facing the wall."

Sam immediately did what Ian told him, palms pressing into the wall, hips tilting back and butt muscles tensing up. He looked like prey—trying so hard to hold still he was nearly quivering with it.

Ian took his time, rolling on a condom and dropping the lube on the nearby nightstand, watching Sam shiver. He took two steps forward, nearly touching Sam's back, then slowly ran his fingers over Sam's skin to feel the bones underneath. He explored each vertebra while Sam tensed under his hands.

The balance of power had shifted back to him.

Maybe. *Does it matter*? Maybe.

When he reached between Sam's legs, intending to tease behind his balls, he found a surprise. Ian explored with his fingers, taking a second to figure it out, watching all the muscles in Sam's neck and shoulders clench up as he gently flicked the ring hanging there. "What's this?" he whispered, then kissed Sam's neck below his ear. He tugged gently on the new body jewelry.

Sam gasped. "I got rid of the barbell and put a ring in."

"For me?" Ian asked, his breath tripping over itself.

"Yeah," Sam whispered. "Kinda."

Good enough. He stopped teasing and started lubing Sam up and easing him open, trying not to go too fast, leaving the ring alone for now. By the time he finally pressed his cock against Sam's asshole, pushing in a fraction of an inch, they were both sweating. Breathing in unison, fast gulps of air. Ian planted his hands on the wall next to Sam's, caging him in. Sam moaned softly and tilted his hips further out, so Ian took advantage of the offer, fighting Sam's muscles to slide in farther, until he hit that magical point where they stopped trying to force his dick out and sucked him in instead.

He held still, all the way in, feeling Sam's butt muscles tense against his pelvis, body hair meshing, until Sam began to shake. Then Ian started the long, slow process of fucking him into the wall.

He learned more about Sam then. He learned Sam's balls were sensitive as hell, and the new guiche ring was maybe a little more tender than Ian had expected—he might have pushed it a bit at first. He learned that if he fucked Sam with long, quick strokes and then suddenly shoved himself all the way in and held there, Sam would turn into a trembling, squirming mess, begging Ian for more.

He had one arm across Sam's chest, fingers toying with a hard nipple, and one hand between his legs, gently caressing Sam's sac. His wrist rubbed accidentally against Sam's dick. "Don't move," he barked when Sam tried to take a hand off the wall. Sam let out a moaning sob, squirming more. Ian took his hand off Sam's chest and slapped his hip, hard. "I said don't move," he growled. He felt Sam's dick jerk against his wrist, then wetness oozed onto his arm, so he took Sam's shaft in his free hand to find out his dick was slippery and coated with pre-cum.

That was just too fucking much. "Jesus, Sam," he groaned, and started the quick strokes again, shoving Sam into the wall and Sam's dick into his hand. "Gonna ride your ass until you come for me, kiddo."

Sam groaned loudly and shoved himself back into Ian's hips, widening his stance. Ian watched his fingers curl against the wall, all the long muscles in his back tense and shaking.

"C'mon," Ian muttered, dropping his head onto Sam's neck. That was damn close to begging, but fuck, if Sam didn't come soon, Ian was going to—

Hot, liquid silk spilled into his hand, and Sam's body shuddered while he sobbed and groaned. Ian was so relieved that he thrust into Sam too hard, his hand colliding with the wall, but he was coming and just didn't care. Sam wasn't complaining. Ian couldn't move anyway, shoved inside Sam as deep as possible. For the first time in memory, he wished he could feel himself shooting into someone and not just into the damned latex. He gripped Sam's hip tighter and tried to imagine he was.

Sam sagged into his arms and his hair tangled in Ian's whiskers. Ian thought about propping him up against the wall, but he held him instead. Waiting until they'd both caught their breath some before he helped Sam the two steps to bed in spite of his own unsteady legs.

When Ian stumbled back from cleaning up in the bathroom, Sam was crashed out on his stomach, spread-eagle across the mattress. It took Ian forever to nudge and prod Sam onto his side, listening to his sleepy, nonsensical murmurs the whole time. It was cute.

Eventually, Ian curled up behind Sam with an arm around his middle. He started to tell himself Sam would like this, being spooned, but he was too tired and sated to deal with his own B.S., so he just hugged Sam tighter and kissed one bony vertebra before drifting off.

When Ian woke up in the morning, he was still wrapped around Sam, just the way he'd been when he'd fallen asleep. The room was full of sunlight. Why did it always shine like that when Sam was here?

Something about lying in bed with all that beautiful skin pressed right up against him made Ian a little drunk. Not his normal self. Sam had the softest skin Ian had ever felt on any guy. It was white, too. Milky. *Milk-fed veal.* He watched the light entwine itself with the almost invisible hairs on the back of Sam's neck. That neck needed to be kissed, didn't it?

He had a feeling he should be alarmed that his whiskers raised a mild pink rash when he rubbed his chin into Sam's neck and shoulders. Instead, he felt some weird emotion he would have called pride in other circumstances. A nice guy would be concerned for Sam's skin; Ian just wanted to mark all the paleness he could reach. Apparently he wasn't much of a nice guy.

It wasn't exactly news to him. Anyway, he was sort of a nice guy. He did his best to kiss it all better after he rubbed the rash in. Sam woke up squirming and giggling, and it was cute as hell. Ian kissed him thoroughly and then went to make him pancakes.

chapter 28

Ian had a waking snuggly episode on Saturday—as opposed to his sleeping ones, which he apparently had no clue about. Even more shocking for Sam, when he got snuggly, he also got chatty. Not just the short flashes of talkative he'd shown before, but chatty—playful and teasing and flirtatious. A little like dinner last night, but with full-body contact.

At first, Sam was concerned that Ian had some previously unmentioned mental health issue, like maybe multiple personality disorder. But by the time Sam had spent an hour lying on the couch, wrapped in Ian's arms while Ian ruffled his hair and dropped periodic kisses on some sensitive, exposed bit of skin, Sam decided that if Ian's mental illness was his cross to bear, he'd do it gladly. He would make the sacrifice and be held until he almost overheated, and listen to that intimate voice that went soft and hoarse. The voice that more often than not was speaking directly into Sam's ear, about anything and everything that popped into Ian's head. He happily suffered Ian's kisses behind his jaw and down his neck, the ones that made him shiver but didn't seem to be designed to turn him on.

It was during the snuggly attack that Sam first allowed himself to think he just might be getting *it*. The romance hero gold standard: a perfect love with his personal prince charming. After a suitable wooing period, of course.

About an hour into his episode, Ian turned his head to look into Sam's eyes, so close Sam could barely focus on him. "What was it like, coming out to your family?"

Sam blinked. "I never came out to my family."

Ian pulled away and peered at him more intently. "They don't know?"

"Of course they know! Sheesh. I mean I never had to *tell* anyone. It was sort of just . . . general knowledge." Sam thought about it while Ian laid his head back on the pillow they were sharing and nuzzled at his cheek. "Well, I guess I told my grandma."

"What did she say?" Ian murmured.

"I got to the part where I was telling her, 'Grandma, I like boys,' but she interrupted me and said, 'What kind of fool do you think I am? We had fancy boys back in my day. I know one when I see one.'"

Ian laughed so hard Sam was torn between squirming pleasure at having amused him and indignation at being the subject of his laughter. Squirming pleasure won when Ian wrapped his arm tighter around Sam and squeezed him against his chest, saying into his ear, "You're so cute."

Sam was a fool for cute.

Ian suddenly pulled back again and gripped Sam's chin in his fingers. "Let's get out of here and go do something."

Ian's idea of "getting out of here" was going to the farmers' market on the riverfront and buying vegetable matter. It was strangely domestic in a way that should have been boring or disappointing but gave Sam a secret thrill instead. Which led to him mostly trying not to overthink what it meant that Ian wanted to shop for food with him.

To think or not to think, that was the question.

Come to think of it, the real problem was just overthinking.

I think.

Possibly he should stop thinking about it now. He looked down at the shopping bag he was holding. It didn't offer much in the way of alternative topics for thought.

We're playing house.

No you aren't, he just needed to go shopping.

Seriously, don't ruin this for me. Let's play house.

He sighed in resignation.

"What are you thinking about?" Ian asked him suddenly. He held apples in his hands—judging the merits of different varieties? Sam didn't know; he'd been too busy playing house with himself to pay attention.

"Nothing," he squeaked when Ian stared at him.

"Huh. Looks like you're so busy thinking about nothing you can't give me your opinion on apples."

"The red ones are better," Sam said hastily.

Ian looked down at the fruit in his hands. "They're both red."

"No, that one's red," Sam waved his hand at the right apple, "and that one's green with red splotches."

Ian grunted curiously, like a caveman who'd just discovered the wheel. He started to put down the red and green apple.

"Wait!" Sam said. "The red and green ones are better. The all-red are too sweet."

Ian scrunched his brow. "Then why'd you say the red one?"

Dammit, he'd been found out. "I wasn't paying attention," he mumbled.

Ian smirked at him. "I knew you were thinking about something else." He looked Sam up and down slowly, making it clear exactly what he thought Sam had been distracted by.

Dammit. Now Sam was thinking about sex. He frowned at Ian in what he hoped was a quelling manner.

Ian grinned at him and waggled his eyebrows. Sam had always thought waggling eyebrows was sort of lame and dorky, but somehow Ian made even that look like sex. When he couldn't squelch a tiny grin, Ian seemed satisfied, finally turning back to his apples.

Oh God, how sweet, he's indulging in unspoken flirtation with me. As if they had real intimacy and a history. A history longer than a couple of weeks.

Sam was so far gone. This had better turn out all right or his damn heart was going to hemorrhage. *Don't think about it.* "Why are we doing this again?" he asked quickly.

Ian made a face, digging out his wallet to pay. He handed the fruit to the stand attendant for weighing. "Because I promised myself I'd stay healthy and eat better."

"That's three fifty-eight," the girl running the scale said.

For four apples? Sam was about to ask her if she'd maybe made a mistake on her big, huge calculator with the big, huge buttons when Ian muttered, "Damn organic fruit."

"Whoa, you're really trying to eat better." He almost poked Ian in his nonexistent gut, but he still hadn't figured out if touching was okay in public and if so, how much.

Ian's teeth flashed in a quick smile while he dug through his wallet. "Yeah, well don't do it if you aren't going to do it right." From where he stood, Sam could see the corner of his eye crinkling in little laugh lines he'd never noticed before. Oh, and an elusive dimple.

Sheesh, that was sexier than the eyebrow waggling.

At the exotic fruit stand—did they fly it in from some small Hawaiian farm to this little, local farmers' market? It was messing with his definition of "local"—Sam was looking at pineapples when he felt Ian just behind his shoulder. Ian's hip nudged Sam's ass, and his hand landed on Sam's biceps, then made a slow trip down his arm, his thumb tickling Sam's palm for a split-second before he whispered throatily in Sam's ear, "Why don't you let me carry that bag?"

Apparently, covert touching was okay. Sam heartily supported that.

At the weird knickknacky stand that sold just . . . stuff, Ian cornered him in the back of the stall, behind some kind of concealing sculptural object. He placed a hand on the small of Sam's back, slipping a couple fingers into his waistband and teasing the skin just above the crack of his ass. "What do you think of that?" he asked Sam in a low voice, breath brushing the nape of his neck.

Sam tried to focus on some strange sculptural thing. "What is it?" It was made out of cut-up plastic soda bottles. Maybe.

"I don't know," Ian murmured, leaning in close enough to nip his skin. "Does it matter?"

"No," Sam whispered, trying not to melt.

Ian chuckled and withdrew his hand, leaving Sam feeling flushed and dizzy.

Guh. Who knew shopping could be foreplay?

By the time they were done buying all of Ian's fruits and vegetables (how many could he eat in a week?), Sam was abuzz. Drunk on Ian and on being with Ian in public—a straight-people-abound public—and on being touched by Ian. His skin was fairly humming with the possibility of being touched more—their little gay sex secret, surrounded by all those ignorant straight people.

It was possibly pathetic, but he'd never been on this kind of date. He and his first boyfriend Bryce had dated much like prey animals on the African savannah must—amidst a vast herd of their kind, hoping the cheetahs would find someone weaker to pick on. They'd never ventured out to the waterhole alone.

Marley had never taken him on a date, or vice versa. Unless visiting Marley's pot dealer counted as a date. That guy was straight, and as far as Sam could figure, 90 percent of his clientele was equally hetero.

Not that he'd gone there with Marley much, just a couple of times in the beginning. Marley had called him a "drag" because he wouldn't smoke up with them, and he never wanted to hang out. Sam hadn't understood why they needed to hang out and offer to smoke some of the marijuana with the dealer from whom Marley had just bought it.

That question had earned him a lecture on the etiquette of buying drugs. That had been Sam's last trip to the dealer's house.

An errant Frisbee hit Sam in the chest, bringing him back to the present with Ian. It dropped onto the path at his feet, and Ian laughed.

"Still thinking about nothing?" he teased, bending to pick up the Frisbee. Sam watched his shirt ride up just enough to show a brief slice of skin. *Yummy.*

Focus. "That thing just hit me," Sam said, tuning in to what was going on outside of Ian's pants.

Ian stood up, smiling. "Yeah, it did, kiddo. I better figure out who this belongs to. You want to keep heading back to the truck, and I'll catch up?"

They were standing in the middle of the walking path, a large sloping stretch of grass to their right and the river to their left. It was a nice day, so people were around, but not too many. "I'll wait," Sam said.

Ian nodded, looking uphill at a guy jogging toward them. "That must be the owner of the Frisbee, anyway." The dude had on sandals and shorts, and a dog with a bandana around its neck trotted in front of him. Your standard Frisbee-playing neo-hippie.

"Hey, you wanna play, man?" he yelled at Ian.

Did people just do that? Ask strange men to play Frisbee? No one had ever asked Sam. He turned back to Ian and realized why—Ian looked like the kind of guy who might toss things around for fun in a park on a nice day. Sam probably looked like the kind of guy who couldn't catch. He sighed.

"You care?" Ian asked, looking like a hopeful little boy.

That little boy look would get Ian far. Sam shrugged and smiled. "It's fine with me." He found a bench to sit on and watched while Ian jogged over to the guy. Then he had the entirely novel experience of watching his completely hot . . . well, the completely hot guy who was doing him play catch in the park.

It was surreal and quickly got Sam to the point where he was fantasizing about chasing Ian down like a Frisbee and tackling him, ripping open his fly and reaching into his bulging briefs to wrap fingers around—

"Well, if it isn't Sam, sitting in the park watching all the sexy boys who'll never give him a second look."

Sam closed his eyes. *Un-fucking-real.* He knew that voice coming from the path behind him very well. Maybe if he pretended to be deaf, Marley would just go away.

"Hey, Sam, I know ya can hear me, you skinny little fuck," Marley slurred.

Sam dug his phone out of his pocket and checked it, carefully ignoring Marley. Just after one in the afternoon, and Marley was drunk. Some things never changed. Had he ever sobered up in the past two years?

Marley snuffled closer, blowing foul breath over Sam's shoulder. *Ugh.* How could he have forgotten that Marley was a dedicated mouth-breather? And sheesh, his hygiene had gone downhill precipitously. Sam held his breath; it helped with both the stench and the not-speaking thing.

"You 'noring me, Sammy-boy?" Marley asked, his tone edging into menace. "Can't have that." He came around the end of the bench and sat too damn close to Sam, right up against his thigh. Sam's skin tried to crawl away, even with the layer of denim between them.

He checked Marley out in his peripheral vision. Oh God, he was even fatter and sloppier. Sam could see a slice of skin where Marley's shirt rode up over his expanded beer gut, and it was so completely the opposite of the skin he'd spied on Ian.

Marley hadn't been anywhere near this repulsive when Sam had been seeing him. In the beginning, he'd even showered regularly. Not even *Sam's* self-esteem was low enough to date a guy like the current Marley.

Marley dropped a fleshy hand on Sam's knee, breathing loudly too damn close to his ear.

That's it. Sam grabbed the shopping bag and stood up, shaking Marley's hand off. Ian could find him at the truck. Sam took one last glance at him, just leaping to catch the Frisbee, joyously playing some simple game, making the disc sail into the air with a negligent flick. Sam's heart sank.

He's not my kind. He faced Marley, who was struggling to get his bulk off the bench. *But I'd rather be alone if he's my kind.*

Sam turned and headed toward the truck.

Ian didn't know what the hell had happened. One minute he was having mindless fun at the park, and the next he was seeing Sam walk off with what looked like some obese, homeless guy harassing him. The guy had dreads, a holey T-shirt, and a ratty pair of shorts in danger of slipping off his ass. He was right behind Sam, practically tripping on his heels, not quite up to Sam's shoulder, but menacing just the same. Ian's instincts were screaming at him, and he trusted his instincts.

"Gotta go, man!" he shouted at the Frisbee kid, then hurried to catch Sam and the malingering asshole.

When he was a couple feet behind them, he heard the bum say, "Have you had yer watertight boy-pussy reamed lately, Sammy? You used to love it when I did you, dintchoo? C'mon, Sammy-boy, you wanna g—"

Ian grabbed the guy's shoulder and spun him around, barely stopping himself from raising his fist and smashing the prick's face in. "Sam," he said between his teeth. "Who the fuck is this?"

Sam was a good ten feet up the path by then, walking fast, but he stopped cold and slowly turned around. "He's my ex, Marley," he said shakily.

Ian almost punched the guy on principle. Not the principle of him being an asshole, although that was reason enough, but the fact that he'd dated Sam and treated him like shit. He took a deep breath and leaned down, right in the guy's face, despite the fumes wafting off him and Ian's watering eyes. "Get. The fuck. Out of here. I never want to see you near Sam again."

Marley the Ex stumbled off with gratifying speed, nearly going down when he turned to scurry away. Ian should have punched him— he'd claim the guy fell on his fist and the cops would go for it, he was sure.

You aren't that kind of guy. Anymore.

When he turned and got a look at Sam's pale face and his trembling hands, he wished he was. "Let's go home," he said softly.

When they finally made it back to his pickup, Ian's adrenaline rush was leaving him. He felt as if his frown had set in concrete. Sam wasn't in any better a mood—he hadn't said a word to Ian the whole way back, which had the effect of pissing Ian off even more. When they reached the passenger side, he unlocked Sam's door and yanked it open impatiently, then stalked around to the driver's side to do the same.

Once they were settled in the cab, he put the key in the ignition but didn't start it. He could feel Sam's mood drifting into his space like a dark cloud. Not an angry dark cloud, a depressed one, and Ian had a pretty good idea why. "I can't believe you went out with a loser like that," he spat out. Damn, he sounded angry. He needed to tone it down for Sam's sake. "You *lived* with him?"

Hell, that wasn't any better.

Sam turned his face away. Ian could almost see the cloud settling heavier on his head, his body slumping down with it. "Yeah," he said quietly.

Ian waited for more, but Sam stayed still and silent, his shoulders hunched forward as if for protection. That annoyed Ian too. "Want to tell me why the fuck you'd move in with a prick like that?"

Sam cleared his throat, but didn't look at him. "He wasn't as bad when we first met. He wasn't so overweight, and he took better care of himself."

Ian closed his eyes a second and, with supreme effort, softened his voice. "That's not what I mean. I want to know if he treated you like that back then."

Sam slid further down in the seat, hunching even more, but at least now Ian could see his profile.

"What the fuck were you thinking?" Ian's voice filled the cab. He struggled to rein it in again.

Sam took a deep breath and straightened up in his seat. It looked like it took a lot of effort. His back straight as a ruler, now, and his shoulders almost back where they belonged, he clasped his hands in his lap tightly. "I don't know."

Ian stared. That was it? He didn't know? But now he looked angry, at least, which was better than depressed—half the reason for Ian's annoyance, if he was honest. A depressed Sam twisted something under his sternum, giving him a violent need to get rid of the feeling.

Except now Sam was staring out the front windshield like he could melt the glass with his laser-beam eyes. Ian inspected the side of his face, trying to get a clue on how badly he'd fucked up. Because he obviously had.

Hell.

Fine, they'd head back to his place. They could both cool off on the drive, and he'd get some answers there.

Sighing, Ian turned the key and backed out.

chapter 29

Sam should have just let loose and told Ian what a bastard he was, but he didn't have the energy. Or the balls. Maybe both.

They rode silently back to Ian's place. Sam got out as soon as Ian had parked, before he even shut off the engine, just wanting to get away from him. He stalked over and waited at Ian's door. Yeah, he had a key, but he wasn't going to use it now.

When Ian let him in, Sam went straight for his backpack on one of the living room chairs. He clutched the straps of his bag tightly in his fist and walked into the bedroom, finding scattered clothes and shoving them in without folding them first.

Not that he would have folded them even if he weren't so mad he was shaking.

"What are you doing?" Ian asked quietly from behind him.

Ha! As if he didn't know. Sam snatched up a sock and said, as calmly as possible, "I'm going back to my place." He marched into the bathroom, catching sight of Ian's confused expression out of the corner of his eye.

Ian followed him to the door and stood there. Sam swore he heard him swallow. "Do you have to go?"

"Yes."

"Because you have to work tonight?"

"That too," Sam snapped.

"I thought maybe I could pick you up after work . . ."

Sam sighed, annoyed, and dropped his pack on the bathroom floor. Where had he left his dumb toothbrush? "Why would you want me to come back? You made it clear you think I'm a loser. I thought you'd be happy to get rid of me."

Okay, fine, annoyed and incredibly hurt. And maybe ashamed of himself. He glanced up and saw Ian's reflection gaping at him in the mirror. What, he didn't expect Sam to call him on it?

"I didn't say that," Ian sputtered. "I said *he's* a loser, not you!"

"Yeah, and I lived with him. So I'm a loser too." Suddenly Sam was exhausted. He wished he could lie down on Ian's bed. Maybe he'd get lucky on the bus home and have two seats to himself, so he could stretch out. He turned to Ian, ready to get this over with. "It's not like I'm surprised, Ian. I mean, I knew I wasn't your kind before this started. I just sort of forgot for a bit." Sam looked away, cringing inside but trying to hide it. "It was nice, pretending you'd want to be with a guy—"

"Would you *stop* that shit?" Ian yelled. He took a deep breath and continued in a more controlled voice. "Yes, fine, I'm a shallow bastard who couldn't see you for what you were when we met. I'm sorry, okay? Things are different now."

"But you told me I wasn't—"

"I was wrong. You *are* my type."

Sam swallowed and tried again. "But you aren't attracted to me, not really, Ian."

Ian stared at him. "I am too, Sam. I'm crazy attracted to you, can't you see that?"

"Well, you think my mouth—"

"All of you." Ian moved toward him, reaching out for him, but Sam stepped back with a sneak attack of nausea. "I just . . . I see *you* now." Ian came forward again, trying to trap him against the sink, but Sam slipped off to the side. He couldn't let Ian catch him and convince him he meant what he was saying.

But maybe we'd like to know what he thinks. Sam tried to shove the questioning part of himself back into its little room and slam the door.

It didn't work. "How . . . how do you see me?" He wanted to hit himself in the forehead as soon as the words were out. Did he really want to know how Ian saw him? His digestive system felt like it had worms in it already. Sam closed his eyes and hung his head. God, he was pathetic.

He felt Ian's breath on his face and Ian's body heat, suddenly too close. He opened his eyes to see Ian's jaw and his arms reaching for Sam. When Sam took another step back, he realized Ian had trapped him against the wall. "Will you let me show you instead of telling you?" Ian ducked his head, attempting to meet Sam's eyes.

Sam's stomach lurched. "Right now?" he squeaked.

"You have to go to work soon, right?"

Sam nodded slowly, risking a glance up. Ian was inches from him, all the anger and disgust from earlier gone from his face. Had it really all been about Marley? His green eyes looked so sincere.

"After work," Ian said.

Hesitantly, Sam shrugged. Could he actually do that?

"Do you want me to take you home so you can think about it? You could call me from work, and I'll come get you. Or you could wait awhile if you need to." Ian paused, then added, "But Sam, I need you to trust me." He gripped Sam's shoulder, squeezing once but not letting go.

"My safeword is grapefruit," Sam responded. If this was just about *that* kind of trust, then he could—

"Not like that. I mean, that's good, but I want you to believe me when I show you how I see you. I'm not going to hurt you. I'm not blowing smoke up your ass."

Maybe that was supposed to be a joke, but Sam didn't feel like smiling yet. When Ian promised not to hurt him, they weren't talking about physical pain; they were talking about Sam's biggest weakness. "I don't know," he whispered.

Ian stroked hair off Sam's forehead. "Are you scared?"

"Yeah." And close to puking.

Ian breathed out slowly, a controlled sigh. "But you'll think about it?"

Sam swallowed with difficulty. "Okay."

The ride to Sam's apartment was silent again, but in a different way. The air was still tense, but not angrily so. More like expectantly. As if Ian was waiting for him to say something. Sam couldn't think of anything, not until they parked in a visitor spot at his complex and Ian reached across the console, taking Sam's hand in his and stroking it with his thumb.

"Sam . . ."

"Why were you so mad?"

He felt Ian staring at the side of his face, but kept watching Ian's thumb caressing his skin. Ian shifted in his seat. "You mean so mad about Marley?"

"Yeah."

"Because . . . you think you aren't worth more than him. That prick wanted you to think that, and he used your self-image against you. And you let him."

"Oh." After another minute of staring at Ian's thumb on the back of his hand, Sam pulled away to get out of the pickup.

"Call me," Ian said.

Sam looked at him, then shut the door.

Sam walked in his door, dropped his pack on the floor, flopped on his unmade bed, and hit speed dial on his cell. Nik answered on the second ring. "Ian's attracted to me," Sam blurted as soon as he heard Nik's breath.

Nik didn't miss a beat. "Well, I would hope so, considering the time he's devoted to getting into your pants."

"That's what he says, I mean, that he's attracted to me. But . . ." Sam paused, wishing for the bad old days when he had a curly phone cord to twist around one finger. He twisted his hair instead, but it wasn't the same. "Do you think he's lying?" Sam whispered.

"He's not lying. Why would he lie about that?"

"I don't know," Sam nearly wailed. He shot up from the bed and started pacing, kitchen counter to empty laundry basket (ringed by dirty clothes on the floor) and back.

"Why is this so hard to get through your head, Sam? Guys will and do find you attractive. Deal with it."

Nik's exasperation was a little bit comforting, just not quite enough. "But he didn't find me attractive at first," Sam pointed out.

Nik sighed loudly. "When I met Jurgen, I thought he was an asshole, and now he's *my* big, dumb asshole. It's a complete one-eighty. But I suppose you're feeling emotionally needy, and I should be drawing from my carefully guarded sympathy reserves?"

Sam nodded vigorously, hoping it would translate over the phone line. "Yes, that. Pretend you're being graded on it and give me your best caring friend impersonation."

"Okay, give me a minute," Nik grumbled. Sam heard him set down the phone.

It took several minutes, actually, during which Sam chewed his lip and paced some more. Occasionally, he yanked on his hair for variety. Then Nik came back on the line, sounding downright excited. "I've got something, I think. Do you remember when Jurgen came up from Whitetail Rock after I returned to school in the fall and fucked me on my desk while I was wearing his handcuffs?"

Wait a second. "I knew about the handcuffs, but on your desk? In your office? At school? Omigod, Nik, you never told me that! That's kinda hot, isn't it? Although I'm glad I didn't inherit that desk because it doesn't have a lot of clearance in the leg hole, and I wouldn't want to hit my—"

"Sam! Don't get distracted."

"I can't help it, you never told me about the desk part before."

Sam could all but hear Nik's hand land on his hip. "I never meant to, either. It's a sign of how excited I am to successfully offer sympathy to my best friend."

Dammit. He'd been distracted for a minute or so until Nik reminded him he had worries. "Sorry, go on."

"When he left after that first time and I told you about it, do you remember what you said?"

Oh no, a pop quiz. "Umm, did I say it was hot? Because if I didn't, I should have."

"Yes, of *course* you said it was hot, but what else did you say?"

"Umm . . ."

Nik made a small, exasperated noise. "Sam! You asked me if I was still hung up on him being white and me *not* being white."

"Oh, yeah . . ."

Silence stretched between them.

"Do you see what I mean?" Nik asked.

Sam cast his eyes around the room, hoping for some inspiration. Nothing. "No."

"Oh my God. This is why I never do this sympathy thing. I'm not very good at it. It's really not my forte and I'm all right with—"

"Maybe if you just told me more explicitly what you're trying to say, instead of dropping hints, I might understand the point."

Nik took what sounded like a deep, calming breath. Very evenly, he said, "I had problems believing Jurgen was attracted to me for *me*, and you have problems believing Ian is attracted to you for *you*. Maybe if you give him a chance, he'll show you that you can believe him, just like Jurgen showed me."

"Ooh," Sam whispered, finally getting it.

Nik gave him a respectful few seconds before asking, "Okay, are we done? My well of sympathy is drying up."

"Almost. But wait, I have a question . . ."

"Ask it! Like sand in an hourglass, my sympathy is running—"

"Why was it less scary to have Marley use my self-image to hurt me than it is to have Ian want me to think I'm attractive?"

"Oh," Nik said thoughtfully. "That's a tough one."

"Yeah."

"You want my advice?" Sam was about to decline, but Nik didn't wait for him to answer. "Don't think about it too much, just go with it."

"Thanks," Sam said uncertainly.

"Anytime. So we're done, right?"

It wasn't until his last break that Sam managed to phone Ian. At first he'd still been waffling . . . or freaking out, more like. Then Fatty's had gotten busy, and he couldn't take the time. Plus he had to shake Tineke off his tail long enough to call—her eerie sixth sense for relationship milestones or troubles had kicked in again, and she suffered under the delusion that she was entitled to know about them.

Finally, at nine thirty, Sam took his break while Tineke was busy with a garrulous old lady taken out far past her bedtime by her lame-ass son. The lady felt someone needed to share her displeasure, and Tineke was in the line of fire. Was it wrong that Sam had purposely seated the old lady in Tineke's section, hoping this would be the result? Did he care?

Ian answered on the first ring. "Yeah?" he said gruffly.

"Hi," Sam said uncertainly.

"Hi, kiddo," Ian responded, still gruff. Had he been waiting for Sam to call? *He answered on the first ring.*

"Um, would you still pick me up after work?"

"Yes," Ian said immediately. His voice softened. "I want you to come over."

chapter **30**

By the time Sam finally called at 9:33, Ian was convinced he wasn't interested in seeing him again. He steeled himself for it when he answered the phone.

It wouldn't be so bad, right? Sam was his first attempt at emotional connectedness. There would be more opportunities.

I want this *opportunity*.

And thank fuck, he got it. He hung up the phone and immediately started making plans. The first order of business was to make the place welcoming for Sam.

He couldn't see any way to avoid it; he called Jurgen.

Jurgen answered after two rings. "Hey."

"Hey."

After a few seconds of silence, Jurgen asked, "S'up?"

Ian took a deep breath. "Uh, I was wondering what kind of wine Nik likes to drink." That'd probably be what Sam drank, right?

"Why do you care what kind of wine Nik drinks?" Jurgen asked.

He had to cough a blockage out of his throat before he could answer. "Just want to have it handy in case you guys stop by."

"Hang on," Jurgen said. Ian heard him ask, "What kind of wine does Sam drink?"

"Hell," Ian muttered. Not that he should have expected to fool Jurgen.

Distantly, he heard Nik call back, "Tell him any chardonnay over seven dollars from 2011 will be fine. And chill it!"

"You get that?" Jurgen asked. "Neither one of us has to work on Tuesday, so we'll be stopping by for dinner about six thirty. Don't forget the wine. Make sure Sam's there, too."

"What is this, an inspection?"

"Yep," Jurgen said. Then the smart-ass hung up.

Ian found the wine at the local grocery store.

"It's good," the dude working there said for about the third time when Ian asked. He was pretty sure the guy added "Jesus," under his breath.

It was ten dollars, so it must be okay wine, right? He'd never pay that for a six-pack. Ian bought it, took it home, put it in the fridge, and immediately left again.

In the pickup he started the engine, and the digital clock on the dashboard lit up. It was only ten thirty. Sam didn't get off work for an hour. He really should go back inside and wait. Watch some television. Maybe men's gymnastics was on.

Fuck that.

He drove slowly. Then, when he got to Fatty's, he circled the block a few times, pretending to look for a parking spot—completely ignoring Fatty's lot. That ate up about five minutes. He gave in and ended up in customer parking: a space near the employee entrance, one where his pickup was fully illuminated in the light from the fixture mounted over the door.

A half hour wasn't *that* early.

While he waited for Sam, he mentally reviewed his plan while watching his thumbnail trace the grooves in the gearshift knob.

Wine for Sam: check.

Beer for him: check.

Lube and condoms: check.

Half-formed, half-assed plan for what he wanted to do with Sam once he had him tipsy and lubed up: check.

Sam: not yet.

His heartbeat was a bit off-kilter.

Yeah, so maybe he was a little agitated.

Obviously, he felt *something* for Sam—even if he hadn't figured out exactly what that feeling was. And so what if it made his lungs constrict every time he thought about—someday—telling Sam what he felt? That'd go away eventually, right? Sam deserved to know the truth. Ian had been such a bastard in the beginning, and Sam deserved to know things were changing inside him now.

Emotional-type things.

He should start out slowly though, for both their sakes, so tonight would be only about his physical craving for Sam. Just looking at him made Ian ache, a full-body, internal, gotta-be-with-him-now throb. Yeah, he liked what was inside the Sam package, but somewhere along the way, even Sam's awkward skinniness had become attractive. Hot.

Ian got that Sam was scared. He may not get what exactly Sam was scared of, but if Marley was anything to judge by, Sam had never been with someone he could really trust. Ian would be damned if he was going to be another guy like that.

He heard a noise and jerked his head up, staring at the door of Fatty's as it opened and a woman about Ian's age walked out, followed by Sam. The waitress from the other night, he thought. She saw his truck first, and looked at it—and him through the windshield—carefully, as if she could determine his moral and financial worth by visual inspection.

Sam grabbed her arm when she started over to the pickup, and she turned and had what looked like a debate with him. Finally, though, Sam let her go and she stayed put while he walked over to Ian, hitching his pack onto one shoulder and grasping the strap tightly with both hands.

Ian stopped paying attention to the woman. His heart echoed every step Sam took toward him. For the first time, he wasn't chasing Sam; Sam was choosing to be with him.

Everything stilled for a split second while something important happened under his ribs. Whatever it was felt amazing. Made him feel alive.

Sam didn't look at him as got in the cab, nor once he'd settled his pack on the floor between his feet. Ian wanted to reach for him, pull him across the console and—

"I don't want to talk about Marley," Sam said quietly.

Thank fuck, because neither did he. "Okay."

Sam nodded slowly, pulling his seatbelt on. "So tonight, um . . ."

"Tonight's about how much I want you."

Sam looked at him then, eyes wide and lips parted. "That sounds . . . carnal."

Ian leaned toward him and took Sam's chin in his hand, tracing Sam's lips with the tip of his finger. "It will be." He pulled Sam forward with the hand on his chin, until he could brush Sam's lips with his while he spoke. "I don't just like to see your lips wrapped around my cock or feel you suck my balls. I like to kiss you. Feel your lips against mine." He slipped the tip of one finger into the heat of Sam's mouth, and Sam immediately licked at it, twining his tongue around it. "I like to feel your mouth respond to me. I like to know it's going straight to your dick when I stroke inside it just right." He pulled his finger out, leaving a slick trail on Sam's skin.

"It does," Sam breathed.

Ian took Sam's upper lip between his teeth and tugged, then licked to soothe any sting. "Good." He brought his other hand up and held Sam's head, fingers tunneling into his hair. "I want you, Sam." Then Ian kissed him, trying to make it like the first time, losing control in his mouth.

Judging by the dazed look on Sam's face when Ian pulled away, he'd managed it. Ian let go of him, feeling light-headed himself, heart pounding in his eardrums. He adjusted his dick and started the truck.

Sam was nervous when they got to Ian's place. It was obvious in the way he stood by the door, playing with the strap of his backpack. Ian kissed him quickly. "Put your pack down, and I'll get you a glass of wine."

Sam jerked his head up. "You have wine?"

Ian ducked his head and smiled. "Yeah. Let me get you some. Take off your shoes and your coat."

When he came back from the kitchen, Sam had lost his shoes and jacket. Ian gave him a glass of wine and had Sam sit on the floor between his legs while he sat on the couch. He took a sip of the beer he'd gotten for himself, pulled Sam gently back until he was leaning against the couch, and then he started rubbing his shoulders.

Sam froze for a second, then settled into Ian's hands. It took half a glass of wine and a thorough massage of Sam's shoulders, neck, and head before Ian felt that Sam was relaxed enough. He stroked up Sam's neck, running fingers through his hair until Sam tipped his head forward, sighing. Then Ian suggested they go into the bedroom.

He'd left one dim light turned on next to the bed. "Lie down," he said softly, and Sam did, on his side, looking at him with a mixture of curiosity and apprehension. Ian lay down next to him and started slowly kissing him, seducing him, making him desperate to lose each article of clothing before helping him out of it. He didn't waste words on explaining to Sam why he found him attractive. Instead, he tried to show how much he liked Sam's reactions. The way his flat, pinkish-brown nipples hardened for Ian's fingers, or the way his skin shivered under Ian's touch. Sam's abs tensed when Ian nibbled his way down his concave belly, and it made Ian want to rub against him like he was marking him with his scent.

Ian had hoped Sam would lose the power of speech by the time they were both naked and he was pulling Sam over him, but Sam wasn't that far gone.

"You want me to be on top?" Sam asked.

"Yeah, I do. Hop on, kiddo." Jesus, even that pouty lip was sexy, but Ian wouldn't let himself sink his teeth into it until Sam did what he asked.

Sam sighed and hesitated, but finally climbed astride Ian, all arms and legs and prominent joints and bones. "I don't know why you like to look at me like this," he said.

"You're sexy," Ian told him, watching Sam's long muscles move under his skin. "I like to watch you fuck yourself on me." He curled up, pulling Sam's head down for a kiss. Sam pulled back and looked him in the eyes, still pouting.

Ian could feel him, only half-hard against his belly now. He gyrated a little, letting Sam's cock drag across his tensed abs. For a few seconds, Sam got distracted, furrowing his brow and closing his eyes. Ian could *see* him feeling it, skin slipping across skin, some slide and stutter as Ian pressed against him harder.

But it didn't last. Sam cracked his lids and whispered, "But I'm skinny and gangly and *awkward*."

Ian used the hand on the back of Sam's neck to pull him closer again. He nipped Sam's bottom lip very lightly. "It's a very sexy kind of awkward."

Sam pushed his lip out more. Pouting again, or wanting more teeth? "How can awkward be sexy?"

Ian couldn't suppress his smile. Sam was just too cute sometimes. "It's sexy because you let me see you, even though you want to hide. You expose yourself for me." He paused for a short, clinging kiss. "Just me," he whispered.

Sam's lips parted and he rocked his hips slightly, leaving a slick trail across Ian's abdomen. "Just you." Sam nodded. "You really like that?"

Ian held his gaze. "Seeing you vulnerable is sexy."

"I couldn't do this for anyone else. Be like this."

"I know, kiddo." Sam was talking about far more than just being on top with a light on. Ian brought his other hand up from the bed and squeezed Sam's ass. "Just me," he repeated. Sam nodded.

Ian lay back down, trailing his fingers across Sam's skin. From his butt cheek around his hip to his thigh, stroking high up on the inside with his thumb, close to Sam's nuts, until Sam's eyes started to go glassy. Ian let go of his neck, letting him straighten up, tracing across his clavicle and the stringy, taut pectoral muscle. His nipples beaded under the scrape of Ian's fingernails.

"You ready to take me inside, kiddo?" 'Cause he was more than ready to feel Sam wrapped around his cock. Wanted to watch Sam's face, to feel Sam's hands on his chest pushing for leverage, to see Sam arching back, cock bouncing. To hear Sam shouting his name, if Ian did it right. "Want that," he said, more to himself than to Sam.

He slid his hand higher up along Sam's thigh and worked his thumb under his scrotum, looking for the guiche ring. Playing with it made Sam jerk and rise up on his knees. Ian let his fingers slide back to Sam's asshole, tracing little circles around it. The feel of it was seductive enough that he kept playing.

Sam braced his hands on Ian's thighs, eyes closed and brow wrinkled in concentration. Ian pushed in with his fingers, making Sam gasp. With his free hand, he transferred Sam's palms to his chest, one at a time, trapping them just over his heart, which tried to beat itself out of his chest. Sam opened his eyes and looked down into Ian's in a daze. Ian smiled and let his fingers stroke, little movements, slow and soft as he could make it, until Sam was rocking against his hand.

Then Ian hooked his thumb back into Sam's guiche ring and pulled. Sam jerked against his hold. "Oh, God," he gasped.

"Want more, kiddo?"

Ian found his prostate and pressed lightly with his fingers, making Sam groan and push his whole body back into Ian's hand. "Ian."

"Yeah?" Ian kept his voice as even as he could manage. Couldn't do anything about his panting. He wanted Sam out of control, wanted to make him lose it, and he needed to concentrate on Sam for that, not get lost in this himself. He massaged Sam inside and out, watching Sam pant and rock his whole body, listening to the noises he made.

Fucking amazing.

Sam whimpered, a drop of sweat rolling down his forehead. "I wanna come."

"Can you come like this, kiddo? Just on my fingers?"

"Yes."

"I'm still going to fuck you."

"Okay," Sam panted.

Ian started tugging on the ring lightly in rhythm with the fingers inside Sam. "Here's how it's going to happen. I'm going to make you come like this, just my fingers and your ass and this guiche ring."

Sam nodded frantically.

"Then I'm going to roll you on your side and pull your leg up, spread you open for me." Sam whimpered again. Ian sped up his rhythm, tugging Sam's guiche ring harder, making him squeak. "Then I'm going to shove my cock in you, and you're going to take it. Aren't you, Sam?"

A long, shuddering moan and more nodding. A drop of sweat fell from Sam's chin to Ian's chest.

"Say it, Sam."

Sam cut off a cry, nodding desperately. "Yes, Ian." His eyelids slid completely closed and that groove above his nose deepened. His arms trembled.

"Then I'm going to ride you hard. Fuck you sore."

"OhGodohGodohGod," Sam chanted, rocking back and forth faster, brow wrinkling, arms shaking.

Ian didn't know how much longer Sam could support himself. He leaned up, dislodging Sam's hands, wrapped his arm around Sam's waist and his leg around Sam's thigh, then flipped them both, laying Sam on his back.

He spoke against Sam's cheekbone. "You may not like it, maybe won't be ready for me in your ass after coming as hard as I'm going to make you, but it doesn't matter. You'll do it because I want you to. Your asshole is mine to fuck, kiddo, isn't it?"

Sam didn't need prodding this time. "Yes, Ian." He was nearly sobbing, sweat-soaked and arching up and shaking.

Ian fought Sam's fingernails digging into the back of his neck so he could push himself up enough to see Sam's face. "Come now."

Ian got what he wanted; Sam screamed his name. The expression on his face was beautiful, so purely sweet it was nearly painful. Ian thought he was having an out-of-body experience because it felt like he was the one writhing and coming uncontrollably—but then he realized he was coming against Sam's thigh while Sam's muscles pulsed around his fingers and his hips snapped up into Ian's hand.

He lay half on Sam afterward, feeling his muscles twitch, the whole room vibrating in his ears. Sam moaned, his skin prickly with goose bumps when Ian swept a hand up and down his side. He rolled off him and tucked Sam against his body, covering him and then cleaning them both up while whispering to him—he didn't know what, but Sam probably didn't either. Ian kissed him lazily until Sam was nearly asleep, long slow kisses until he could barely respond, then Ian let him rest. He rubbed Sam's back, petting him while he drifted off to wherever he was going. Sam murmured something about rolling over.

"You're fine where you are kiddo. Just rest." Ian kissed his temple and listened to Sam's breathing even out. It was better if he fell asleep, because Ian had some thinking to do.

chapter 31

When Ian woke up wrapped around Sam yet again the next day, he forgot his plan to show Sam all the things about him that made Ian addicted to him.

He just did it without thinking.

Wandering back from the bathroom after his morning piss, he looked at Sam, sprawled out on the bed. Sam had moved as soon as Ian unwound himself from him, rolling onto his stomach and spreading out.

All that skin would look so hot against my black sheets if I tied him spread-eagle to the corner posts. Ian's dick, only recently coaxed out of a morning hard-on, liked that idea. Unfortunately, Ian had an inkling Sam wasn't quite ready for that level of play. Besides, the black sheets were in the closet. But Sam looked pretty tempting even on light blue. *I bet it brings out the blue in his eyes.* He wasn't even covered by the top sheet. Ian should cover him, because Sam always got cold, and if he did, he'd wake up soon. It would suck for the kid to get up early on one of the few days he could sleep in.

Unless he woke up for a good reason.

Ian slid his briefs down his legs, looking at Sam's pale, tight ass. He had nice muscles, rounded except for those hollows: like some kind of moons. Which sounded about right—they were almost the color of the moon. Ian smiled and looked down as he kicked off his briefs. His own skin was tan and covered in brownish-gold hair. Next to Sam, he looked almost rough. He loved that contrast.

Somehow, Ian ended up naked and in bed, lying next to an unconscious Sam. He ran his hand over Sam's back, looking at their differences.

"Mmmmmm?" Sam moved lazily. A big sigh in and out, then he turned his head to the other side, facing Ian. His eyes were still closed.

"Mmmmmm." Ian gripped a butt cheek briefly, then went back to rubbing Sam. Petting him.

"Feels good," Sam mumbled.

"Your skin's soft."

Sam's eyes snapped open. "Soft? I'm a guy. I can't have soft skin."

"You do, kiddo." Ian smiled.

Sam stared at him for a few seconds. Then he groaned, "Oh, God," and pulled a pillow over his head. "I have girl's skin," he said from under it.

Ian pulled him closer so he could feel Sam's skin all along his body. "I like it. Feels good."

"I'm a girl," Sam whined.

"You aren't a girl. Your dick is distinctly male." Ian pushed himself up on his elbow, then planted the other elbow on the opposite side of Sam to hold himself over him. "So are your butt cheeks." He scooted down Sam's body and gripped one cheek in each hand. Sam tilted his hips up into Ian's palms, so Ian pulled his cheeks apart and tongued his guiche, then licked from his ring to the end of his spine. "You don't taste like a girl." Ian sampled him again, taking a swirling detour around his asshole just to hear Sam's response.

"Oh, God," Sam groaned. He started to pull the pillow off his head.

Ian stopped licking. "Leave the pillow over your head." He ran his tongue along Sam's skin again, a long, slow, slick stroke, getting him extra wet.

Sam dropped his hand. "What if I can't breathe?"

Ian tongued the base of his spine. "You can breathe."

"'Kay," Sam said faintly. Ian started kissing and nibbling up his back, until he lay all along Sam's body. He thrust his cock into Sam's slicked-up crack, working a hand under him to fist Sam's dick, then he slowly rocked them both to orgasm. Sam seemed to appreciate it, and Ian's eyes nearly rolled back in his head when he shot all over the small of Sam's back, watching his cum spill out onto all that skin he was worshipping.

Sam's hands fisted the sheets and his muscles spasmed as he moaned and rocked under Ian. Ian ripped the pillow off his head and kissed him through his orgasm, gripping Sam's chin tightly and cranking his head too far back, feeling wet heat hit his palm.

Then he lay panting half-on and half-off Sam, hand crammed under the weight of both their bodies. Sam smiled sleepily and blinked at him, until he closed his heavy eyelids and didn't open them. "Sorry

I woke you up," Ian murmured, kissing Sam's ear as he finally rolled off of him.

Sam lifted his head and yawned until his jaw cracked. He leaned over and kissed Ian on the cheek, then lay back down, wiggling until they were skin-to-skin from shoulder to toes. "I'm not," he mumbled before he fell back asleep.

Ian didn't wake Sam again before Tierney picked him up for their Sunday rugby game. He knew what he was doing. Sort of. He had a good idea how things were going to go, and it happened pretty much the way he expected.

Just after Tierney knocked, Sam stumbled into the living room, wearing a T-shirt and boxers. Ian looked over at Sam, waiting until he saw comprehension in his eyes, then opened the front door and swung it wide.

"Nice of you to answer on the first knock this time," Tierney bitched, stepping into the room. "Are you all ready to . . . Dude?" He spoke to Ian, but stared at Sam.

Ian took a slow breath. "Just a sec. Almost ready." He sounded steady to his own ears; God knew if he sounded steady to anyone else, but Sam and Tierney weren't paying much attention to him. He turned his back on Tierney and walked across the room toward Sam, who looked at him with wide eyes.

Ian stopped just in front of him. "There's stuff for breakfast in the kitchen, kiddo. I'll be back in a few hours."

"I really should go home. I have homework and a class to prepare for . . . Are you sure about this?" Sam asked quietly.

Ian shrugged with his eyebrows. "Not really, but it's better than hiding," he murmured. "I'll call you, okay?"

Sam laid his palm on Ian's chest and nodded. "Okay."

His eyes got even bigger when Ian grabbed his hand, pressing it into his chest, and leaned forward to kiss him. It was a quick kiss, and Ian's slamming heartbeat distracted him so much he barely felt it, but that wasn't the point.

"Be careful," Sam whispered.

"I will."

Tierney's shock lasted awhile. Ian had to prod him to get him moving, and then Tierney nearly stumbled over his own feet. He followed Ian out to his pickup and got in without protesting once that he wanted to drive.

That's when Ian realized just how much his big, gay display had knocked Tierney on his ass. He purposely drove by the T-boner-mobile to get a reaction out of him. Nothing. Tierney didn't even glance at it.

Ian drove in silence. At some point, Tierney had lost his dazed look; now he looked like steam would start boiling out of his ears any second. Whenever Ian had to stop for a light, he'd glance over and see some new muscle twitching in Tierney's face, or his pulse pounding in some usually hidden vein.

As soon as Ian came to a rolling stop at the field, Tierney slammed out of the truck. Ian parked carefully, wondering just how bad T's reaction would get. So far, it seemed over-the-top, even for him.

Ian had gone into this figuring he could pretty much write off their friendship. Maybe these rugby games, too, since Tierney would never keep his damn mouth shut about Ian's queerness. He'd take every opportunity to deride Ian as a faggot and worse from now on.

It wasn't like T was such a great guy. What kept them hanging out was history and Tierney's stubborn refusal to let the relationship fade, unlike most of Ian's college friendships.

This level of anger—T so mad he was shaking with rage, so mad he couldn't even speak—was more than Ian had expected. Did their friendship mean more to Tierney than he'd realized? When he finally left the relative safety of the truck to walk toward the guys—stalling as long as he could—he felt like he might be walking into an ambush.

As usual, the players had left their packs on the side of the field, along with the sweats they wore over their shorts. Most of them were out warming up already. A couple of guys were still on the sidelines, watching with wide eyes while Tierney paced and muttered to himself. He hadn't taken off his sweats, and was running agitated hands through his hair. From twenty feet away, Ian could see him getting red in the face.

It really brings out the auburn in his hair, he thought. As if it mattered.

Guys were starting to drift in from the field, likely sensing something was not right. Maybe hoping for a fight; they played rugby for fun after all, and fights were a not-so-secret pleasure for all of them.

Tierney stopped his pacing and turned to stare at Ian, lip curled in disgust and possibly hatred. The guys came up behind him, as if they were on his side.

It all reminded Ian why he hadn't ever wanted to come out before, because of this possibility. Being the odd man out on the team, any team. It was so easy for him to pass for straight, and he could get along with all these guys without anyone wondering about him. No one questioned that he never brought a girlfriend or wife along to watch— neither did they. Even at the fire department, no one had thought it weird when he'd just given up bringing along a token female to social things in his late twenties. They'd figured he didn't like to get tied down.

If Ian hadn't kissed Sam this morning in front of Tierney, he could have been that undercover queer guy for the rest of his life and never raise a blip on any hetero radar. Never have to face this. Hide who he was.

Sam could never hide it. He'd lived with being odd man out since puberty, probably before.

Fuck 'em.

Ian walked the last couple feet into Tierney's seething silence. About ten guys were standing around him, more coming up to circle them. Ian dropped his pack to the side, not looking away from Tierney's glare.

Bring it.

"You motherfucking traitor," Tierney snarled.

That surprised a sharp laugh out of Ian. "Traitor to *what*?"

"To *men*. Straight men."

That caused a few eyes to widen among their audience. Ian kept his breathing steady by force of will. "Why's that, Tierney? 'Cause I never told you? Maybe I thought you'd act just like this." Well, not quite this over-the-top, unless he'd been drinking. Tierney could really tie one on, though. Maybe he'd been hitting the alcohol this morning?

Tierney's face was nearly purple. "So it's true? You're fucking that fairy?" he choked out, spit flying.

Seriously? Ian's face must have been answer enough.

Tierney blanched, and then took a step toward Ian. Ian stood his ground. Tierney stopped about five feet away. He looked so unhinged Ian thought his eyes might start spinning independently of each other any second.

"Just tell me one thing," T said hoarsely. "Why him?"

Because he makes me feel good. "Why not? Me being with him should mean fuck-all to you."

Tierney looked like Ian had gut-punched him, gasping for breath as his eyes went wide. It was almost as satisfying as the actual thing. But it was Tierney who first punched Ian in the gut, literally. Well, head-butted him, same thing. Lying on the ground with grass tickling the back of his neck, Ian could hear shouting over the ringing in his ears, but it was a distant concern, far behind his need to suck in some oxygen.

One voice came through loud and clear. "Get up, you fucking faggot! Bet you can't fight a real man since that little nellie boy got you up his ass, can you? How is he, huh, Ian? Does he squeal like a pig when you—"

Ian hooked Tierney's legs with his knee and yanked them out from under him. Then he wrenched Tierney's sweatshirt in his hand, yanking him close enough for Ian's fist to connect with his face.

After that it was all about rolling around on the ground, trying to punch T harder than he was getting it. By the time the guys finally separated them, Ian's left eye was throbbing, and Tierney's cheek was swelling, blood seeping out of his nose. Ian shrugged everyone off after a minute. The guys who held Tierney still had to restrain him— he was lunging for Ian. Ian grabbed his pack, breathing heavily with adrenaline and exhilaration, and backed off. Everyone was silent; the only sound was Tierney's occasional grunt of exertion as he tried to break free.

"See you guys around," Ian said, meeting as many eyes as he could. A couple nodded at him blankly. He turned and walked off, confident no one else would go after him.

In the truck, it took him a few tries to get his key in the ignition. Then he slumped back in his seat, closing his eyes. Tierney must have hit his lip, because it hurt when he suddenly smiled.

chapter 32

Sam didn't leave Ian's. He had everything he needed to get ready for tomorrow, and he could prep on Monday for his Tuesday morning class. Instead he ate toast and drank coffee, worrying about Ian.

He had a feeling Ian was going through something worse than the swirlies Sam had suffered in high school for being gay.

He'd just managed to settle down enough to start on his homework when his cell rang. He lunged for it, dumping his backpack upside-down to find it, digging through the pile of papers, pens, notebooks, and candy wrappers that had cascaded out (thank God he'd already taken out his laptop). He found it on the third ring and checked the display.

It was Ian.

"Are you all right?" Sam asked as soon as he hit the button to answer.

"I defended your honor," Ian said. It sounded like he was driving, judging by the background noise.

"Are you in the pickup?"

"Yeah, I'm on my way home. Have you left yet?"

"It's illegal to talk on the phone while you're driving," Sam pointed out. "It's dangerous."

"It's not illegal if you have one of those headsets."

"Do you have one?"

"No," Ian said cheerfully. "Did you hear what I said?"

"About you driving and talking on your phone? Yes. I don't think you shoul—"

"No, about me defending your honor."

"Wait, you what?"

"Defended your honor," Ian enunciated carefully.

Sam pulled the phone away and stared at it for a second, then put it back to his ear. "I'm not sure whether to be annoyed about that or happy."

"Why would you be annoyed? You read all those romance novels; doesn't that shit happen all the time?"

"Yeah, it happens. To *girls*. Wait, are you saying you got into a *fight*?"

"Yep."

"With Tierney?" *Not the whole rugby team, please.* Of course, then he'd be calling from the hospital, right?

"Yep." Sheesh, he was cheerful about it. Sam had always thought fights looked painful. "I even got a black eye, I think. And maybe a swollen lip."

Sam gulped. "A fight about what?"

Ian sighed. "Hello? Defending your honor?"

"Oh, um, did Tierney besmirch my honor?"

"He certainly did!"

"Oh my God," Sam muttered, dropping his forehead into his free hand. "Maybe I didn't need you to defend my honor," he pointed out.

Ian made a noise that sounded like he was motorboating his lips. Sam had the hardest time imagining that, but he couldn't figure out what else it would be. "You can defend your own honor next time," Ian said. Wow, fighting really put him in a good mood. Not that Sam thought he should do it more or anything, it was just an observation. But, wow. "Besides, you defended your own honor with Marley. It was my turn."

"What?" A warm little glow kindled in Sam's chest, but still. *Fighting is bad. Hot, but bad.* "No I didn't. You're the one who scared him off. I was just walking away."

"Sometimes that's the right answer." Ian's voice had gone from cheerful to serious. "Taking on that asshole or provoking him would have made it worse."

"But . . . but you said I let him push me around!"

"I'm sorry. I was being a jerk. He just—all that shit he said about you just made me crazy, kiddo," Ian said, almost indiscernible over the background hum of his pickup.

"Oh." They were both silent a couple seconds. "Thank you," Sam said.

"I want to see you tonight."

"I have an early class . . . but I want to see you, too."

"Do you want me to pick you up later?"

"Well . . . actually I never left."

He swore he heard Ian smile. "Good. I'll be home in five minutes. Be waiting for me."

"Oh." Sam's heart jumped and his stomach tightened up into a ball. "Okay."

Ian clicked the phone off.

Fighting, Sam discovered, not only put Ian in a good mood, but also made him crazy horny. Not just horny, but passionate. Sam thought he might be devoured alive on Ian's living room floor, but he was okay with that. Ian nearly ripped Sam's boxers off and swallowed him whole, jerking himself while he sucked Sam like it was an Olympic event. Sam came like he'd won the gold, then Ian lunged up and shot all over his stomach. He licked it up until Sam was almost ready to go again.

Afterward, naked on one of Ian's rugs, with a tiny afghan wrapped around as much of them as possible, Ian told him about Tierney. First the fight, which—in spite of all Sam's best intentions to disapprove— was hot enough to keep him from falling asleep like usual, and then how Ian and Tierney had become friends during college in the first place.

"We were in the same dorm, and he thought we were alike. I kept trying to find a girl who could do it for me, and he kept trying to find a girl to do. I don't know, he just hung around. After a while he just seemed like part of the landscape, I guess."

"That's not a lot to build a friendship on, is it?" He and Nik had a lot more in common.

Ian shrugged, jostling Sam's head where it rested on his shoulder. "I guess not, but it sort of stuck. He stuck." Ian rolled onto his side and pillowed Sam's head on his biceps. It wasn't actually that comfortable, and it left Sam's feet uncovered, but Ian was looking at him intently, so Sam settled in and listened.

"You know how I figured out I like guys?"

Sam shook his head. He finally noticed Ian's swelling eye, and his fingers itched to touch it. "Shouldn't we put something on that? Like a steak or something?" And hadn't he said something about a bloody lip? Sam couldn't see any evidence of it, but Ian's lips were kinda puffy now anyway . . .

Sheesh, that was hot. Sam wiggled closer to Ian, running his palm over Ian's chest hair to feel the almost-tickle that made him shiver.

Ian ignored him, caught up in his story. "Tierney and I got drunk one night, and he dragged me down to this basement bathroom on campus and introduced me to a glory hole."

Sam bounced up like he had a spring-loaded elbow. "You're fucking kidding me!"

Ian laughed. "Serious. He had to know there was a guy on the other side, I mean you could see half the dude's face and his five o'clock shadow. Tierney let the guy suck him off after me, too. I was sitting on the floor outside the stall, completely losing my shit because I'd just gotten harder than I ever had in my life and then came until I saw stars, and I was watching Tierney and boning up again. Tierney was looking at me, too. It's fucking weird he didn't figure me out."

Huh. "Maybe he did," Sam said, lying back down and tracing Ian's cheekbone with his finger. His lip wasn't that bad. Actually, it was barely swollen at all. Or that might still be the dick lips. *Mmm.*

Ian stared at the ceiling, apparently lost in thought. "Shit, I never thought of that," he said slowly. He focused on Sam again. "You think he could be gay?"

Sam nodded. "It's possible. They say a lot of homophobes are at least bi-curious."

They both fell silent, Sam running his fingers through Ian's chest hair, then down his happy trail. He dragged one finger down along Ian's cock, causing a stir of interest there. Ian's foreskin was pulled back. That always made it look like his dick was wearing a turtleneck sweater. Sam kept that to himself. "What did you do after the glory hole incident? Have a slutty period?"

"I got a girlfriend."

Sam jerked his head up, although he probably shouldn't have been shocked.

"Jurgen was so mad at me when I finally told him I was pretty sure I liked guys more than chicks. I was still seeing her, Sherri. He said I was using her, and I needed to man up."

Sam sighed and looked back down at Ian's belly. "Jurgen is really rigid about some things." Then he snickered. "Rigid."

Ian huffed a laugh and kissed Sam on the temple while Sam swirled his fingers in Ian's belly hair. "Did you man up?"

"Not for a while after that. I did eventually. I never told her why I didn't want to be with her anymore, but there was no way to avoid hurting her . . . I don't think. What do I know?"

He totally shouldn't be asking this, but Sam knew it was pointless to try stopping himself. He watched his fingers tangle in Ian's pubic hair and asked, "Did you love her?"

Ian kissed him on the temple again. "I wasn't in love with her. I've never been in love before."

The *now* that Ian hadn't tacked onto the end of the sentence rang in Sam's ears. His heart lightened so much and so fast he nearly floated away. He rewarded Ian by wrapping tight fingers around his shaft and slowly stroking. Ian *mmm*ed in his ear and rested his thigh on Sam's. With all that room, Sam could fondle Ian's nuts, weighing them in his other hand and feeling the way the skin wrinkled in reaction to his touch and how the hair there seemed to tangle around his fingers like it was reaching for him.

"You really have a thing for balls, don't you?" Ian murmured.

Sam smiled, more to himself than for Ian. "Yeah," he said. "I don't know why. I like the way they dangle and the way they look kinda heavy. You have beautiful nuts. When you're standing up and they're relaxed, the way they hang down just below the tip of your cock . . ." Sam wiggled with the shiver that crawled up his spine. He was getting hard just thinking about it.

Ian reached for his balls, cupping him carefully. Sam sighed and arched his back, shoving his hips toward Ian. It was getting crowded down there, with both their hands and all that excited genitalia, and now he wanted it to get sloppy too.

"You like it when I play with yours." Ian very slightly increased his grip around Sam.

Sam gasped. "Yeah, but mine aren't sexy."

"I think they're sexy."

Sam made a grunt of disagreement. "They aren't. It's not fair. I'm this tall, gawky, gangling guy, but the one part of me I want to gangle is tight and small."

Ian frowned against his ear, then kissed it before asking, "Is gangle a word?"

"For the purposes of speaking about my testicles, yes," Sam said between breaths. Ian was making him crazy with the way his fingers were mapping out the shape of his testes through his skin. Sam strained toward him, wanting to get his hips as close as possible.

"Let's go lie down in bed," Ian murmured in his ear, then took the lobe between his teeth and tugged lightly, tickling Sam with his breath.

"Yeah, bed," Sam whispered. "I think I owe you a blowjob."

"No, I want a handjob, with your dick against mine," Ian murmured against his neck.

Sam shuddered and thrust his hips toward Ian harder. "Not here," Ian said, then nipped at his skin. "I'm not as young as I used to be. I need a mattress."

Sam fell asleep after coming again, and when he woke up, Ian was wrapped around him and snoring softly in his ear. Fights must also tire him out. Sam extricated himself carefully, trying not to wake Ian or instigate an episode of the usual grabby arms. He finally made it out of bed and turned to look back at Ian.

Okay, the black eye was kind of sexy. It made him look like the kind of guy Sam shouldn't be with. The kind of guy Sam never thought he *would* be with (even if he'd kinda, sorta wanted to), and the kind of guy Sam had taken Ian for at first.

But he wasn't a bad boy, not really. Ian was amazing; loving and careful of Sam's feelings and his insecurities. *He defended my honor.*

Sam rolled his eyes and sighed, reluctant to leave, troubled by the faint rumblings in his heart. There was a revolt brewing there. In spite of his best intentions, he'd fallen in love, and his heart was planning to make him acknowledge it.

Oh sheesh, he didn't really want to fight a losing battle, anyway. Maybe it wasn't going to turn out well, and maybe he was going to get his heart stomped on, broken, then drawn and quartered and hanged, but dammit, he wasn't going to be a coward and run from it, right?

Right.

You win, heart. I love him.

Sam was so absorbed in his book, he didn't notice when Ian got up. He was lying on the couch, head pillowed on one end and feet propped on the other, a paperback clutched tightly in his hands. He'd reached an exciting scene. He was preoccupied. Sue him.

"Got a thing for studs in kilts, kiddo?"

Ian's voice exploded in his ears, and Sam jerked in surprise, nearly falling off the couch, pulling the book up to cover most of his face. He peeked at Ian over the top of it. "No," he said, voice muffled by his paperback. After a second he added, "Yes."

Ian grinned at him.

"Maybe," Sam continued.

"I thought you were supposed to be doing homework," Ian said, prowling—*walking* (he really did read too many romance novels)—over to the couch. Sam lifted his legs to make room. Ian sat and pulled Sam's feet into his lap.

He inspected Ian over the top of his book a few more seconds before finally dropping it with a sigh. His face felt hot. "I finished my homework and you weren't awake yet, so I started my new book."

"Your new romance novel," Ian corrected, then grabbed it before Sam realized what he was doing, making him yelp.

Sam pouted. "Give it back."

Ian ignored him and looked at the back cover. "A Highlander, huh?"

"Oh God," Sam groaned, covering his face. "Please don't make fun of me."

Ian dropped the book on his stomach. "Sorry." He felt Ian rubbing his feet. He looked out from between his fingers suspiciously. "I think it's cute," Ian said.

"Oh," Sam said, dropping his hands. Ian *seemed* sincere. He wiggled his toes so Ian would pay more attention to them, maybe rub each one individually. "The first time I saw you, you looked like a Highlander to me," he blurted. *Dammit.*

Ian looked at him blankly a few seconds. Then he said, "At that rugby game?"

Sam nodded and fidgeted with his book, running his fingertips around the edges of the pages and fanning the corners. "They're in all these novels, they're practically their own sub-genre. I thought ..." Sam took a breath. "Later I thought ... um, fantasized you were chasing me, and when you caught me you'd ..." He circled his hand in the air, making a "you know" kind of gesture.

Ian's grin about swallowed his face. "Ravish you, kiddo? Throw you down and take your ass?"

Sam squeaked, then nodded, pressing his lips together and cringing in shame.

Ian lifted Sam's feet off his lap, then stretched out next to him on the couch, nudging Sam until he made room. Ian nuzzled his ear and cheek. "I'd love to do that sometime," he said softly, his breath on Sam's neck making his skin prickle. "But I'm not as young as I used to be, and I beat up some guy this morning." Sam frowned, trying to turn his head enough to look at Ian's face, but they were too close together. "And yeah, I got beat up some myself. I think I might be tapped out for a while, kiddo."

Weird, but Ian sounded almost worried about that. Sam struggled to turn and face Ian, nearly knocking him off the couch. He saw a slightly darker spot forming along Ian's jaw. Was that another bruise?

Sam caressed Ian's cheek with his thumb, just above the potential bruise. "It's okay, I don't care. I'm happy like this." He kissed Ian's nose, then gently kissed Ian's bruised eye. It really wasn't that dark, not like he'd expected a black eye to be. More like a charcoal-gray eye.

They lay there a long time, not really talking or making out, just being together as the room got steadily darker. Sam felt enveloped in a special Ian bubble. It made his heart ache in a happy-sad way. *God I hope this lasts awhile.*

Then Sam's stomach growled. He groaned, and Ian laughed. "I'll make us dinner. You read your book, kiddo." He let go of Sam and rolled off the couch, catching himself on his arm, then standing up. "You staying again tonight?"

"I'd like to if you want me."

"I want you."

Sam stayed Sunday, but he couldn't stay Monday. Unless Ian really, really wanted him to.

Or just really wanted him to.

In the morning, Ian stood at the bathroom sink and knotted his tie while Sam shaved. Ian was done shaving, since he had an electric razor. Sam should get an electric razor, but since he could go two days between shaves before anyone noticed, he didn't think it was worth it. Disposable razors were a pain, though.

"I have a late meeting tonight, but I want to see you tomorrow," Ian said.

Sam stared at Ian's hands on the red silk of his tie. He was slowly discovering that Ian was a closet hedonist. Five-hundred-thread-count sheets and silk ties, not to mention cashmere sweaters in his drawer.

He'd only seen those accidentally. That drawer had come open almost on its own. He'd barely done more than brush past it.

Ian's hands stopped messing with his tie. "Sam?"

"Huh?" Sam dropped his razor in the sink. He was done anyway. "What?"

"Can I see you tomorrow?"

"Of course," he blurted. He thought about backpedaling and making it look less like a foregone conclusion, but it seemed pointless. Besides, Ian smiled at him in the mirror and kissed his cheek, then walked out of the room.

Sam rinsed the few bits of foam off his face and walked into the bedroom. He was still in boxers and a T-shirt, and Ian was shrugging on his suit jacket. "Do you have to leave soon?" he asked, as if it wasn't obvious.

"Yep," Ian answered absently, shoving stuff from his dresser into various pockets.

That sucked. If he had a little less on and Ian had a little more time, they could play corporate raider and houseboy.

Ian walked behind him and patted him on the butt. "C'mon, kiddo. You hurry up, and I'll have time to drop you at campus before I go to work. We can make out in the pickup behind the English building."

"Oh, okay," Sam said, and dived across the bed for his backpack.

chapter 33

Tuesday morning, and Ian felt like he'd already put in three days at work. He'd barely had the energy to call Sam last night when he got home from his meeting, but he had.

It had been totally worth it. He may not be comfortable admitting everything he may or may not be feeling for Sam, but he could admit that talking to Sam relaxed him. He needed to be able to relax. He had a fuckton of work to do.

Most immediately, he had to chair a huge interagency roundtable meeting and navigate the tricky political waters of district boundaries, protocol overlaps, procedural clashes, and insurance payment share disputes among the fire, police, and ambulance agencies in a three-county area.

His main issue right now was convincing all these yahoos—oh, excuse him, *agency representatives*—that, seeing as the emergency backup radio frequencies for the first responders were transit's primary frequencies, yes, they needed to be included in the good ol' boys' network.

He could talk that way about these guys; he was one. Totally all right.

Sigh.

Who in hell ever thought he'd be any good at this? He didn't tend to suffer bullshit and posturing well, and meetings like this were nothing but. He knew from experience; he'd attended enough of them as a representative of the fire district.

Yet somehow, he actually—kinda, sorta—liked this job. He liked figuring out how to make it all run smoothly. He even sort of liked the chess-playing air of it all, figuring out what leverage applied by who to whom would get him support. This was the suckiest part, meetings with multiple parties who thought the simple desire to fuck with each other was reasonable motivation to go ahead and do so.

So why the hell was he in such a good mood?

Like you don't know.

He smiled guiltily to himself, sitting at his desk, thinking about his boyfriend.

Yeah, he'd thought the word. "Boyfriend," he whispered out loud. There, he'd said it, too. Suddenly it occurred to him he might need to talk to Sam about that. Hell, how did that work? Was he supposed to clear it with Sam before he used the "b" word? Ian sighed. One more thing to ask his therapist.

He heard Dalton's disembodied voice say at his elbow, "Mr. Cully? You have a call from Jurgen Dammerung on line one."

"Dalton, call me Ian," he called out his open office door.

"Sorry, sir," Dalton's voice said at his elbow.

Ian shook his head and picked up the phone. "Hey."

"Hey," Jurgen said. "Guess we're coming up tonight."

"Yeah, to make sure I'm treating my boyfriend well." Holy hell, he'd just called Sam his boyfriend to someone else.

"Did you hear what you just said?"

"When I accused you of being all up in my shit? Yeah."

"Ha," Jurgen grumbled. "So he's your boyfriend now."

"Yeah." *I just need to tell him.*

Jurgen was silent a second, probably judging Ian's sincerity. "We'll stay home tonight then."

Ian smirked.

"Shut up," Jurgen growled. "We're coming up on Friday. Nik got us all tickets for Exposed Innerds."

"That band? Sam loves them." Ian could probably stomach it for a night. He'd bring earplugs.

Jurgen sighed. "Yeah, so does Nik." He sounded about as excited as Ian felt. "He says you and I have to come up with a date for Miller Harpe," he added grouchily.

"Make it a good one!" Nik yelled in the background.

"That guy whose head you fucked with last summer because you were jealous?"

"You helped," Jurgen snapped. "And I wasn't jealous, I was trying to *fix* things."

"You asked me to help you. You're my cousin—I helped."

"Shut up," Jurgen said. "Just come up with a date for him."

"Where the fuck am I supposed to find a date for him? You're the one who tried to *fix* things. You find one."

After a painful pause, Jurgen admitted, "Nik says all my suggestions are inappropriate."

"Hell," Ian grumbled. The idea of Tierney flashed through his head, nearly making him laugh.

Then Dalton appeared in his doorway. "Mr. Cully?" he whispered.

"Call me Ian," he responded automatically. "Oh, hey. Do you like the Exposed Innerds?"

Dalton's eyes lit up. "I love that band."

"I think I got a live one," he whispered into the phone. "We're good."

Once he hung up, he realized what he could do tonight with his suddenly free time. He just had to run a small, personal errand first.

Unfortunately, before Ian could run his errand, he had to finish this damn agenda. He was sitting at his desk, working on it and eating the pineapple he'd brought from home when Andy walked into his office, holding her ever-present cup of coffee. He glanced up. "Hey," he said, then went right back to the stupid fucking agenda he was trying to draft for the stupid fucking meeting.

"Hey." She stopped next to his desk. "Your eye looks better."

"Huh."

"I think I found our last employee. When can you do a final interview?"

"Can it be after this stupid meeting?"

She snorted delicately. "Next week? I think not."

Ian sighed and dropped his pen to rub his good eye. "I don't know. Talk to Dalton about my schedule."

He could feel the sheer wattage of her shit-eating grin heating the back of his head. There was no way he was looking up at her. "Aren't you glad I made you hire my little brother?" she asked.

Yes. He grunted noncommittally and made a show of ignoring her in favor of spearing another piece of pineapple.

"Jeez, you eat a lot of fruit," she said.

"Fruit for the fruit." He could tell by the way her whole body jerked in his peripheral vision that she'd almost spit out a sip of coffee. He smirked up at her.

"Wow," Andy said, wiping a few stray drops of coffee off her chin. "Since you started seeing your *friend* you're sure more lively, aren't you?" She gave him a sly wink and sauntered off toward the door.

It took him a few seconds to think of a comeback. "Shut up," he grumbled just before she walked out.

She laughed all the way back to her office.

Later, when he went to see Andy to tell her he had personal business this afternoon, a book shoved into the side of her briefcase caught his attention. The cover looked familiar. A wild-haired chick clutched to the semi-bare chest of some rough-looking dude with long, brownish hair. There was a castle on a distant hill behind Rough Dude's plaid-draped shoulder and some stormy looking skies.

Ha.

"Sooo," he said, "you read a lot of those Highlander romance novels?"

Her head snapped up, then she looked over at her briefcase. "Oh, shit," she said, dropping her papers on her desk.

His grin was so wide his cheeks hurt. "Andy, I think we need to talk," he said, sitting down in the chair in front of her desk. "Now, these Highlander romance thingies, let's talk about that, uh, what do you call it? Oh, yeah—trope. I need to conduct a little research."

She eyed him suspiciously for a second, then arched an eyebrow. "This research, does it have anything to do with your boyfriend?"

Hell. "Maybe."

"I'll consider that a yes. Now, I think I have just the scenario for you . . ."

chapter 34

In the middle of class, Sam got a text. He slapped a hand over his vibrating front pocket before things got out of hand, then snuck the phone out. He didn't *know* it was from Ian, and he shouldn't check it in class, but . . .

It was Ian.

I want you to be at my place by 6:30.

Sam swallowed. Some of his blood got excited and started rushing around in his ears. Fuck, that was hot, being texted in the middle of class with instructions from his . . . friend. His fingers shook a little as he typed under the desk. *Okay.*

I'd like that. Ian texted back immediately.

Me too.

I have a present for you. You might need your safeword, kiddo.

He couldn't stifle a small whimper. Eva—sitting next to him yet again—looked over sharply, and Sam snapped his mouth shut.

K.

He was forced to leave class early due to pressing concerns. Like, he was concerned his zipper would press permanent tracks in his dick, even through his boxers.

Sam got to Ian's apartment just after six, horny as he could remember being in recent . . . well, ever. He'd been crazy since Ian had texted him.

Suddenly, though, his body wasn't quite as eager as it had been on the way over. When he fumbled with the key in the lock of Ian's front door, he mostly felt the nerves he'd been fighting. His chest and stomach buzzed with tension, sending a slight tremor from his fingers through his whole body.

Planned sex. This was about him trusting Ian to want him.

The door swung open. Ian stood on the other side, bare chested and bare legged, wearing—

Holy shit. A kilt.

Insta hard-on; just add tartan.

Oh, God, those thighs Ian had. So meaty and hairy. What if he'd gone commando under the kilt? Sam could just *see* his dick bobbing, his hairy balls swaying gently under the scratchy wool as he walked. Sam stood in a daze on the wrong side of the door, head swimming, breathing in short, tight gasps. He swallowed, trying to get a handle on things.

Ian gripped Sam's wrist tightly, pulled him into the apartment, and shut the door. He backed Sam up to it, face hard and set, staring into Sam's eyes. He almost looked mad. Or like a pissed-off Highland laird, angry over the young (yet nubile) member of the enemy clan trespassing on his land.

Someone *definitely* needed to be punished for this.

Sam shivered, breath coming faster. "You're wearing a kilt," he whispered.

Ian's face lost the pissed-off laird look. "Lots of firefighters have them, kiddo."

Sam swallowed. "Oh," he whispered. "Are we going to play angry laird and trespassing enemy?"

Ian smiled—it had to be said—*wolfishly*, reaching to grip Sam's ass cheek hard in one hand, cupping his groin with the other, squeezing him roughly for a second. "We're playing victorious laird and his war prize." He loosened his hands and leaned in closer to whisper, "You're my booty."

Sam squeaked and dropped his keys on the floor, reaching to grip Ian's biceps. "Oh." His head fell back against the door. "You've read some of those books," he said faintly.

"Quiet, boy!" Ian barked. "I might have done some research," he added in his normal voice. "Don't break character again."

"'Kay." Sam nodded enthusiastically.

"Now," Ian said in his mean laird voice, yanking Sam away from the wall. "I'm going to inspect and then mark my property." He slapped Sam on the butt, hard, making him gasp. "Get your ass in the bedroom and get naked."

Ian followed him in, dogging Sam's steps and making it impossible for Sam to think about anything other than what "mark my property" might mean, or what exactly being "war booty" might entail. He found both of those ideas extremely, *ahem*, stimulating.

The full implication of "inspection" didn't sink in until they reached the bedroom, and Sam saw that Ian had made preparations—it was easy to see he had, because every light in the room had been left on. He'd taken all the blankets off the bed. A bottle of lube was sitting on the bedside table, along with some other stuff. Clearly, the laird had plans for his booty, and those plans were well illuminated.

Ian had said he liked to look at Sam naked. He'd said he wanted Sam's trust—and he had it, mostly. Just, when it was like this . . . disrobing in the light of, um, light fixtures turned up all the way . . .

Sam would be getting naked for *inspection*. Not in the heat of the moment or in a sort of surprising "Oh, we were just kissing and fooling around and would you look at that? I'm naked" kind of way.

Gulp.

Sam would be pale and gangly and bony and Ian would be disgusted, right?

Shut. Up.

Something quailed inside of Sam. He almost turned and told Ian he couldn't do it this way. Maybe Ian could rip his clothing off in semi-darkness instead? Not make Sam choose to bare himself in front of him, not like this, with all his flaws on display.

Would Ian be disappointed? Sam stared at the bed.

Dammit.

"Sam?" Ian asked quietly from behind him. "We don't have to—"

Sam turned around to face Ian. Slowly, he unsnapped the fly on his jeans. He couldn't hold Ian's gaze, but when he glanced away he saw himself in the mirror. He looked down quickly to avoid that sight and concentrated on getting his clothes off with minimum panic.

He could feel Ian watching him the whole time—he caught a flash of pale skin in the mirror just before his shirt engulfed his head, and felt a split second of complete insecurity when he was tangled in the cloth but his chest was exposed to the cool air and Ian's gaze, nipples tightening up.

When he bent to take his leg out of his jeans, he caught another glimpse of himself and ducked his head again, but the afterimage wouldn't go away. Bare back rounded, spine poking out, boxers tight across his flexing butt, just a sliver of skin at the top of his thigh.

He looked vulnerable. *Shiver*.

Sam glanced up at Ian for a split second. His lips were parted, eyes wide and focused intently on Sam.

That made the blood pound harder in his ears, and his dick began to perk up a little. Not getting hard again, exactly. More like it had stopped searching for a place to hide.

Vulnerability was just a little bit sexy, even when you were the vulnerable one. Maybe *especially* then, if you trusted your partner.

Trust was sexy, too. Trusting Ian to still want him, letting Ian do what he wanted to Sam's body. That was gut-tighteningly exciting. Sam stood up, naked, hands staying at his sides by force of will, and let Ian look at him.

"Look at yourself in the mirror," Ian said quietly, eyes tracing down and up Sam's body.

Sam licked his lips as Ian stepped around behind him, turning them slightly so they both faced the mirror.

He was too skinny. Gangly. Pasty. He quickly jerked his eyes up to his face. His bottom lip was reddened and swollen. Had he been chewing on it? He licked it to soothe it, and for a split second, when the pointed tip of his tongue swiped at his lip, he had something of a different perspective on things.

If he were a guy who liked to get his cock sucked (and who wasn't?), he'd want to stick it in his mouth. His mouth was—holy shit—*sinful*. Just like any main character's mouth in a romance novel should be.

Sam couldn't stop staring at his lips. He didn't look at his body again, but he felt a strange wave of something sweeping through him from his mouth down, tightening his nipples and encouraging him to get harder. That warm tingly sensation . . . was that *confidence*? Whatever it was, it was slowly heating and relaxing his muscles. He sucked in a breath and reveled in the strange melty-ness filling his body.

Standing just behind him, Ian reached for Sam's hand and pulled it back to his groin, pressing Sam's palm against the scratchy wool covering Ian's erection. "That's because of you," he said in Sam's ear.

Then Ian dropped his hand and stepped back. "Don't move," he ordered, voice hard and low, switching back to a laird on inspection. *Yummy.* Sam watched his face in the mirror, looking for disgust or anything remotely like it, but it wasn't there. Ian's palm swept down his back to his butt, squeezing.

"I took you from another clan I'm feuding with, and now I'm going to mark my property. Then I get to break your ass in."

"Oh," Sam gasped. "That works." He nodded agreeably.

Ian's face got harder, intimidating. "Your virgin ass, kid, and I don't care what you want. You're my sex slave now."

"Yes. Yes I am," Sam said faintly. Ian winked at him, but otherwise didn't break character. He stared at Sam, then walked over to the nightstand, picking up the lube and something else, walking back until he stood in front of Sam.

"Get in the shower," Ian ordered him. "There's a razor in there. Shave your balls." He handed Sam what he was carrying. "Get yourself off and come out with that in your ass."

"Oh fuck," Sam whimpered, staring at the lube and plug in his hands.

"Quiet, boy! Now get moving." In his normal voice, Ian added, "And don't fall asleep in the shower."

With Ian waiting out here in nothing but a kilt and body hair? Not a chance.

Sam was a dripping, sodden lump of eager sex toy, leaning weakly against a wall next to the bathroom door, legs spread for his post-shaving inspection. He didn't think he could get excited again this fast, as hard as he'd come in the shower, but when Ian traced a fingertip across his smooth, naked balls, Sam shuddered.

"Good boy," Ian whispered. He lifted his eyes to look into Sam's, smiling as he teased him with that finger.

"Oh God," Sam breathed. Ian chuckled. If Sam didn't love it so much when Ian teased him, he'd hate that sound. Ian knelt on the floor, somehow still completely in control of the scene. Maybe because of the way he stared at Sam, green eyes trapping his. Or possibly it was the way he gripped Sam's sac firmly in his hand.

"Watch," Ian ordered him, reaching for something on the floor. It looked like a cock ring. Then Ian pulled down gently on Sam's sac, shooting sharp jolts up into his stomach and making him gasp. Something in his gut was alarmed at the feel of his testicles being handled this way, but that sensation he always had—that he was sort of tensed up—felt like it was unraveling. Like a cramped muscle finally getting stretched out.

The leather strap snapped snug around the top of Sam's balls, next to his body. He jerked his head off the wall and bowed his back like a pissed-off cat. "Fuck!"

"Just give it a minute," Ian said, rubbing circles on Sam's thighs. "Let yourself get used to it."

Sam trembled and waited, eyes closed, trying to concentrate on Ian's hands massaging him and failing miserably. Shocks still arced through him, not so much pain as alarms that soon started settling down, tapering off. Becoming more a heightened awareness. The feeling of unraveling and relaxing got stronger at the same time, leaving him with a sense of frozen tension, hypersensitizing his nerves.

When Ian breathed softly on his nuts, Sam nearly came out of his skin. "Don't stop," he begged when Ian stood up.

"Slaves don't give orders," Ian growled, and Sam cracked his eyelids to see Ian staring at him stonily.

"Oh," Sam whispered. "Yeah, I'm your property." He arched his back, focused on the strange feeling in his testicles, which vibrated with so much sensation he felt like they might start spontaneously resonating.

Ian looked like he was trying not to smile. "Now I get to claim you."

With supreme effort, Sam held still. "God, please," he groaned.

"Should I tie you down, boy? You might run if I don't."

Sam whimpered. In fear, of course. "I'm thinking about running." *So you can chase me.*

Ian stepped back. "Run!"

Sam blinked in surprise, then pushed off the wall and darted for the door.

Even with a head start, Sam only made it to the hall before Ian tackled him, his full weight pressing Sam into the cool, wood floor. He grabbed Sam's wrists and stretched his arms over his head, then trapped Sam's legs with his own, grinding into Sam's ass. Sam could feel rough wool against part of his ass and his lower back. Through the scratchy fabric, Ian's dick was rock hard and rubbing across one of Sam's cheeks. Sam pushed back with his hips.

"Good boy," Ian rasped in his ear. Shivers ran down Sam's back. Ian transferred both wrists to one hand, then shoved his free hand between them, yanking up his kilt enough to slide skin against skin, adding to the overall sensory charge. He moved his hips in slow circles, then paused a second to shove his hand under Sam's pelvis and grip Sam's cock. The contrast of Ian's hot hand on his dick and the smooth, cool floor tugging on his balls made Sam's eyes cross.

Ian groaned and stilled. Sam shoved back into him, arching his back. "Ian," he begged, terrified Ian was stopping. "Please."

"Shut up, boy," Ian growled. And in his regular voice, "We can't do this here, kiddo."

"Once you catch me you have to fuck me, no delays," Sam panted, drooling on the floorboards under his cheek, thrusting his dick against Ian's palm as much as he could. Feeling the skin of Ian's cock pulling and shifting against his ass. "It's a rule."

Ian laughed in surprise and let go of Sam's shaft. Sam had a moment of eye-popping panic until Ian pulled his hand out and worked his fingers in between Sam's ass cheeks, pulling on the plug. Sam moaned from his gut as Ian slid it out, then quivered when Ian lined up his cock. Shuddered and tensed when he felt the touch of Ian's glans against him, slipping in the excessive lube he'd used.

When Ian slid through Sam's sphincter, there wasn't any pain, just that fucking fantastic stretching feeling. Sam keened for more, but Ian clamped his hips down and held Sam still. "Wait," he panted. "You've never done this before."

Sam laughed, and Ian leaned down and kissed his cheek. "Pretend," he whispered in Sam's ear.

"'Kay," Sam whispered back. "Burns. Feels so good. I never knew—"

"Quiet boy," Ian said in his laird voice. He worked himself deeper into Sam, who moaned and wailed and tried to push back onto Ian's cock, but the way Ian's legs pinned his thighs made it impossible. When Ian's head rubbed against Sam's prostate, Sam lost his breath.

"Deeper, Ian," he moaned when he got it back.

"Call me master," Ian said. For a second Sam, froze. They'd never done that, and he didn't know if he wanted to go there. "Pretend," Ian reminded him. He held still above Sam, his voice coming through clenched teeth, halfway in Sam's ass. Sam could feel his own heartbeat thudding around Ian's cock.

Sam swallowed. "Deeper, master." When he said the word, his muscles clenched around Ian, who shuddered and pushed in deeper, finally sliding in the last inch or two all at once. They lay there panting together, Ian's body weighing Sam down. The floor wasn't cold anymore, it was hot and slick with sweat, but Sam was shaking. "So deep."

"Too deep? Don't let me hurt you," Ian said in his ear, then bit his lobe lightly.

Sam shivered. "No. Fuck me," he whined, rocking his hips.

Ian rasped Sam's cheek with the whiskers on his chin. "Gonna, kiddo. Just hang on, I'll take care of you. Gonna give you what you need." He started grinding, circling his hips. Pushing himself in and out by fractions of an inch. Sam gasped and clenched his hands in Ian's grip, arching his hips off the floor, fighting to get his legs free because he needed it as deep as Ian could go. Needed to expose himself totally.

He must have said that out loud, because Ian was making promises again. "Gonna make you scream, Sam. Make you beg. Fuck you so deep." Ian released Sam's legs, letting him spread them wide to feel Ian deeper. Hotter and slicker than ever, every single movement sending shock waves out from his ass, resonating in his balls.

When he struggled to get his knees under him and thrust his ass up for Ian, wanting to be completely open, Ian said in a growly sort of purr, "There's my slutty boy. You're my slut, Sam, aren't you?"

Sam gasped, muscles clenching, and shoved himself back into Ian. "I'm your slut. Harder, Ian. More."

Ian started to pump his hips, his balls swinging and crashing into Sam's and making him wail. The cry spurred Ian on. He thrust harder, hitting Sam's guiche. Sam couldn't even catch his breath to beg, but whatever he was managing was enough for Ian. Ian's hand slid down from Sam's hip around to his dick, sweeping up the pre-cum and sweat, gripping him hard, letting him slide in and out of Ian's fist

"Turn your head," Ian panted. "Wanna see your face." Sam did, laying his cheek on the floor and thrusting his hips back, trying to tell Ian to take what he wanted. All of it. Fill him up. "Yeah, kiddo. Love that. You're so close." Ian thrust harder, his balls slapping, friction from his cock in Sam's ass hot enough to start a fire. Sam's orgasm built behind his nuts, fed by the two of them slapping together.

He started mindless, begging babble. "PleaseIanohfuckpleaseIan."

"There you go, kiddo, come for me," Ian said, twisting his hand and shoving in deeper than Sam thought possible.

Sam screamed his lungs out, shooting cum out onto the floor and Ian's hand, toes curling, ass convulsing. He had that crazy, unraveling feeling in his balls, ricocheting through his dick and his ass, his whole body getting in on the act, everything coming together to let go. Thrusting himself back instinctively, trying to get Ian deeper for that last, extra sensation.

Ian fucked him hard and fast through it, then shoved into him once more and held there. "Jesus, Sam," he groaned, grinding his hips right up against Sam's ass. Sam felt the rush of warm cum inside him, and it felt better than ever. Ian stroked lazily a few times while Sam gasped with aftershocks, his legs jerking.

Fuck, that felt amazing.

Slowly, they came down, Ian murmuring to him. The kilt trapped between them became itchy rather than stimulating. "Oh, fuck, Sam, that was . . . Oh fuck." Ian kept whispering variations on that theme for a minute or two, then they lay there quietly, Ian rasping the back of Sam's neck with his cheek and chin, then kissing and licking him.

"Need to take that ball stretcher off," Ian mumbled. "Not good to leave that thing on you too long your first time." When he pulled out, it *really* felt different. Ian unsnapped the leather strap, and Sam yelped when the nerve endings in his nuts started lodging protests. He scrunched his eyes shut and sucked in a deep breath, trying not to curl up into a ball.

The sensation settled down soon. It felt like his foot waking up after falling asleep, except it wasn't his foot, it was his testicles. Big difference. Ian rubbed gentle circles on his back until Sam relaxed again. "You okay, kiddo?"

Sam exhaled long and slow. "Yeah, think so. Just sorta shocking."

"You ever gonna want to wear that again?"

Sam opened his eyes and turned to look at Ian's face. He looked like it might really matter to him. "I could do that again. The feeling when it's on is worth it." Even after everything they'd just done, he blushed admitting it.

Ian smiled at him. "Good. You looked sexy with it on. Next time I want you to see yourself in the mirror." Ian kissed his cheek. "You gangle."

"'Kay," Sam sighed happily, laying his cheek back down on the floor and closing his eyes. Ian chuckled, but lay next to him, half on him and half off, rubbing his back.

And sheesh, his nuts really *did* feel different. Was it the hairless thing? Sam thought about it, trying to pin down the sensation.

Ian kissed between his eyebrows. "You must be thinking hard," he murmured. "You have that line between your brows."

"I'm trying to figure out why it feels *so* different. Maybe it's the cum drying on my—Ian!" Sam's eyes popped open, and his head shot off the floor.

Ian froze at his cry. "What?" he asked, alert and still. Like maybe Sam had seen a burglar. Or a mouse.

Sam groaned and pounded his forehead against the floor once. "No condom."

Ian went suddenly limp. "Fuck."

They didn't talk about it, not right away. Sam couldn't make himself look as Ian pushed himself off the floor, then pulled Sam up by his wrist, leading him to bed. "Get in, kiddo," he said softly, watching as Sam lay down and pulled the blankets up. Then he walked around the bed, losing his kilt on the way, and crawled in on the other side. Sam felt him scooting under the blankets until he was there and warm and wrapping Sam up. Pulling Sam's head onto his shoulder.

It was hard not to feel loved when Ian did this. Sam had to fight it with everything in him. He could have the romance novel sex fantasies ('cause Ian was clearly superlative at fulfilling those), but he had to keep reminding himself that while Ian may have feelings, he might never come through on the Big Declaration. Sam couldn't count on, "I love you, I can't live without you. You complete me." Or even just, "You'll do."

So this no condom thing? That was a potential problem. Not like a romance novel problem. There would be no unplanned pregnancy that would force Ian to offer marriage and keep them in close proximity until the scales fell from his eyes and he realized Sam made his heart beat.

There was no HIV trope. Sam wracked his brain, but he couldn't come up with a single literary example of a sexually transmitted disease morphing into true love. He was pretty sure sexually transmitted diseases were a no-no in Romancelandia, even for evil exes.

That was what he should be worried about, right? The possibility of getting something from Ian. Except he knew Ian hadn't been with anyone for a long time before they got together, and he was all but positive Ian hadn't been with anyone since they'd met. Sam certainly didn't have anything to give to Ian. Not only was he practically a monk for months before they met, but he'd been tested twice since he and Marley broke up.

"I haven't been with anyone except you since before my accident," Ian said.

"I know," Sam whispered, swirling his fingers in Ian's chest hair. He sighed.

They lay there quietly a few seconds until Ian jostled him, like he was expecting something from Sam. He lifted his head and looked at Ian.

Ian swallowed. "What about you?"

Sam blinked. *Holy shit*, Ian was worried *he'd* been with someone else? "I haven't been with anyone for over a year. I blew a guy at a party after Marley and I broke up, but I used a condom."

"So," Ian took a breath. "No one except me?"

Sam put his hand on Ian's cheek and stroked his thumb across Ian's lips. "No," he said, then kissed him. "I was tested a few months ago; I'm clean."

Ian closed his eyes in apparent relief. "Me too." He reached for the back of Sam's head and fisted his hair gently.

Sam's heart beat a little harder. "We could . . . not use condoms. Promise not to be with other people."

"Yeah." Ian stared at him. "We could do that." He slid his fingers around Sam's chin and pulled him closer for another kiss. "I want that with you," he said into Sam's mouth.

Sam cracked the door in his heart and let himself feel a bit loved. Not just liked or desired—and yes, he believed Ian desired him—but loved.

It was possible.

chapter 35

Ian lay awake wondering if Sam had liked his present. And the role-playing. After everything that had just happened—forgetting the condom, and then their conversation about not being with anyone else—he shouldn't care about this.

But he did. He'd spent an hour trying not to bug Sam about it, and trying not to wonder why Sam hadn't said anything. Sam could say something later. In the morning, because he was asleep now, as usual. He'd been asleep since about ten minutes after their conversation ended, which was a long time for Sam to stay awake after coming. Ian should be sleeping too.

But he wasn't. Because ten minutes was long enough for Sam to tell him if he'd enjoyed himself.

You aren't a guy who worries about this shit.

Except, apparently, he was now. He sighed and pulled Sam closer. Thank God he'd given up pretending he didn't like to cuddle. Sam snuffled and breathed heavily against his shoulder, throwing a limp arm across Ian's diaphragm. Ian winced.

Hell with it. He untangled himself and got up, wandering into the kitchen for a glass of water, then into the living room to sit on his couch and brood. He'd never brooded about a guy before, but how hard could it be? He kept the lights off because he thought it might help.

It was harder than he'd thought. Plus, he had no clue if he was doing it right.

"What are you doing out here?" Sam's sleepy voice asked behind him. Ian turned to look. Sam stood there naked in the light coming in the window, rubbing at his eyes and yawning.

"What woke you up?"

Sam hugged himself and came around to the front of the couch. "I got cold 'cause you weren't there."

Ian lifted his arm when Sam sat down next to him so Sam could get under it and start to warm up. "I made sure you were covered up."

"S'not the same," he said, yawning until his jaw cracked. He settled in under Ian's biceps, head on his shoulder, breath evening out. Ian almost thought he'd fallen asleep again until Sam moved to kiss him on the neck. "Thank you."

"For keeping you warm?"

Sam squirmed, turning more into Ian and trying to pull his legs up on the couch. "Toes're cold," he muttered, but they didn't fit between them. He dropped his legs back on the floor. "I was thanking you for the present."

Ian shifted so he could lie back, pulling Sam with him. He had to be practically on top of Ian for them to fit on this couch. "You liked it?"

"Best present ever," Sam said.

Thank fuck. Ian squeezed him tightly, then caught Sam's toes between his feet, trying to warm them up. "Squirrel."

Sam lifted his head and stared down at Ian in the dark. Ian couldn't read his expression, but he could guess at it. He probably had that little lip curl of confusion. "What?"

"That's what I'm going to call you."

After a second or two of staring, Sam laid his head back down on Ian's shoulder. "That's . . . weird. Can't you just keep calling me kiddo?"

"I call you kiddo?"

Sam huffed a soft laugh. "Yeah, all the time."

Ian ran a hand through Sam's shaggy hair. "Isn't that kind of, I don't know, condescending?"

"Um, hello? It's better than squirrel. Why would you want to call me that?"

"'Cause you like nuts." Ian squeezed him.

Sam was silent a few seconds. "Why do you need to call me anything at all? I mean, other than Sam." He didn't sound annoyed, he sounded apprehensive. Tension started to invade his neck muscles again.

"Shouldn't I have a pet name for my boyfriend?" Ian said and held his breath.

Sam rolled over on top of him completely, feeling his way along Ian's arms to intertwine their fingers. Ian could sense his intent stare, even if he couldn't see it. It was in the closeness of his face and the way he gripped him. "Am I your boyfriend?"

Hell. "Yeah, if you want."

"I want," Sam said immediately. Then he kissed him, tongue insinuating itself into Ian's mouth, and Ian let him have control. Partly because Sam wanted it, but also because Ian needed him to have it. Sam was getting hard again, rubbing against Ian, capturing Ian's thighs between his and using the hold for leverage.

Ian was suddenly so hard he ached. He lifted his hips into Sam's, wanting to give him what he was already taking. Sam's hands gripped tighter, trapping Ian's. When Ian came, he came for Sam, out of control and moaning into Sam's mouth, letting Sam draw it out of him. Sam came right after, and Ian understood in that moment what Sam was giving him. He couldn't explain it later, but for a few seconds it was crystal clear.

When Sam finally let go of his hands, Ian couldn't stop running them up and down Sam's back, feeling the sweat he'd worked up. Jesus, even *that* was for him, wasn't it? This feeling had to be why people sometimes cried after sex. He blinked hard against the urge, but Sam somehow knew and kissed his eyelids closed. He couldn't miss the wetness there. He didn't say anything though, he just held Ian's head between his hands and kissed him softly, over and over, until Ian felt almost normal and lost that weird urge to open his mouth and say things he didn't know if he really meant.

He couldn't stop feeling that Sam was holding his heart between his hands.

Finally Sam rolled over partway, almost falling off the couch, but Ian caught him. Sam grabbed the afghan off the back of the couch. "Is this washable?"

Ian had to clear his throat. "Yeah."

Sam wiped them both off with it, then threw it on the floor.

Ian might have dozed off for a few minutes, lying there with Sam's arm pillowing his head. When he woke up—after trying to move a half inch and discovering he had no room—Sam was still awake, snuggled under Ian's chin and running fingers through his chest hair.

"I loved that. When you did that for me. The kilt and the war prize and . . . you know. Played romance novel with me."

Ian's heart did a somersault, but he managed a normal tone. "We can do it again, it was hot."

Sam stretched an inch or two, not quite enough to knock him off the couch. "Good. So, I guess I should have a pet name for you."

"You could call me laird," Ian suggested, even though he wasn't feeling like one right now.

Sam swirled fingers in his chest hair, then tugged lightly on it. "Can I call you laird bear?"

"Hell no."

Ian felt Sam smile against his neck.

"No," he repeated.

"Okay," Sam said agreeably, still smiling.

"Fuck," Ian muttered.

Sam giggled. It was cute.

"Let's go to bed," he said, nudging Sam with his arm. "This couch is too small."

"Okay, laird. Bear."

"Ha. Ha."

chapter 36

The bench at the bus shelter outside Fatty's was uncomfortable. Actually, the benches in all the bus shelters in the city were uncomfortable, but since Sam was currently sitting on the one outside Fatty's, it was the one he cared about now.

Fortunately, he had a book to distract him from his throbbing ass. *Too bad it's throbbing because of this damn seat*. If it was throbbing in a good, Ian-induced way, he'd be fine with it. But it was Wednesday night, and he and Ian were responsible adults who had to get up early and needed their sleep, so Sam had no plans to go over to Ian's place now that his shift at Fatty's had ended.

That had seemed like a good decision this morning, when they were making out in the cab of Ian's pickup in their secluded spot behind the English building.

Right now, Sam's romance novel was a pretty poor substitute for Ian. A sci-fi romance he'd read at least three times before, and one of his favorites. It was het romance, about two spaceship captains on opposing sides of a war. The hero was in love with the heroine—crazily, madly in love—he kept a journal about his abject devotion to her. The heroine was scornful of the hero. By the end of the book, of course, he'd won her over, the war had ended, and they warped off to the edge of the galaxy in sexual and romantic bliss.

The best thing about the book—what pushed it into Sam's "favorites" category—was the hero's geekiness and social ineptitude. He was misunderstood and disliked by his crew, while the heroine's crew (and the hero's, for that matter) *loved* her. But somehow they got together anyway, and she fell in love with him in spite of knowing just how pathetically desperate he was for her (because she'd infiltrated his computer system and read his email).

It was very, very satisfying, not to mention it had lots of potential for him and Ian to "play." Plus it was romantic enough that Sam occasionally caught himself clutching at his heart. Sometimes with a simultaneous hard-on.

Which was his state when a vehicle pulled up alongside the bus shelter. Sam froze. *Shit*. He hated when this happened. He sighed heavily. "Really," he said loudly over the growl of the running engine, refusing to look up, "I'm just waiting for the bus. I'm not looking for a 'date.'" At some previous point in his life, he might have been flattered to be mistaken for a rentboy. Until he was actually mistaken for one and realized how low-rent rentboys were. Seriously, he wore an apron and held a battered backpack in his lap. How did that make him look like he had sex for money?

"If that's the way you want it, squirrel," Ian's amused voice replied.

Sam stood up and his backpack fell on the ground. "What are you doing here?" Did he sound short of breath? He felt short of breath. Ian was stretching across the cab of his truck, the passenger window rolled down. His caramel-colored hair was shining bluish in the streetlight, and he was smiling. He kept on smiling, leaning over and looking into Sam's eyes.

"Hey, kiddo," he said. He reached for the passenger door from the inside and opened it. "Hop in."

Sam picked up his pack and climbed in. "What are you doing here?" he asked again, smiling back at Ian.

Ian still leaned toward the passenger side, like he had some important business to take care of on Sam's side of the cab. "I came to see if you needed a ride." He moved closer, gripping Sam's chin and kissing him. Not an explicit, we're-so-gonna-fuck-when-we-get-home kiss. Just a kiss—a boyfriend kind of kiss. Just, "Hi there. I'm glad you're here."

"I could've taken the bus."

"You'd have to transfer twice to get to my place from here." Ian's fingers dug into his jaw slightly.

"I'm going to your place?" Sam managed to contain his happy wiggle.

"I want you to."

Sam bit his lip, and Ian's eyes dropped to his mouth. "I want to."

This time when Ian kissed him, it was a full-on, explicit, we're-so-gonna-get-it-on kiss. "Good," he whispered against Sam's lips. Sam couldn't help but trail fingers across his cheekbone. Ian let go of his chin, finally—with reluctance?—and sat up straight, putting the truck in gear.

"Do you need to go by your place first and get your stuff?"

"Oh. Um, no. I brought clothes and my razor and stuff I'll need in the morning with me. Just in case. You know."

"Yeah, I know," Ian said, looking at him before pulling away from the curb.

chapter 37

Ian probably should have let Sam shower alone, but Sam didn't object when Ian got in with him and started soaping him up. He didn't object when Ian dragged him out, toweled him off, and herded him toward the bed. He really didn't object when Ian pulled Sam on top of himself in the bed—in fact, he went so far as to lube and stretch himself, which had to be the hottest thing Ian had ever seen.

Afterward, Ian let Sam doze, but he couldn't keep his hands off of him. He spooned Sam tightly, caressing his skin, even though it was ridiculously early in the morning and they should both be asleep. But Ian couldn't seem to stop, and after about twenty minutes of his usual postcoital nap, Sam woke up. He yawned and stretched, then hugged his corner of the pillow they shared. "Did I fall asleep?" he mumbled into it.

Ian kissed a vertebra on the back of his neck. "Yeah."

"Mmm." Sam rolled over and wormed his arm under Ian's waist. "Sorry."

"It's okay."

Sam yawned again. "Marley used to give me crap for falling asleep after I came."

It was the first time Sam had volunteered anything about his ex-asshole, and Ian had been looking for an opening. He hadn't wanted to talk about Marley the other night, but he sure as hell would pursue it now.

"Tell me about him," he said, bringing Sam even closer to him, pulling one thigh up over his so he could do a little exploring while Sam spoke. He slid curious, hungry fingers up the back of Sam's leg, getting his skin fix. He stopped at the sensitive place where Sam's buttock met his thigh, stroking lightly, waiting for Sam to squirm.

Nothing. Sam kept his leg where it was, one arm trapped under Ian's waist and his other fingers swirling in Ian's chest hair. Ian pushed his upper body back far enough to see Sam's face. He looked unhappy. Ian stroked the skin under his fingers, trying to comfort.

But okay, it hurt a little. "You don't want to tell me about him?"

"It's not that I don't . . . I don't want to talk about him at all."

"Okay," Ian said. He was sort of at a loss, now.

"Why do you want to know?" Sam asked hesitantly.

Carefully, Ian picked through his thoughts. "I think he's the reason you're skittish about trust and control."

Sam swallowed and nodded, still focused on Ian's chest hair. "He wasn't very good to me. I never had a safeword, and he didn't really . . . care."

"Did he hurt you?"

Sam's eyes flew up to meet his. "Not really. Not physically. He liked to, um, humiliate me. Have more control over me than I wanted to give him."

"Humiliation isn't your thing." Ian was certain of that.

"No." Sam shook his head, hair shushing against the bedding. Ian had been right; Sam looked perfect lying on his black sheets

He pulled Sam closer, kissing his forehead. He didn't like it, but he wasn't going to press Sam to say more. Sam sighed, and some of the tension melted out of his body, so Ian let his fingers explore again.

He tickled the back of Sam's thigh until he could feel goose bumps and hear the slightest shudder in his breath. He loved that he could cup Sam's ass, one whole cheek fitting comfortably in his hand. His thumb could rest on Sam's hipbone while his pinky finger could slide between his buttocks. Sam's ass was small and tight and it did something to him when he held it or watched Sam walk. His cheeks looked like his glutes were always tensed, like he held the tightest piece of heaven between them, and if Ian coaxed him just right, he'd share it.

It wasn't false advertising.

Ian let his pinky slide down slowly, off of Sam's tailbone, into the valley below it. Dragging through slightly tacky lube left over from earlier, he circled that tiny hole. Sam squeaked and jerked his hips toward Ian, eyelids falling closed and lips falling open.

Ian pushed himself up on his elbow, looming over Sam. "Are you too sore to let me fuck you again?" he whispered in Sam's ear.

Sam wrapped his leg tighter around Ian's, grinding his hardening dick into Ian's thigh. "It'll be fine," he panted, then tried to pull Ian in for a kiss. So Ian gave him one—a long, tongue-fucking, dominating one—then pulled away to nip his neck.

"Love your ass, Sam. I wanna fuck you on your stomach and watch my dick slide in and out of you," he murmured, pressing and rubbing against Sam's hole with his finger.

"Oh, God, yes." Then Sam moaned in protest when Ian pulled his hand away, so he kissed him again.

"I wanna spread you out over the bed so I have all your skin under me." He pushed gently on Sam's shoulder, moving and positioning them both, until Sam was face down on the black sheets and Ian was kneeing his legs apart, watching Sam's hips lifting for him. He lay on one of Sam's legs, chest against his back, rolling Sam's nuts gently between his fingers. "I wanna taste you. Wanna eat your ass," he murmured into the back of Sam's neck, stroking his thumb over Sam's asshole.

Sam froze. He had his head hidden in the crook of his arm, and Ian heard him whisper something.

"What?" Ian's heart pounded. Partly from being turned on, partly from worrying he'd freaked out Sam. But he'd rimmed Sam before, so what was the problem?

"I want you to do that," Sam whispered just loud enough for Ian to hear, his voice reaching inside Ian and grabbing hold of something tight, and it wasn't his nads. Sam took a small, gasping breath. "I want you to tongue fuck me until I'm loose enough for you." He said it quickly, like he had to push it out.

"Yeah?" Ian could hear Sam gulp as he nodded. "Would you let me tie you spread-eagle to the bed for it?"

Sam froze again, muscles so tense he was trembling. Ian wondered if he shouldn't have gone here now, but the idea of Sam tied down and writhing on his tongue wouldn't let go of him, making his dick ache and his blood pound. He leaned to nip at Sam's shoulder. "You have a safeword."

Sam didn't respond. *Hell.* "Did Marley ever tie you up?" Ian watched the back of Sam's head nod. "We don't have to." Ian kept the disappointment out of his voice pretty well. The sinking feeling in his gut Sam wouldn't know about.

"I want to," Sam said.

Oh, fuck yes. "You sure?" Ian asked, but he was already rolling toward the nightstand, where he had some soft rope. Which, yeah, he was keeping there hoping for a moment with Sam just like this. The throbbing ache returned, stronger, spreading through his gut and his groin, seeping into his limbs. He could even feel it in his fingers as he reached for the drawer.

"You'll let me free as soon as we're done?"

Ian stopped what he was doing and looked at Sam. He could still only see the back of his head. "That son of a bitch wouldn't untie you?" he asked. What kind of asshole *was* Marley?

Sam shook his head. Then he turned it to peek at Ian over his elbow. "But you will."

Ian nodded, the ache filling his heart now. "I will." He rolled back toward Sam without the rope, because this was so much more important. "You want this?" he asked about three inches from Sam's face.

"Yes." He sounded certain.

"I'll make this good, I promise."

"I know."

Ian pushed up on his arm and kissed a line down Sam's back, trailing his tongue. Sam shivered. Ian lifted himself up off the bed, got the rope and then grabbed some pillows and a black towel to cover them with. He shoved the pillows and towel under Sam's hips until his ass tilted into the air. Ian let his eyes wander all over Sam's skin on the dark sheets while he stood beside the bed. Finally, he took one of Sam's pale, bony wrists in his hand, stroking it before wrapping it carefully in soft nylon rope.

He tied Sam at both wrists and ankles until his body was spread out, all his pale, seductive skin on display. Just the sight of Sam's fingers gripping the ropes made Ian's blood pound harder and spots dance in front of his eyes. He sat down heavily on the edge of the mattress and laid his hand on Sam's back, stroking it in long sweeps.

Now that he had Sam like this, he was almost too excited to go through with it. Afraid he'd come while he had his tongue inside Sam, tasting him and (hopefully) making Sam yank on his bonds and sob in pleasure.

"Ian, please," Sam whispered, and then it didn't matter to him if he did come that way, as long as Sam was happy. Crazily, out-of-his-mind happy. Ian trailed fingers down his long spine and watched Sam's toes curl and his calves flex.

"Oh, kiddo," Ian whispered, watching other muscles in Sam's body tense at his touch. Could Sam hear the beat of his heart? Was it loud enough? He wouldn't be surprised. "Just hang on."

He tried to go slow, but he might have hurried the trip his mouth took from the nape of Sam's neck to the end of his spine. Ian couldn't wait to get there, and guessing by the soft noise Sam made every time he exhaled, neither could he. Ian's fingers trembled when they pulled Sam's cheeks apart, and he couldn't make himself tease anymore. He tasted, swirling around Sam's hole and making his body jerk. Under the slight bitterness of old lube, Sam tasted like growing things. Which was a weird thought, but seemed so perfectly him.

"Fuck, that's nice," Ian groaned, the whiskers of his chin scraping Sam's skin, leaving his mark on Sam. *Oh fuck.*

Moving slowly, Ian worked his way inside Sam, and soon he had Sam moaning. Ian fucked Sam's hole with his tongue, and lost himself in it for a while. He felt Sam's glutes tense next to his face, like he was trying to trap Ian there and never let him go, to keep him fucking and sucking on his ass forever. Ian rolled Sam's nuts between the fingers of one hand, using the other to stroke Sam's lower back. He soaked in the taste of Sam and the smell of him in the air and the sounds they made—Sam's noises and the sucking, licking sound of Ian working him with his lips and tongue, and the occasional scrape of teeth.

Sam was tied too tightly to thrust his hips more than a little, but soon he was nearly sobbing. His every other word was "please," and most of the rest were incoherent. Then Ian heard him cry, "I'm gonna—" and he looked up to see Sam's shoulder blades lifting from his back like wings trying to burst from his skin.

I'm going to make him fly.

Ian stopped.

Sam groaned, gripping the ropes until his hands were white. Ian couldn't crawl up his body fast enough, or lube his dick quickly enough—he'd give thanks for the no-condom thing later, when he had the time. His cock met barely any resistance pushing into Sam's ass, and he watched Sam's back muscles strain, trying to reach out for Ian and bring him inside.

It was hard as hell, but Ian slowed himself down. Making Sam vibrate with need, his arms taut and his shoulder blades vividly outlined under his skin. Sam was whimpering incoherently by the time Ian had sunk all the way in, his balls pressed up tight against Sam's.

He stayed still, propped on his elbows over Sam, shaking and gulping air. "I don't know how long I can—"

"Oh God," Sam groaned. "*Please.*"

Ian fucked him. Each stroke in reverberated through him, like shocks from an earthquake or a tidal wave, forcing his lungs to gasp out air and his toes to curl and his hips to jerk. And Sam to cry out.

Ian made it for about a minute, and then—thank fuck—he could feel the first spasms of Sam's muscles contracting around his cock, and Sam started screaming himself hoarse.

Ian's eyes rolled back in his head and his nuts shrunk up tighter than peas. He slammed into Sam, trying to force Sam to take him all, pelvis and hips and everything. His whole body was one giant ache and it all ignited at once, making him shout. Then everything—all that sensation—drained out of him, leaving him completely sated.

They lay there, panting and twitching, sweat sealing them together, until Ian worked up enough muscle control to shakily reach for the bandage shears and cut through the ropes on Sam's wrists. Sam's arms flopped on the bed, and he groaned from his belly.

"Okay?" Ian panted.

"Oh fuck yes," Sam answered. Ian worked up to freeing his ankles and yanking the pillows out from under his hips. Eventually he curled around Sam, kissing him endlessly, feeling Sam's consciousness sink away from him with each heartbeat.

This time, Ian fell asleep too.

chapter **38**

Sam popped into consciousness in the morning with that tingly sense that something specific had woken him. Ian had, by staring at him. Sam blinked until he brought Ian into focus, giving him time to look away.

Ian blinked back. He reached out with his finger and lightly stroked Sam's nose. The side of his face was smashed into the pillow, sunlight lining the other cheek. His lips parted, close enough for Sam to feel his breath. He followed his finger with his eyes, stroking Sam's nose, then ran his finger across Sam's cheekbone. He pushed off from his pillow, and Sam rolled onto his back as Ian came over him, pressing him into the bed, forcing his thighs to make room.

"Missed you," Ian whispered right before he kissed Sam, and somehow it made sense, even though Sam had lain next to him all night.

Missed you, too, Sam thought. He couldn't say it because Ian was keeping his mouth busy, full of his tongue and taste and breath. Sam couldn't even gasp at the sensation of Ian's foreskin slipping in the groove between Sam's groin and his leg. He fought Ian's hold—his arms were everywhere, caging Sam in—to slide hands around to Ian's ass and feel his muscles flex while he rocked against him. When Sam gripped him and squeezed, just to feel the resilience there, Ian tore his mouth away from Sam's and gasped. He bit at the tendon at the base of Sam's neck—Sam's turn to gasp. Not just from teeth but from scratchy whiskers and heat and the feeling that Ian was trying to consume him. Gnawing up his neck to Sam's ear, then panting in rhythm with his hips as he ground against Sam. Sam pushed back, helping Ian along, giving him resistance to thrust against.

Ian wrapped one arm around Sam's neck, fingers clamped on his shoulder, holding him still for leverage. "Oh God," he whispered, and Sam realized how close Ian was. In a rush, he was there, too, right on that edge.

"Ian," Sam whispered for encouragement. Ian moaned low in his ear, and Sam gripped his cheeks harder, rubbing his finger against that tender spot between them.

"Oh God," Ian whispered. Sam wrapped him in his legs, trying to pull him closer, and felt goose bumps sweep across Ian's skin under his hands. He held Ian tighter, kneading his ass and rubbing hard and steadily.

"IthinkIloveyou," Ian gasped when he shuddered and came, slippery heat flowing between them. Sam nearly let go, but he gripped Ian tighter instead and gave it up himself. Coming hard, the emotional tension of the moment and last night amplifying the physical feeling of Ian's cum on his body and Ian's hair rubbing against his dick. He arched up and hung on tight with his entire body, trembling.

Ian shook afterward, panting in Sam's ear, a dead weight on his ribs, but Sam couldn't care. He stroked Ian's naked back, sifted fingers through his hair, smiling so big his cheeks hurt. The room was filled with sunlight, and Sam was certain he'd never felt so *aglow* in his life.

"I can't believe I did that," Ian groaned.

Sam's heart fell through the bed and bounced once on the floor.

"That wasn't how I was going to tell you," Ian muttered.

Sam's heart climbed back into his chest. Ian lifted his head and looked down at him. "I meant to make it special, but I sort of lost control," he said, stroking Sam's face with one fingertip. "I'm sorry."

"Don't be sorry. Just be sure about it."

Ian nodded. "I'm as sure as I can be."

Sam decided that was good enough for now, and he'd worry about whether this could possibly be real later. For now he felt the glow.

chapter 39

The redistricting plan was completely fucking with Ian's proposed interagency radio communication protocols, and he had less than a week to figure out all the angles and redraft his plan—while making all parties happy, of course. The trick was to make each one think they were somehow getting an advantage the others weren't.

So far, he hadn't quite figured out how to do that. He ran a hand through his hair, looking at his chart. If the city fire department got the extra fifty addresses from the county fire district, that made them th—

"Ian?" Dalton's voice broke his concentration. He looked up from the document and rubbed his eyes, blurry from effort.

"Yeah?"

"A Chief Carl Cully's on the phone? He says he's your father," Dalton said in a hushed voice.

Ian slumped in his chair. *Hell.* The chief. Fucking lovely. Had he given his father this number? That was stupid. Ian took a slow, calming breath, puffing his cheeks out as he released it.

It didn't work. He tried another.

That one wasn't any more effective, so he gave up. "Thanks, Dalton," he said tiredly as he reached for his handset. If Carl wanted to talk, Ian probably couldn't avoid it.

"Dad," he said in greeting.

"Ian!" his father said, sounding like he was hailing a buddy from across a crowded bar.

He silently implored the ceiling for fortitude. "Yep, it's me."

"How's the new job? Must be boring as hell, driving a desk after being on a rig for fifteen years," Carl said jovially.

"Eleven years. Actually, I like this job."

That knocked his father on his ass for a few seconds. "Huh. Must've gotten some of your mother's genes," he finally said.

"Must have," Ian agreed. He waited silently for his father's next volley.

"So, meet any nice women up there?"

For fuck's sake. Way to be subtle, Carl. "Oh, yeah." He faked cheerful. "Lots of nice women."

"Good, good," Carl encouraged, a note of relief in his voice.

"But since I'm attracted to men, the women don't really do much for me." Ian felt tension invading his muscles as his adrenaline spiked—just like it did every time they had this conversation.

Silence. The first pleasant thing Carl had said.

Ian went for broke. "I met someone, though. Sam." He straightened his spine, pressing the button on the end of his pen up and down. *Click click.*

"I don't suppose Sam's short for Samantha?" Carl said.

Jesus. "Nope. It's short for Samuel." Wasn't it? He should probably check that.

"Ian . . ." His father's voice took on that pitiful, deflated balloon quality. *Fuck.* He dropped the pen and pinched the bridge of his nose, fighting the urge to jump out of his seat and pace around the room.

"Think of your poor mother—"

He slammed his palm down on the desk, then took a breath to calm himself and enunciated carefully. "Mom wouldn't care." Another breath, trying not to shout. "You know what I remember when she died? I remember sitting beside her bed in the hospital, and she took that fucking oxygen mask off and told me to be happy no matter what. *You're* the one who wants me to be straight."

"I want you happy!" Carl thundered. He breathed audibly in Ian's ear. "You're my youngest son, I want to see you married like your brothers. I want you to have someone who takes care of you. You think you'll ever get that with another man? Men aren't like that, Ian. You should know, you've been with enough of them and none of them worked out, did they? This Sam, he's just another lay. You keep looking for something you'll never find. You can't marry another man, you can only fuck him."

The fight drained out of Ian, leaving a sick feeling in his gut. "The sex is your real problem, isn't it?" he asked. "You don't like it that I've been with men. You can't see past that." He felt weak and lightheaded, but he didn't let any of that invade his tone. "Mom wouldn't have cared." Hell, his voice shook a little there. *Barely a quaver.*

"She would have been as disgusted as I am!"

Ian slumped in his seat. "Fuck you," he said tiredly, then hung up the phone.

The weather matched Ian's mood. They were finally moving out of the Indian summer and into the stormy season. Right now it was gray and threatening rain, and Ian figured that was pretty much perfect. As soon as he stepped foot outside the health division building, he knew it would start raining on him.

So much for not letting the chief get to him anymore.

Ian tried to do the thing Janet had been teaching him: identify his emotions and label them, figure out what was what and who was who. But it was all a painful mishmash, and the only thing he could reliably identify was the twisting ball of fear whenever he thought of Sam. *Fuck*. He thought about calling Janet, but he had an appointment in the morning. He could hang on that long, right?

Besides, if he didn't leave right now, he'd be late to pick up Sam. They were supposed to go back to Ian's place so he could change, then go out to some movie Sam wanted to see. Probably get dinner somewhere.

The fear fisted around Ian's stomach, giving him heartburn or something. He wasn't hungry. Didn't want to see that movie, anyway; it sounded dumb.

This is all about your father. Things had been so easy lately, his life and his job. Sam. Everything had been clear, but after talking to Carl it was all murky again. It was the way his father saw things that was screwed up. Didn't mean that's the way things actually were.

Logic wasn't helping him—he still felt confused.

When he saw Sam, things would fall back into place inside him.

Sam never said he loved you.

He did love Ian, though, he just needed more time, or maybe more proof of Ian's feelings for him first. This could work. It *would*. It had to.

He just needed to get his head screwed on straight. Seeing Sam when he had all these stupid doubts . . . that seemed like a bad idea.

chapter **40**

Something about this sudden rainstorm wasn't right. The wrongness of it settled in Sam's gut and filled him with anxiety. The weather in romance novels always reflected the plot point. Thunder and lightning? The Too Stupid to Live heroine was about to run out on the rocky cliff in the dark, wearing only her nightdress. Sudden rainstorm on an otherwise nice day? They were about to have a serious, possibly relationship-ending incident.

Maybe he was imagining things.

Maybe he felt that sense of impending doom because Ian was fifteen minutes late to pick him up. Sam stood at the glass doors of the student union, watching cars sweep by, looking for Ian's pickup, but he was officially tardy enough to start worrying about things like car accidents and hospitals.

Maybe he didn't get done with work on time, and he forgot to charge his phone. And didn't notice until after he'd left, so he couldn't call from the office.

Sixteen minutes. Officially, Ian was late enough that Sam could start worrying about his boyfriend having some kind of freak out about being in an honest-to-God relationship for the first time in his life.

Since Tuesday night, in the back of his mind—or maybe his heart—Sam had been waiting for the plot to go awry. For Ian to react badly to calling Sam his boyfriend, or to the level of commitment they'd reached when they decided not to use condoms. Oh, Sam hadn't *known* he was waiting for Ian's impending freak out, but now that it was here he realized he'd been expecting it.

God, and then this morning, when Ian had blurted out *I love you* while he came. What if he really *had* just said it without meaning to?

You should have told him you loved him too. But Sam hadn't wanted to do it that way. He didn't want Ian to think he'd just said it because he felt like he had to; he wanted Ian to *know* it.

Seventeen minutes late. *He isn't coming.*

Sam stared blindly into the traffic passing by outside, wondering how it had come to this. Really, he couldn't blame Ian; the man had been honest with him, at least up until this morning. He'd truly believed all that stuff he'd said about wanting to have a relationship. Wanting to *try*. This heartbreak was all on Sam. He hadn't done enough to guard his heart, had he? *Failed again*.

Time to let his heart shatter into a million tiny pieces, like it had been destined to do all along—

His phone rang in his pocket, startling him. Of course it would be Ian, and when Sam looked at the screen he found exactly what he'd expected. *My boyfriend*. He tried very, very hard to be relieved and hopeful, not dreading what he was about to hear.

"Hello?" He held his breath.

"Sam?" That was all Ian said for a few seconds, but really, it was all Sam needed to hear. His stomach felt hollow and empty. Ian took a breath before speaking again. "Listen . . . I can't pick you up."

Sam swallowed and blinked hard. "Why not?"

"I, um . . . my father called today."

"Oh." In Sam's experience, all trauma began with family interference.

"I'm not sure I can explain, but I need some time to myself to think, kiddo."

Don't call me that. Sam swallowed the lump in his throat. "Ian . . ." *You said you* loved *me*.

"I just need to get my head screwed on straight. Please don't be mad?" He didn't feel mad, he felt sad. Why couldn't Ian get his head screwed on straight *with* him? Or was it gay? Get his head screwed on gay. Ian continued before Sam was ready—as if that were an actual possibility. "This isn't about you kiddo, it's other stuff. It's me. I'll call you as soon as I figure this out."

"Okay," Sam whispered, squeezing his eyes shut and resting his forehead against the cold glass of the door.

Ian hesitated. Like he didn't really want to end this. "Will you be all right?"

"I'll be fine, Ian. I'll talk to you s—whenever you're ready." Weak. But Sam *had* to keep that possibility open. Even if it was only to fool himself a little bit longer.

"Sam? I swear, this isn't about you, it's about me," Ian said.

"Yeah. I know."

"Maybe—"

"Ian, don't drag this out." Sam said. His voice was on that edge of raw where he knew he'd break down and beg if they talked any longer. He should just say goodbye and end this, but some vindictive part inside him wanted to make Ian do it. It was his idea; he could take responsibility for all of it.

There was a very long pause in which Sam heard Ian's breathing, even over the noise of the traffic outside. Was that a gulp? "Sam, I'm—"

"Ian."

"Sorry. Bye." He hung up immediately, and Sam let himself think it was because Ian knew if he didn't do it fast—if he heard Sam's voice one more time—he wouldn't be able to.

Bastard.

He sort of remembered getting on the bus. He sat next to a window and stared out, watching it get wetter and darker, looking at all the miserable people trapped in the rain. His heart was in free fall, and his main parachute had failed.

Sam dredged up his backup parachute—*IthinkIloveyou*.

It failed too.

He only had one choice left. The Hail Mary pass—and yes, he was mixing metaphors, but at a time like this, did it matter? He fished his phone out of his pocket and dialed up his first-string.

"Nik? It's me."

"I'll be there in an hour," Nik said, tipped off by something in Sam's voice. "Just hang on, honey."

"Bring wine," Sam croaked.

chapter **41**

When Nik knocked, Sam answered the door in his comfort jeans and Snoopy T-shirt. Nik looked him over, hugging four bottles of wine to his chest and clutching a paper bag in one fist. "Are you wearing the Underoos?"

Sam nodded.

Nik pushed his way in. "It's worse than I thought. What did that dumbassed bastard do?" He headed straight for Sam's kitchen and the corkscrew.

"He . . . he said he needed some time to himself to th-think," Sam choked out.

Nik stopped opening the first bottle and looked at Sam in horror, one hand over his mouth. "Oh no," he whispered.

Sam nodded and wiped at the tear that had snuck out onto his cheek. Nik reapplied himself to the wine with vigor. "I'm opening as fast as I can."

Sam nodded dully. "He also said that—" he paused to swallow "—it's not me, it's *h-him*." He swallowed the rest of the sob that had nearly escaped.

Nik stopped rooting through Sam's cupboard for glasses, grabbed the wine, and came for him. He wrapped Sam in his arms, squeezed him tight, then handed him the bottle. "You start on this. I'll open another one for me."

Sam looked at the bottle blankly. "I haven't eaten since lunch."

"I have ice cream in the grocery bag," Nik said. "Drink; it's medicinal."

"I don't remember wine curing me of heartbreak before."

"It doesn't, it just helps you get it all out."

What did he have to lose? He tipped the bottle up and poured some wine down his throat.

That night, he did get it all out. The way the sex with Ian had turned into lovemaking, and how Ian had said he wanted to try having a relationship. As if it were some new and foreign food he thought he might like if he only tasted it.

"Maybe sea urchin roe. What's that stuff called again?" Sam asked Nik, lying next to him on the futon, staring up at the ceiling.

"Uni," Nik answered, shuddering. Sam shuddered too. That stuff was repulsive. "I doubt he sees you as being remotely like the slimy, undifferentiated gonads of a sea creature."

Sam covered his face with his hands and admitted his biggest fear. "But what if I'm just, like, relationship training wheels?" he whispered. "I thought I was the big boy bike."

Nik rolled toward him and hugged Sam hard. "You *are* a big boy bike. If not Ian's, then someone else's."

Sam sighed and patted Nik's forearm. "I guess, but right now Ian's the only one I want riding me."

Nik squeezed him again, then sat up. "Do you think I should open more wine? You're out, and I'm close." He swished around the inch or so of wine left in his bottle, peering at it as if it would answer him.

What did he have to lose? "Yeah," Sam sighed.

"Okay, one bottle or two?"

When Nik came back with fortifications—and ice cream, this time—he said, "Ian thinks you're cute. He even told Jurgen that."

Sam shrugged, trying to tip wine into his mouth without sitting up.

"Jurgen doesn't think I'm cute," Nik said around a mouthful of ice cream.

"What?"

Nik shrugged. "I asked after he told me about Ian and you. Jurgen says I get cute when I'm so mad I'm smiling and using my 'pleasant' voice right before I knife someone in the back. Figuratively speaking."

"Oh."

Nik sighed and said contemplatively, "I think *true* cuteness is an unattainable ideal with Jurgen. I'm okay with that."

"He has many other wonderful qualities," Sam rushed to point out.

Nik sighed again, but in a dreamy way. "Doesn't he?" Then he sort of shook himself. "But we're talking about you, so tell me more."

Sam told Nik more—the boyfriend thing, the no condom thing, the *I missed you* and even the *IthinkIloveyou*. It took nearly another bottle of wine and a lot of ice cream to get through.

Then he threw up. Nik stood in the bathroom doorway, blinking at him and leaning against the jamb. He wrinkled his brow. "Mebbe you should 'ave more ice cream."

Sam retched. Then he laid his cheek on the cool porcelain. "Think th'ice cream's why I'm puking."

"Oh. Could make you toast?" Nik closed one eye, possibly to focus on him.

"D'you think he loves me?"

Nik nodded solemnly. "I do. I thin' he loves you. He's just a dumbass bas'ard."

Sam lifted his head, thinking about that. "So, you think he might ac-tu-ally call me?" he enunciated carefully.

Nik shrugged. "I dunno, Sam."

"Possible, though, right? It's possible."

"Oh yeah, def." Nik nodded so hard he almost fell over.

Sam lay down on the cool bathroom floor. The room was spinning, and he was afraid he was going to puke again.

"You jus' rest there, Sam. I'll get you a blanke'," Nik said in a motherly tone—if Sam had a flaming lush for a mother.

In the morning, life sucked until Nik crawled to the store to get some electrolyte replacement elixir. Once Sam drank that, he began to feel like maybe he'd survive this hangover. Surviving the heartbreak was still debatable.

They went out for a gross, fat-laden breakfast. It was just like old times. Sam stared down at his eggs. "Why did we want to do this again?"

"Tradition," Nik said dully.

"Let's discontinue this one."

"That's what we said last time."

Sam nodded, remembering now. "Okay," he said. "Let's not forget next time."

"Agreed."

Breakfast did help, though. Until Nik brought up the Exposed Innerds concert. Sam groaned. "I forgot that was tonight."

"How could you *forget*?" Nik looked appalled.

Sam gave him a long look.

"Never mind," he said, flapping his hand at Sam. "Well, so maybe when Ian meets us at the club tonight he'll be ready to talk."

"He's not coming," Sam said tiredly, running his fingertip along the edge of the table.

"He might?" Nik offered.

Sam shrugged. "Hopefully Dalton will, or else Miller won't have a date, either."

"Oh, if that happens and Ian doesn't show, you can be Miller's date."

Sam gave him another look.

Nik smiled slightly. "Or not."

"How'd you get Miller to go out on a date with Dalton after that party disaster?"

"I think 'disaster' is a bit strong. I prefer to think of it as 'not a complete success.'"

"Uh-huh. So, he must agree or he wouldn't be willing to go out on this blind date." Sam pushed the issue, because he was suspicious.

"Oh, you might not want to mention Dalton to him. It's a little bit of a surprise."

Ahhhh. "Nik?"

"Yes?"

"Now that I'm single again—"

"If! If you're single again."

Sam sighed again, shoulders sagging. "*If* I'm single again, you don't get to set me up on any dates."

Nik didn't answer, he just pouted.

chapter **42**

"**I** don't know what the fuck I'm doing here." Ian stood next to Janet's office window, looking out over downtown.

"Well, what normally happens is you come in, we chitchat about nothing until I direct you toward something you've decided to work on, or you start telling me about something that's bothering you." Ian could hear the smile in her voice.

"My father called me this week."

"And it was bad?" she asked, serious now.

"One of the worst."

"Why do you think that is?"

"Because I'm done taking his shit."

"Is that it? I thought you were done a while ago."

Hell. Ian traced the shape of a building outside with his fingertip on the glass. "I really let him get to me. It was like . . . I was weak."

"You're not a weak man, Ian," Janet said. "But maybe you're vulnerable?"

"I shouldn't be."

"Why not? Everyone is sometimes. You get no free passes."

"I thought . . . I thought this emotional connectedness stuff was supposed to help me, not make me weak."

"Vulnerable."

"It's the same fucking thing!"

"No, it's not."

He turned to face her. "How not? I was done letting him get to me, I haven't listened to his shit for months, I got the fuck out of there. But now all the sudden I'm breaking a date with my boyfriend because I let that bastard, just, I don't know." He ran hand through his hair. "I let him influence how I feel."

Janet tilted her head and looked at him a silent second. "Let's talk about Sam."

Ian closed his eyes and pinched the bridge of his nose. Whatever. He knew he needed to discuss Sam anyway. "What do you want to know?"

"Is he weak?"

"No!"

"You told me you saw him that way when you met him."

Well, that was a little dose of shame that he totally deserved. Ian shoved a hand in his pocket and paced across the room and back. "That was like someone else. Not the guy I met—me, I was like a different person then."

"That was barely a month ago."

He turned to face Janet. "I changed a lot. He changed me."

"Or did you let yourself change?"

"What's the difference?" Ian flopped on the couch, arms crossed over his chest, and stared at the ceiling. After a few seconds of silence, he checked, and yes, Janet was watching him. "Fine," he muttered. "I let myself." He hated it when she was right.

She returned to her original point, whatever the hell that was. "So you see Sam differently now. What makes him not weak?"

Ian sighed, his head falling back on the couch. It must be his fifteen minutes of shame. "I was a bastard to him in the beginning, but he still took a chance on me. It was like . . . I don't know what I thought. It looks weak that he saw me after that, but it's not. It's strength. He could protect himself enough to open up to me." He jerked his head up and looked at her in horror, sharp pains knifing his chest. "What if he hadn't done that?"

Janet shrugged as if it wasn't important. "Then he wouldn't be the guy for you."

How could she take this so calmly? "He *is* the guy for me. But I could have lost him by being a bastard."

"You didn't, Ian, you did what you needed to do. Sam made himself vulnerable to you, and you honored that. You made yourself vulnerable in turn, didn't you?"

"Yes," he whispered.

"And was it worth it?"

"Yes," he answered louder.

"Do you feel weak for doing it?"

"No."

"Then why is it different when it's your father whom you made yourself vulnerable to, and he fucks it up?"

"Because I didn't want to make myself vulnerable to him! I didn't have control."

She shook her head, smiling. "So you'll learn control, and you'll figure out how to protect yourself. You're like a snake."

"*What*? Can't I be a bear?"

She waved a hand. "No, it doesn't work with my analogy. You're like a snake. You've just shed your skin for a brand new one, so for a few days this new hide will be tender and fragile, and you have to protect it from sharp objects. Your father would be a sharp object here. You'll toughen up your hide and ignore him."

"What if I just don't *want* to deal with him?"

She nodded. "You can make that decision. You can do whatever you need to protect yourself. Sam could have decided not to see you again if he felt he needed to, to protect himself."

Ian had liked where this was going, but now he scowled. "So if I want to be as strong as Sam, I have to talk to the chief?"

"No. It all depends on the threat level. Your father is a much bigger threat to you than you were to Sam at the time."

Ian thought about it awhile, staring up at Janet's ceiling. He thought he got it. "How come everything seems so clear when I'm in here, but when I leave I lose that insight and everything gets confused?"

Janet sighed in resignation. "It happens to everyone. You get clarity or enlightenment or whatever, then you lose track of it for a while and you're wading knee-deep through crap hoping for the truth to reveal itself. Just do the best you can, and try to stick with what you know until you get that clarity back for a while."

"I know I love Sam," Ian said immediately.

"There you go. Have you told him?"

He looked toward the window, remembering. "I did. The other morning when we were, um, in bed."

Janet frowned. "Did you tell him during sex?"

He cleared his throat and nodded.

"You should tell him again, and not during sex. People say things in bed all the time that they don't really mean. I thought that was common knowledge."

Ian stared at her very serious expression. *Hell.* "I need to talk to him."

Calling Sam took more balls than Ian had expected. He knew he'd upset Sam when he broke their date last night, and he needed to explain, but he wanted to do it in person. It wasn't until he got to work, telling himself he had important things to take care of before he could see Sam, that he realized he was avoiding talking to him.

You're scared.

Oh, hell yes I am.

Admitting it may be the first step to solving a problem, but Ian was at a loss as to what the next step might be. Self-fulfillment would be so much easier if everyone could agree on the necessary steps, write down the instructions, and then make sure they were widely available. Drop them from airplanes or something.

And shit, what if he'd really upset Sam? Ian thought it was reasonable, asking for a night alone, but Sam had seemed so, just, *sad*, as if Ian were trying to end things. But how could Sam think that? He went over it again in his head, but he still couldn't see how Sam would get that idea.

Since he hadn't quite worked up to calling Sam, Ian made a plan. He made reservations at the restaurant where they'd had their first date, but late reservations, because he wanted time alone to talk to Sam first. Okay, yeah, and maybe mess around. Make Sam come hard and fast and screaming his name, like that time after he'd messed up at the farmers' market. Something special just for Sam.

Maybe he was imaging things, but lately he thought it made all the difference in the world to Sam that *Ian* was with him. When they had sex now, it *did* something to Ian. Grabbed him by the balls and wouldn't let him go until he came, feeling some little thing inside him—another piece of the "Ian" puzzle—click into place.

At nearly four o'clock, Ian decided he needed to wrap things up and just go. He was pretty sure he knew where Sam would be: at the campus library. Maybe he could just surprise him. That would be so much easi—um, better than calling.

"Ian?" Dalton's voice said at his elbow. "Jurgen Dammerung is on line one for you."

Oh, yeah! He should have thought of that—Nik and Sam both had some app on their phones where they could locate each other by

GPS. He could just ask Nik. "Hey!" he said when he picked up the receiver.

"You fucking dumbass," Jurgen snapped. "I can't believe this shit. What the hell is wrong with you? You love him, and if you fuck this up you're going to regre—"

"What the hell are you talking about?" Ian interrupted. But the sick feeling in his stomach already knew what Jurgen was talking about.

"You know what I'm talking about."

"I just needed to think," Ian whispered.

"Oh my *God*!" Nik's voice broke in.

Wait. "Am I on speakerphone?"

Click. Nik's voice came louder and clearer, without that tin-can quality. "Have you never broken up with *anyone* before? You don't say 'I need time to think' if you actually *just need time to think*. That's relationship code for 'I'm leaving you, and don't call me I'll call you'—which you compounded by telling him you'd call him when you were ready to talk!"

Ian's palms started sweating. "Uh, can I talk to Jurgen?"

"No! He had his turn, now it's mine."

"It was kind of a short turn, and I was on speakerphone."

"Nikky, give me the phone," Jurgen said in the background.

"And since your education in these matters is clearly lacking, let me inform you that 'It's not you, it's me' is also *verboten*."

Ian sucked in a breath. "What does that mean?"

"It means, 'I don't like you, get away from me.' Jesus," Nik added in a mutter. "I'm going to be giving you the verbal ass-kicking you deserve now. We all know it's really Jurgen's job, but he seems to have some of the same communication difficulties you do—is that a family trait?"

"I don't have communication difficulties, now give me the damn phone," Jurgen said, louder.

"Jurgen," Nik said, suddenly sweet. "Did you sit up half the night and drink yourself sick with a brokenhearted, crying Sam? No? In that case, I'm going to be doing the talking for now."

A chill walked down Ian's spine. "Please tell me he didn't cry. I wasn't breaking up with him, I swear."

"I'd love to be able to tell you he wasn't crying," Nik said politely, which somehow made the whole situation scarier.

Ian stood up. "Oh my God, I have to fix this."

"Goddamn right you do. Now, you're supposed to meet us for dinner before the concert in an hour and a half, so—"

"Concert?"

"*Please* tell me you didn't forget about the Exposed Innerds concert tonight?"

Hell. "Okay, I won't tell you."

Nik sighed, as if he needed to gather strength. "Sam's expecting you not to show, but you will, Ian. Won't you?"

Ian nodded firmly, bumping his chin on the receiver. "Yes."

"Okay, then this is what you're going to do. You're going to make reservations for two at a very nice restaurant—"

"Oh, I've done that," he interrupted, relieved.

"—for 6 p.m.," Nik continued.

"I'll change them."

"And then you're going to meet us for dinner at five thirty at the Club Monaco, but *ask* Sam to please have dinner with you, alone."

"Give me the Goddamned phone, Nikky," Jurgen said in a voice so low and sexy not even Ian was completely immune.

It was very disturbing.

Nik's breathing got ragged. "Bye, Ian. Jurgen wants to talk to you now. Oh, and I've upgraded you from bastard to 'dumbassed bastard,'" he added quickly.

"Ian?" Jurgen asked. "Don't fuck this up. Sam's your Nik."

Click.

A half hour later, Ian was just about ready to leave work. He'd called the restaurant and pled for a new reservation, refusing to hang up until he got it. Since it was casual Friday, he didn't need to change; he could just meet Sam at the Monaco. Should he bring flowers? Was that lame? He texted Jurgen quickly, instructing him to ask Nik.

"Hey, Dalton, you're fine driving yourself, right?" he called out the door, stuffing his paperwork in files so he could find it on Monday. "I need to pick up Sam for dinner and—"

"Ian?" Dalton stood in the doorway, looking uncertain. "There's someone here to see you. He seems anxious," he added quietly.

"I can't see anyone *now*," Ian whispered. "Tell him he has to make an appointment."

"I said that," Dalton whispered back. "But he keeps *insisting*."

Someone walked up behind him and looked over his shoulder at Ian. It was Tierney. His eyes were bloodshot, and he looked like he hadn't shaved in a week.

"Dude, I really need to talk to you. I'm, um, I'm sorry. For last weekend."

For fuck's sake. Ian gritted his teeth and exhaled through them. He stared at Tierney a second, then looked at his watch. Four forty. "You have a half hour, dude, that's it."

"Fine. Whatever time you can give me."

Ian closed his eyes and shook his head. "Gimme a minute." He looked up to see Tierney's eyes flicker down the back of Dalton's neck. Something about that look didn't sit right with him, and he said harshly, "Just have a seat out there and wait for me." He stared at Tierney until the man moved. Then he looked at Dalton. "Can you go a little early and wait for them? Then if I'm a couple minutes late . . . please?"

Dalton smiled reassuringly. Ian got the feeling he had some ideas about what was going on. "Of course. I'll leave in five minutes. Don't worry."

"Having a hard time with that," Ian muttered after Dalton turned and left.

chapter **43**

For some unexplained reason, Nik and Jurgen needed to do something alone, so Sam had waited for Miller at his place, then gave directions while Miller drove them to the Monaco. It took forever to find a place to park, about five blocks from the club. They trekked toward it mostly in silence. As well as feeling sort of numb to everything, Sam didn't feel much like talking. He only roused himself to tell Miller when it was time to cross a street or something.

"Turn here, it's a shortcut," Sam said, indicating an alleyway between two buildings. He saw the club entrance across the street at the other end. Some blond guy was standing there, looking around. Waiting for his friends, Sam guessed. Miller nodded and turned. He seemed a little nervous and had been since he'd picked Sam up. Sam was starting to have suspicions about that.

"I don't think Nik is trying to set us up," he blurted. He immediately felt his ears heat. Of course he'd said that, because he was a dorky, awkward social misfit who'd never have a boyfriend again and hadn't been cute enough or sexy enough or *something* enough to keep around the one chance he had at—

"Nik's kinda weird, you know?" Miller said. "He thinks we're both in *need*, and maybe if he hooks us up we can help each other out. He doesn't get it. Whatever it is you need, I ain't it, and vice versa. No offense."

"None taken." Sam said, before beginning his defense of his best friend. Then he thought it over. "Yeah, he hasn't really figured out giving emotional support yet. He's much better at receiving it."

"He tries, though. More than he used to be able to do."

"He's really changed since meeting Jurgen, hasn't he?"

Sam didn't expect Miller to have much of an answer. After all, other than high school, Miller hadn't had a lot of contact with Nik. But Miller stopped halfway down the alleyway, turning to Sam. "Seems different to me. When I met him again last summer, he seemed just like he was ten years before. Snippy but so damned cute it about made my eyes cross. Sorta like one of those snarly lapdogs little old ladies carry around in their purse."

Sam laughed so hard he snorted something out his nose. Thank God there was a handy brick wall for him to lean his shoulders against until the tears stopped rolling down his face and he could catch his breath.

Miller stood in front of him, grinning. "Guess that was kinda funny."

And I really needed to laugh. "Tell me," Sam gasped, "how he's—" *giggle* "—different." He wiped his eyes.

"He doesn't walk like he owns the world anymore. More like the world owns him. Not in a bad way, but like he found his place or something." Miller looked thoughtfully down the alley toward the street.

"Oh," Sam said, sobering up. "That's . . . about right."

"You know, as much of a brat as he could be in high school, he was pretty good to me. He put up with my stupid crush, and he never told anyone. I made a fool of myself 'bout fifty times over with him, but he never got sick enough of my B.S. to hurt me or tell everyone."

"The city I grew up in wasn't very big, but I never got the kind of shit Nik did. I can't even imagine what hell they would have put you through if you'd been out, since you were sort of 'one of them' . . ." Sam trailed off. Miller was still looking at the street, but his whole face had changed from thoughtful to alarming.

"Speak of the devil," he said softly.

Sam looked, expecting to see Nik and Jurgen. It wasn't them. "Miller?"

"Yeah?"

"Is that an *actual* pickup truck full of gay-bashing rednecks?"

"Sam, you need to run. They're here for me," Miller said, turning to face the threat squarely.

"But how did they—"

"I might have done something stupid a day or two ago."

"Miller, is that your *boooyfriend*?" the driver shouted out the window. Sam could hear the *screech* of the parking brake when the guy set it. He opened the door, and Sam watched his gut spill out in front of him as he climbed down. The guy in the passenger seat was getting out, too, coming around the front.

"Get the fuck outta here, Sam," Miller said quietly. Sam heard the threads of fear in his voice.

He swallowed. "No," he said shakily. "It's my first gay-bashing. I wouldn't want to miss it." He wasn't as scared as he would have expected. The numbness that had settled over him earlier was good for *something*.

"That's not funny," Miller hissed.

Sam ignored him, watching the guys vault out of the bed of the truck like good ol' red-blooded—straight—American boys. Some of them had difficulty—they'd stopped going to football practice or whatever about ten years ago, and Sam bet there'd been a lot of beer and potato chips between then and now.

Predictably, the one who looked like he worked out was the one with the baseball bat.

"If I live through this, it'll make a really good scene in a book," Sam whispered.

Miller turned toward him, eyes huge. "For God's sake Sam, get the hell outta here! You can't help me, and these guys could actually *kill* you."

The rednecks overheard Miller. "Oh, we won't kill your girlfriend, Miller. S'not nice to pick on someone weaker, don't cha know. Not like he can hurt any of us," the driver sneered. The other bashers laughed at his wit. The driver looked pleased with himself and hitched his waistband up a couple inches. It immediately slunk back below his belly, and his gut popped back out, taking its rightful place in the world.

Sam felt a white-hot flash of fear and adrenaline that burned away all his numbness. He'd seen Marley's waistband do that about a million times, right after Marley insulted him. "I can't, huh?" He sneered right back, reaching for his back pocket, so mad his fingers trembled.

Everyone froze, and Sam could feel the tension in the air. And— *yes!*—the fear. These fuckers were afraid of him!

But why?

"You got a *gun*?" Miller mumbled out the side of his mouth.

"No! Where would I get a gun?" Sam whispered, pulling out his cell phone.

It was like waving a red flag at a group of bulls. The redneck herd charged them. Sam had never texted so fast in his life. *Thumbs of fury*, he thought, giggling hysterically while listening to feet pound toward him.

He got off a message to Nik, the last person he'd texted. *Getting bashed in alley behind drugstore*. Shit, what if he thought it was a line from an Exposed Innerds song? No time to worry about that. He only got partway through texting Ian when someone punched him in the chest so hard his feet left the ground, and he landed on his back.

Oh, so this *is what it's like to get the breath knocked out of you*. He lay on his side, blinking, trying to remember how to breathe while he watched Miller get his ass kicked.

Miller wasn't a huge guy, but the height he did have was muscle-bound. Sam was no expert, but it looked like Miller did some damage before the five guys surrounding him got him on the ground and started kicking him. He was pretty sure that meant Miller was losing.

It was incredibly brutal. Sam may have been the original ninety-pound weakling, but he couldn't just watch a guy get kicked in the gut and kidneys by an endless stream of pointy-toed cowboy boots and not *do* something. He struggled up on his arms as soon as he got his breath back. He was on wobbly legs when the guy with the baseball bat raised it over his head, ready to crack open Miller's skull.

Sam didn't think—he just jumped the guy, grabbing the arm with the bat. He got thrown off immediately, but at least he'd distracted the batter. He could tell because the batter now turned and came for him. *Oh, that was fucking stupid*. Except not, because otherwise Miller could have died.

On the other hand, now the guy with the bat wanted to smash Sam's head in. The rest of the redneck horde had stopped kicking Miller to spectate. Sam leapt to his feet and started backing away, hands in front of him, like he was trying to placate a bear. Which he'd rather be doing, given the choice.

"Here, faggot-faggot-faggot," the guy sang out. "Come and get the bat. Maybe, if you're a cooperative little faggot, you can take it up the ass instead of on the *cabeza*."

Like that was some kind of choice? "No fucking way!"

The guy shrugged, holding the bat in a swinger's stance. "Up to you, *boy*."

Shit. What did one do in this situation? Go down fighting? Make peace with one's creator? Backing away slowly seemed like a good option. But every time Sam took a step back, Slugger took a step forward. After about thirty seconds of that, he swung. Sam cringed and squeezed his eyes shut, but nothing smashed in his face. Laughter taunted him.

The dude was *messing* with him, feinting to see Sam freak out. Things just kept getting better.

"Sam!" Oh thank *God*. Nik's voice. Sam turned his head toward the street, taking another step back.

He set his foot down on something that rolled out from under his heel, knocking him off-balance. As he flailed his arms, trying to keep from going down, he saw Jurgen coming for the rednecks, his face the stuff of nightmares. A demon's mask, if demons were in the business of ripping apart gay bashers with their bare hands. Sam didn't get to see that part of it, though. Something hit him in the side of the head, everything went white, and then he felt his brain bounce around in his skull. Unconsciousness welcomed him with red and blue emergency lights.

chapter **44**

Ian picked a bar near his office where lots of professional guys went after work. He'd even seen some gay guys in there, but it wasn't a gay bar, just the kind of place where no one got in your shit. Tierney made for the bartender the second they were through the door, and had ordered two beers and a shot of whiskey before Ian sat on the stool next to him. "You want a shot, too?" he asked Ian, not quite looking at him.

"No, thanks."

They waited silently for their drinks, Tierney rigid and staring straight ahead. No one sat near them, so it was semi-private. When the bartender brought their order, Tierney downed his shot, chugged half his beer, then slumped on his stool. "Gonna need another beer," he told the bartender before the guy was ten feet off.

Ian raised an eyebrow and sipped his beer. Tierney seemed a wee-bit stressed. He felt surprisingly relaxed. Whatever happened, he knew two things: he was already out, and he could still take Tierney in a fight.

Not that it would come to that. But just in case it did.

Tierney finished his first beer and started on his second, drinking it slower. "I'm sorry, man," he said, fingers twirling a beer coaster on the bar.

Well, hell. "Guess I can see why you took it hard."

Tierney snorted. "Kind of a surprise, yeah."

"Sorry." Ian wasn't sure what he was apologizing for, but it seemed like the best thing. He didn't have to mean it. "Your reaction was worse than I expected."

T cleared his throat. "You been planning that for a while?"

"Telling you? Not really. I mean, I knew I had to, but I didn't plan it out. Just seemed like it was time."

"'Cause of that kid?" he asked in a strangled voice.

"I was going to come out no matter what." *But even if I hadn't planned to, I would have for Sam.*

Tierney hunched over, staring into his beer.

Ian surreptitiously checked his watch. Tierney had eighteen minutes left. He probably shouldn't go there, but he didn't have anything to lose and he needed to move this along. "I figured telling you would be the end of our friendship. Even thought you might try taking a swing at me. But T, man, you kinda lost your shit."

Tierney didn't puff up and get pissed. He took another long drink of his beer. "Yeah, well . . . So I guess it's serious, you and that kid."

"Sam. Yeah, I think it's kind of permanent." Adrenaline rushed through him as he said it, but this time it was more exhilarating than terrifying. He could fix things, right?

"Well that just fucking figures," Tierney muttered.

"Not like I'm going to go straight again," Ian said.

"I don't fucking care about you being gay!" Tierney nearly shouted. People near them looked in surprise, but then most politely turned away. After giving Ian and Tierney a hairy eyeball or two. Ian had picked this bar carefully for tolerance, not acceptance.

Ian turned his head, giving Tierney a few seconds to compose himself. "Okay," he finally said. "Then what the fuck was that about on Sunday?"

"I'm jealous," Tierney hissed. "Can't you fucking see that? I'm jealous, okay?" He ran a hand through his hair, straightening up and chugging the rest of his beer, then motioning with his glass for another.

Ian stared at the side of his face as T slumped back on his barstool. "Shit," he breathed. "It's true? You're gay."

"Aw fuck," Tierney groaned.

Ian leaned over the bar toward T, trying to get in his face. "Then what the *fuck* is with all the homophobia?"

Tierney rested his temples on the palms of his hands, shaking his head. "I don't know, man. I mean, it started when I was a teenager, I guess because I was trying to hide it if you believe all the psych, and it just never stopped. I *can't* stop, or someone might figure me out. And without a good reason to be out, I mean, like a *really* good reason, I just can't face that." He lifted his head, blinking his bloodshot eyes. His face was so pale he looked like a ghost. "Welcome to my world, man. It's a scary place."

Ian straightened up, trying to think. For fuck's sake, what was he supposed to say to that? "I get it. Okay, and so you're jealous . . . of what? Me coming out and having a boyfriend?" Ian kept his voice low as the bartender walked toward them with another full pint.

Tierney snorted and accepted his next beer from the bartender, who immediately walked off. "Yeah. That. I'm jealous because you have a boyfriend. You're the guy who's got everything I want."

It was disorienting as hell. Ian felt like he'd been looking at Tierney wrong, and had been for years. He had to make some sort of effort to help the guy, though. "You could have it, too, you know. You're a good-looking guy, T, and there's gotta be someone out there . . ." *Fuck*. He needed to find a P.C. way to say this.

"Who'll put up with me?" Tierney laughed meanly. "That's the least of my worries, dude. Only one guy I ever wanted like that, and I gave up on him years ago. Besides, you've met my family. You think Father or Mother would put up with a gay son? Fuck, no. That son of a bitch would kick me right out of the company *and* the will."

Ian's cell phone buzzed on his belt. Hell with it, he was after hours and Tierney needed something from him. Help or something. Some kind of gay brotherhood support bullshit. *I'm in so far over my head.*

Dammit, he wished Sam were here. Or he wished he were with Sam. He couldn't think of a fucking thing to say.

"This is it for me, dude. I'm gonna be a pathetic, closeted drunk fucker who spouts homophobia in public and gets his rocks off through a hole in a bathroom wall for the rest of my life. I've been sucked off in so many bathrooms, I bone up when I flush the toilet."

Ian's phone buzzed at him again, but he ignored it. "T, it doesn't have to be like that. There are guys who have relationships and stay in the closet." There had to be, right? Jesus, this was depressing as shit.

"Didn't you hear what I said?" Tierney said, picking up his glass and lifting it to his mouth. "I said there's only been one guy for me, ever, and he's never going to want me." He chugged the rest of his beer, then tried to catch the bartender's eye by waving the glass.

"Dude, maybe you need to lay off the—dammit." Ian yanked his phone out of his pocket. Whoever the fuck kept texting him didn't want to be ignored, so if he wanted to deal with Tierney's shit— which, point of fact, he didn't, but it looked like he had to—he had to answer and shut the fucker up. Then he could maybe get to Sam.

It was from Dalton. *They hit him in the head with a baseball bat.*

Ian nearly dropped the phone. *Hit who?* But he had a horrible feeling about who it was. He scrolled back to Dalton's previous messages.

911 I think Sam's getting bashed behind the club.

Sam's down. Get over here NOW.

The blood drained from Ian's head and fingers, leaving him suddenly cold but sweating. He stared at the screen, then jumped out of his seat and was halfway across the bar before he heard Tierney yell. "Ian! What the fuck, dude?"

Ian hit the door running.

chapter 45

Someone was driving a nail into his arm. Sam tried to pull it away, but he was tied down to the table. Why had Ian tied him to the table? It was uncomfortable as hell. He tried to move his head, but even his forehead was strapped down. "Ian," he complained, but his voice wasn't strong enough to express his annoyance. "Grapefruit," he said. That came out a little louder.

"Ohthankgod," Ian babbled.

Garlic breath. "Uh," Sam complained. God, Ian was just a torture fiend tonight, wasn't he?

"Sam?" Nik's voice shouted. "Sam, can you hear me?"

What was Nik doing here? How did he make his voice echo like that? "Wha...?"

"Sam?"

Sam swallowed. What was the thing around his neck? Nothing made sense. "Where's Ian?"

"He's coming, Sam. He's coming, I swear."

"He usually waits for me to come first." Sam tried to screw up his face in confusion, but it hurt like hell. "What are you doing here?"

"Sam, can you open your eyes?"

It took a few tries, but he got them open. The world burst on him in painful detail. Lights and people and footsteps and Nik hovering anxiously over him, Jurgen standing nearby looking hellaciously pissed. For a second, Sam had a flicker of memory about Jurgen, but then it was gone. "Where's Ian?"

A woman in a blue shirt moved Nik out of the way, her fingers running across Sam's scalp and behind his neck. Was this a massage? She needed to rub a lot harder.

"Hi Sam, I'm Lydia. Do you remember what happened?"

"What happened when? Who are you?"

"My name's Lydia. I'm a paramedic. You were hit in the head by a bat—"

"You got bashed," Nik interrupted, voice strident. Lydia smiled at him soothingly.

"What? I what? Why would I get hit by a bat?" Sam asked her, frowning. His brows rubbed against the thing across the forehead. "Why am I tied down?"

"We had to make sure you didn't move."

Sam closed one eye to focus on her. "What is going *on*?"

"I'm just making sure you're all right. I'm going to check your pupils now." She was flicking a light on and off in his peripheral vision.

"What are you going to—gah!" She stabbed him in the eye with the laser light thingy, then did the other one. "Nik! Jurgen! Help!"

"It's okay, it's okay, she's a paramedic." He felt Nik petting his hand.

"I'm all done," she soothed.

"Fuck," Sam muttered. Something about the laser dagger had set off a pounding in his head. It got worse with each beat. "Warn a guy before you stab him in the eye." A bluish-black blob filled his sight. "Are my eyes open?"

"Your vision will come back in a few seconds."

Somehow, Sam thought someone who'd just blinded him would be more sympathetic. He didn't like her much. He tried to throw her a dirty look, but since he *couldn't see her* he didn't know if it hit its mark.

She followed up the maiming of his eyes by poking around his head some more, meanwhile asking him questions.

"Do you know your name?"

She'd just used it, could she really not remember? "It's Sam," he said clearly. He tried to lift his head and his headache ratcheted up another notch when the thing around his forehead pulled him back.

"Good job." What was this, kindergarten? "Do you know what year it is?"

Oh for God's sake, was this necessary right now? "Yes, it's, um . . . Nik, what's the date?"

Nik didn't answer, but the woman didn't ask him any more questions, so Sam dropped it. "Fuck, my head hurts," he moaned.

"I'm going to give you something for that," the woman said. She started fiddling with the nail in his arm.

"I don't think aspirin will be enough," Sam told her.

"Oh, it's going to be a *little* stronger than aspirin. You enjoy your trip in la-la-land."

"Wait!" Nik screeched. "You're giving him drugs? I thought you weren't supposed to do that with head injuries."

She was giving him drugs? He didn't know drug dealers made deliveries. Was it an extra charge?

"Nikky, let her do her job," Jurgen said.

"That's a common misconception. In most East Coast protocols you can't, but on the West Coast we're much more aggressive with drugs."

"Yeah, the voting public makes that obvious," Jurgen interjected, sounding almost normal.

"At the hospital they'll give him a CT scan to check him for head trauma."

Hospital? What? "Where'm I going?" Sam asked her, but she didn't answer. Instead Nik was back, hanging over his face.

"You don't remember what happened? You got hit in the head with a baseball bat."

Sam's body felt weird, a little bit like he was on a carnival ride. "Are we in an airplane?"

"No," Nik snapped. "The paramedics are moving you to the ambulance. You got bashed by a bunch of rednecks! You and Miller."

"Miller's here, too? Oooh, head rush!" Sam giggled. "Did I have something to drink at the bashing?" If he had, he needed to remember what it was, because it was making the headache recede. Not really go away, more like it was sitting in the corner and watching him rather than jumping up and down on his brain stem. Oh, the airplane was flying over gravel, he could hear it.

"Nikky," Jurgen's voice said from somewhere down a tunnel. "You need to take it easy on him." Sam couldn't see Jurgen, though. Dammit, that woman *had* blinded him!

Oh, wait, he'd shut his eyes again. "Nik, I think this's my Dark Moment. D'you think my prince'll come?"

Nik gulped and gasped. Sam felt shaking fingers on his cheek. "You're not 'im," he mumbled. He didn't want Nik to get the wrong idea.

Nik sounded like he'd swallowed a cough. "I know." He paused, then took a deep breath and spoke in a calmer voice. "Sam, you were beaten up and so was Miller. Do you remember that?"

"I might, actually . . ." Sam tried to grasp the elusive memory, but it slipped away on the back of a bubble, except it left a few scraps behind. He gasped, eyes flying open. "I got beat up by rednecks, 's tragic."

"Why didn't you run!"

"Shhh, there's no need to yell." Sam focused on Nik. He was sort of bobbing up and down. "I didn't run 'cause I'm Too Stupid to Live," Sam answered, watching red and blue lights twirl slowly by behind Nik's head. "I suffered from the foolhardy notion that I could help, like any good romance character should."

Someone grasped his hand, holding it too tightly. "*What the fuck* are you talking about?" they shouted in his face, and it sounded like Ian. Sam blinked a few times, trying to focus on the head bobbing and weaving on the other side of him.

It *was* Ian.

"Oh, you're here, thank God," Sam said with a sigh. "But your voice is too loud," he whispered, trying to encourage Ian to do the same. Having Ian here was a relief, but he was just so tired . . . The airplane came to a halt. Could they do that in midair? Wouldn't they plummet to the earth? Oh, there it was jerking, but then flying again. This time when he came to a stop, there was a *click*. The airplane had been tethered, now. No more flying for it. Poor airplane was trapped.

"Sam, please, just . . . be all right, okay? I'll come with you to the hospital and—" Ian interrupted himself with a weird, gulping noise, and something wet hit Sam's forehead.

"We're going to the hospital? Why?" He opened his eyes. Ian was blurry, now. "Can't really see you," Sam mumbled.

Ian turned his head and Sam heard Nik repeat what he'd said in a frantic voice. Another voice answered, a woman's. Was there a woman here? "It's okay. We're leaving in a minute. Do you have a ride to the hospital?"

"Yes!" Ian yelled.

"Shhh," Sam encouraged. He couldn't tell for sure, but he thought Ian turned back to him. Sam tried to smile, but he couldn't concentrate enough to be sure he managed it.

He felt something next to his ear, then Ian's voice whispered, "I'll be there for you, kiddo."

chapter 46

Hospitals were incredibly boring, it turned out. Sam was stuck in a little curtained alcove, his head was pounding, and Ian wasn't there. The walls were gently rocking from side to side, but Sam didn't find the movement as soothing as it seemed like it should be.

It would have been nice if he could have lost consciousness, but he'd managed to stay awake—albeit incredibly high—the whole ride to the hospital, and during the stuff that happened once he got there. Some of it was blurry in his mind, but he remembered a guy saying something about "concussion" to the lady in the blue shirt. Then they took him for a ride on the wheeled bed and stuck his head into a gigantic steel donut. The whole time, someone kept erupting into giggles; he suspected himself.

He'd also begun to suspect the hospital was some alternate plane of reality.

Eventually, all the people who had swarmed around him before had left him alone in this curtained closet, with the lights dimmed and the drugs wearing off. He was still plenty high, but he could now recall some of what had happened with Miller.

Then he remembered Ian had broken up with him.

Except Sam wondered now if maybe that plane of existence—the one where Ian didn't love him and didn't want to be with him—had been more nightmare than reality.

A guy in those pajamas people wore in medical dramas pushed aside a curtain wall and walked into Sam's little cubicle, interrupting his train of thought. Whatever he'd been thinking floated off like bubbles.

"You actually wear those?" Sam asked, too loudly. It made him wince.

The guy stopped beside him and beamed. "You're making more sense," he answered. Well, not actually answered, per se.

"Yeah, my head hurts," Sam whispered.

"My name's Urban. I'm your nurse." He looked at Sam's arm where the IV went in.

"My name's Sam. My head hurts," he said just above a whisper.

Urban smiled at him some more. "Well, once you see the doctor you can have more of the good stuff, and then it'll feel better." He started checking other things, writing on Sam's chart, looking at various bits of equipment. Sam had no clue what Urban was doing and found he was strangely uninterested.

"Think I'm still on the good stuff." He sure felt like he was on *something*.

"Yeah, that's why I said you can have *more*." His nurse winked at him.

Huh. "Are you flirting with me?" Sam asked.

Urban raised his eyebrows. "I am if you want me to be."

"Could you maybe find my boyfriend and bring him here?"

"And how will I know who your boyfriend is?" he asked coyly.

"He'll be the guy you'd flirt with whether he wants you to or not. Oh, and his name is Ian Cully."

When Ian walked in, he came straight to the bed and grabbed Sam's hand. "Oh, squirrel," he whispered, moving just enough for Urban to lower a rail so he could sit. Then he leaned forward and kissed Sam very gently on the side of his forehead.

"Is that where that guy got me?" Sam asked.

"Yeah." Ian swallowed and gripped Sam's hand tighter. He flicked a look at Urban, on his way out of the curtained cubicle "Kiddo, I'm so, so sorry you thought I was trying to break up with you. That's not what I meant at all when I said I needed to think. I meant I just needed to, you know, *think*. Take some time to sort stuff out. I was . . . I was scared."

Sam cleared his throat. "Because you were freaked out over thinking you might love me?"

"No!" Ian gripped his chin, not too hard. Not as hard as he normally did, which Sam appreciated. "Because of shit with my dad, I swear. It really was about me, not you."

Sam sighed. "You know when you said that stuff it sounded like—"

Ian held up a hand. "Yeah, I got schooled by Nik in what it sounded like to you."

"But you don't want to break up?" Sam whispered.

"No, I swear." Ian leaned forward and kissed him tentatively. "I *really* don't want to break up with you. I just, I have a lot to tell you. There's some stuff I need to say, kiddo." Ian kissed him again, and looked at him as if afraid whatever awful thing he was about to say would make Sam dump him.

Sam could imagine very few things that would cause him to do that. "Like you have a wife and kids?"

"*What*? No, neither!"

"It was a joke," Sam told him. Ian relaxed. "Sort of."

"Okay, kiddo, are you listening?"

Sam lifted his head to listen.

Ian squeezed his hand. "I don't have another boyfriend or a husband, I don't have any STDs, I don't have . . . what else are you worried about?"

"I can't think of anything else."

"Okay, it's nothing like any of those things."

"I think you need to just say it and put yourself out of your misery." He dropped his head back on his pillow with a sigh. *Ow.* "Then I could stop worrying too."

Ian took a deep breath. "I'm seeing a therapist," he spat out.

Sam blinked at him, a couple of times. "And?"

"Hell," he muttered, then added, "I have a screwed-up family."

"Oh," Sam said carefully. Then he reached up to stroke Ian's cheek. "This is what you were so worried about telling me?"

"Not really, it's just where I'm starting."

Sam's fingers moved back, combing through Ian's hair. "How long have you been worried about this?"

"Hello," someone said, barging through the curtain. "I'm Doctor Abanji."

And so began a half hour of torture by the fine doctor Abanji, involving questions about who the president was and the date, then lots of prodding of his head and chest, and finally some of the "good" drugs Urban had been talking about. At which point, Sam began the giggling again. Urban remarked more than once on his trips in and out of the cubicle that it was "darling" the way Sam's giggling made Ian smile and kiss him.

"Go away," Sam giggled. "He's mine."

"Don't worry, honey, I have my own at home. I'm thinking about getting myself hit in the head and seeing if he's as sweet to me as your Ian is to you."

Sam giggled. Urban turned and said something to Ian about police and interviews that Sam didn't quite catch, but managed to make Ian act like a protective bear. "No, he needs to rest," Ian barked at whatever Urban said.

"Oh, it's my bear laird," Sam giggled. Ian went red but kissed him again anyway.

Sam didn't really remember what happened after that. He might have giggled himself off to sleep or something, but he zoned back in when he heard Ian's voice, low but angry. "He can't answer your questions right now. He's not even conscious. Exactly. He giggles every time anyone speaks to him." Sam could see him talking to someone standing just outside the curtain.

"I do?" Sam rasped. His throat felt dry and his head still drummed, but not as painfully.

Ian came back to his side, taking his hand again and kissing his head. "Hey squirrel," he murmured, brushing Sam's hair off his face.

"Can I have some water?" Sam croaked. Someone came up behind Ian and held out a cup. Ian gave the owner of the hand a dirty look, but took it and helped Sam drink from it.

"Sam, this is Detective Johnson. He wants to ask you about what happened, if you can remember," Ian grumped.

It turned out Sam could remember a lot now. He remembered going into the alley with Miller, and the conversation they had—Ian finally cracked a smile when Sam told him about Nik being like a snarly little lapdog—and even the guys getting out of the pickup with the baseball bat.

"He has a bruise on his chest," Ian interrupted when Sam said he was knocked down.

"I do?" Sam tried to look. Oh, he had one of those hospital gowns on. Ian helped him work it open enough to see the huge purple splotch to the right of his sternum, just above his diaphragm. "Whoa," he breathed. "Can we take a picture?"

Ian growled, but Detective Johnson said, "We're going to have to for evidence."

"Evidence?" Sam scrunched his brows, then flinched from the sharp pain that caused.

"Kiddo, you were assaulted. They caught those guys, partly because of Jurgen. I imagine they're all getting charged," Ian said, looking over at Johnson.

"If we can find enough evidence to substantiate it, they'll get charged with a hate crime on top of assault."

"You mean like coming after me with a baseball bat saying 'here, faggot-faggot-faggot'? Oh, and threatening to rape me with it?"

Ian growled again. Sam gripped his hand tightly as Detective Johnson answered. "That'll pretty much do it, yeah."

"The guy with the bat, I think he was about to smash Miller's head in when they had him on the ground. I mean . . . I thought they were going to *kill* him. That's when I got up and jumped on the guy's back."

"Oh for fuck's sake," Ian moaned. Sam squeezed his hand again.

Detective Johnson smiled ferally. "And maybe we can get attempted murder, too," he said, jotting down notes. He was recording this, so Sam wasn't sure what he needed notes for.

It took forever, and by the time his interview with the detective ended, Sam was exhausted. Ian slipped off for a minute, but came back before Sam was completely out. He had something in his hands. "What's that?" Sam mumbled.

"Clothes. I sent Nik and Jurgen to my place to get some for you. They're releasing you from the hospital tonight, as long as you stay with me. Remember the doctor told us that?"

Huh. "Not really." Sam took the clothes though. He wasn't into hospital gowns.

Ian accompanied him into the little bathroom off the cubicle to help him dress. But as soon as the door was shut, Ian grabbed Sam so tightly he could barely breathe. He could feel Ian's arms shaking around him. Sam withstood it as long as he could, but soon he had to say, "Ian, my chest . . ."

Ian let him go so fast Sam swayed. "I'm sorry," he gasped, holding Sam just tightly enough to keep him upright.

"Can we sit down for a minute?"

Ian sat him on the floor, Sam's back to his chest, leaning against a wall. Sam sighed and rested on him, relaxing into Ian's heat.

After a minute, Ian started talking.

chapter 47

"I'm so sorry for yesterday," Ian whispered in Sam's ear.

"I know, Ian. You told me." Sam stroked his hand, trying to comfort him. "I believe you."

"I do love you, Sam. So much."

Sam lifted Ian's hand and kissed it. Now was the moment to say he loved Ian, right? He opened his mouth.

Ian kept talking, though. "I'm not really good enough for you, Sam, I know—Ow!"

Sam had sat up straight, clipping Ian's chin with his shoulder. He struggled out of Ian's hold and turned around, straddling Ian's lap.

"Did I hurt you? I'm sorry." Sam checked Ian's chin, looking for blood and ignoring the throbbing in his own shoulder. He pried Ian's hand off his face to inspect it for damage.

"Sam, I'm all right. You just surprised me."

Sam looked into his eyes. "You surprised me."

"I did?"

"How could you think you aren't good enough for me when you're so good *to* me?"

Ian sucked in a breath. "I'm not good to you. I used you."

Sam shrugged his not-throbbing shoulder. "No, you didn't."

"Yeah, I did."

"Not really." Ian gave him an exaggeratedly stupid look. "Maybe at first," Sam conceded. He had to duck his head to admit it, but, "It wasn't really that . . . I'd never been used for sex before. It was sort of, um, novel. Flattering."

"Oh, kiddo," Ian said softly, kissing him. "But I also wasn't good to you yesterday. I let you think—"

"Ian, it was a mistake. A miscommunication. Oh, hey, we had the Big Mis."

Ian wrinkled his forehead. "What's that?"

"It's short for 'Big Misunderstanding'—a commonly used plot device in romance novels. Never mind, just go on."

"I should have been there for you tonight too. Those pricks might not have—"

Sam slapped his hand over Ian's mouth. "You wouldn't have been there even if we hadn't had the Big Mis. You were at work. No guilt," he said sternly.

Ian raised his eyebrows.

"I mean it," Sam said. "No guilt."

Ian rolled his eyes, then licked Sam's palm. Sam removed his hand.

Unfortunately, Ian still felt he had transgressions to confess. "I told you I loved you during sex. Turns out that's some kind of taboo also."

"But you *do* love me, you just told me so again."

Ian took a deep breath and held it. "I just need to know if you . . . feel like that for me, or if you maybe think you could someday."

Sam stared at him. "Love you?"

Ian nodded, eyes downcast.

"Are you *insane*?" Ian's eyes flew up to look into his. "Of course I love you, Ian. Everyone but you can tell. Nik knows, Jurgen knows, Miller knows, everyone. You're the only one who doesn't seem to know."

Ian swallowed. "So are you saying you *do* love me?"

"Yes. Ian, I'm crazy about you. I love you. You're everything I ever wanted. You—"

Ian interrupted him with a kiss. "Let's go home," he whispered, then gave him another peck.

On the way home, they filled Sam's prescription for yet more "good drugs." By then, Sam's head pounded even worse. "I thought they weren't supposed to give these things to people with concussions," he moaned when Ian returned to the truck from the pharmacy.

Ian handed him a bottle of water and two pills. "That's just a myth."

"Oh, that's good." Sam took his pills.

By the time they made it home—to Ian's place—Sam could barely stand he was so loopy; Ian had to help him stay upright. Nik and Jurgen were there, an empty wine bottle on the coffee table, and an obviously drunk Nik with his head in Jurgen's lap on the couch.

Nik sprang up when they walked in. "Oh my God, I was so worried!" He rushed toward Sam, trying to hug him.

Ian wouldn't let go of him. "He's injured," he barked. "Be gentle with him."

"Oh, that's so sweet. He wants you to be gentle with me," Sam told Nik. "That's my bear laird."

"I will, Sam, I will. I'll be gentle." Nik gripped Sam's hand. "Tell your laird bear that."

"Bear laird," Sam corrected. "I was going to call him laird bear, but he didn't like that one."

"Oh my God," groaned Jurgen. "Nikky, he's home. Let's get your drunk butt to bed."

Nik flapped a hand at his boyfriend. "I'm not done talking to 'im." He turned back to Sam, pulling on his hand. "C'mon, sit with me."

As they sat, Ian helping him aim himself in the right direction, there seemed to be some form of communication going on between Jurgen and Ian. It involved a lot of eye rolling.

Ian glared at Nik. "You have five minutes," he said, then kissed Sam. "I'll be right back, kiddo."

"'Kay." Sam nodded, but it overbalanced him and he fell back against the cushion. Jurgen snorted.

"Tell me all about what happened," Nik said, petting his hand.

Sam tried, but somehow they ended up talking about the size of his nose.

"It's not that big!" Nik exclaimed, waving his hand so vigorously he had to grab Jurgen's knee to keep from falling off the couch. Jurgen sighed.

"Is too," Sam pouted. "It's freakishly big. It's a beak! I got called Big Bird in high school. People were always asking me if Snuffleupagus was a top."

"Tha's weird. You'd think he'd be a bottom." Nik frowned in confusion.

Sam shrugged. "I know. Thought so too."

"Your hips are much smaller than Big Bird's."

Sam sniffed. "Thank you." He sighed and slumped against the arm of the couch, feeling a bit off-kilter.

"So, Bert or Ernie?" Nik asked.

"Ernie for sure. Total top." Sam threw his hand out for emphasis and knocked over the empty wine bottle. Empty bottles could be ignored. Jurgen picked it up.

"Definitely." They nodded at each other in complete agreement for a few seconds. "They both have big noses, you know. And they found a forever kinda love." Nik giggled, singing "forever kinda love." Jurgen snorted.

Sam rolled his eyes. "They're *puppets*. I," he pointed at his chest for emphasis, "am not a *puppet*."

He could see Nik fighting not to point out they were actually Muppets. Sam gave him a narrow-eyed look for moral support. After a few seconds of biting his lips, Nik managed, "I have a big nose."

"But it looks good on you. Your nose has character! My nose is just big, and beaky. Like . . . like *Beaker*!"

Jurgen mumbled and shifted on his small piece of the couch.

Nik stared at Sam. "Who's Beaker again?"

Ian walked in with an exasperated sigh. "C'mon, Sam," he said, stopping in front of him. "Your nose is fine. I like it big." Then he leaned forward and pulled Sam up from the couch.

Sam giggled. "Did you hear? He likes it big," he whispered to Nik.

Jurgen snorted and let his head fall back on the cushion.

"Time for bed," Ian said, picking Sam up and making his head swim.

"But wait!" Nik said. "I have to tell him what happened with Miller."

"Tell him tomorrow," Ian said, walking out of the room.

"Are you carrying me?" Sam peered into his face.

"I am, kiddo." Ian's voice sounded strained.

Sam kissed him on the neck as they left the room, and heard Nik ask Jurgen, "How come you never carry me to bed anymore?" Then he shrieked, "Put me down!"

Sam laid his head on Ian's shoulder and yawned. "I wanna know about Miller."

Ian kissed his forehead. "He'll be all right. You can find out more in the morning. Now you're going to bed."

"Oh. 'Kay." Sam was asleep before his butt touched the mattress.

chapter 48

In the morning, Sam felt surprisingly good. Yes, his head still hurt, but not as much as he would have expected, if he'd actually been sober enough to expect anything. He felt mildly hungover—Ian said it was probably from the "good drugs" and offered Sam more. Sam turned them down. Ian told him to stay in bed and went off to make breakfast.

Then Nik, hungover for an entirely different reason, came into the room and flopped on the bed next to Sam with a groan.

"Are you okay?"

"Fine, I'll be fine." Nik waved a lazy hand in the air. "We're leaving soon, but I wanted to tell you about Miller."

"All right" had been a bit of a white lie. Miller was still in the hospital, and he'd had emergency surgery for internal bleeding.

"He also has a couple broken ribs. I found this out from his parents." Nik hugged his middle, staring at the wall. "They don't seem okay with the possibility that Miller's gay," he added.

"Oh, no."

Nik sighed. "Yeah."

He and Jurgen left soon after that, and Sam ate breakfast in bed. By afternoon he felt better, almost normal. It turned out fighting *did* make one horny. When Ian came to lie down next to him, Sam had a few ideas in mind for working through that.

The look on Ian's face stopped him from suggesting them. For the first time Sam could remember, Ian rolled over and backed into his body, silently asking to be held. Once Sam had his arms around Ian, he started talking about his family.

"My brothers are a lot older than me. They were six and seven when I was born, so when Mom died they were twenty-one and twenty-two. She was diagnosed with breast cancer when I was fourteen, and she didn't even live a year after that."

Sam squeezed Ian tighter to his chest, holding him with everything he had. His penis wanted in on the act, but Sam made it behave. Sort of.

"I didn't even realize my dad was an asshole until after she died," Ian was saying. "I mean, before Mom was diagnosed, I was more into my friends than my family. Then she got sick, and it was all about her, for me."

Sam had been debating how to ask this, but he decided to be blunt. "Did he love your mother?"

Ian nodded immediately, tickling Sam's nose with his hair. "Beth, Jurgen's mom—she's Dad's youngest sister—she told me he fell in love with Mom the minute they met and never stopped loving her. Always looked that way to me."

"I guess even assholes love," Sam said philosophically.

Ian snorted. "Yeah, there's plenty of evidence in the world to support that. My brothers seem to love their wives."

"Your brothers are assholes, too?"

"Not really, I guess. They're just too much like my dad."

Sam kissed the back of Ian's neck for encouragement. And then a couple more times.

"When I was little kid, I loved my mom, you know? But I thought my dad was a hero. He wanted us, me and my brothers, to think that. It was all about how he was a firefighter and he saved people and he had this perfect wife and this perfect life, and we were going to be clones of him. But then his wife died and his youngest son was gay and didn't really want to be a firefighter."

Sam tightened his arm around Ian again. "He knows you're gay?"

"I told him when I was about twenty-six, I guess. I'd known since I was nineteen, or at least I knew I was into guys. Dad was so fucking *disappointed*. Stupid thing is, I knew he would be. I went in there expecting it, but it still killed me. You know where I told him?"

Sam shook his head, even though he was pretty sure that was a rhetorical question. He relaxed again into the heat of Ian's body and laid his palm over Ian's heart. It was very close to his nipple.

"In his fucking office. He'd been the fire chief for about a year, and I got sick of trying to catch him someplace else. Only other place to catch him was drinking with his buddies. I don't know if the dude ever slept at home after he became chief. Maybe they had a cot for him at the bar."

"So he was a drinker, too?" Sam kissed the back of Ian's neck some more, then gave it a little nibble.

"That started a while after Mom died. It didn't get bad until I went off to college and he was in that house alone. I'm sure he's an alcoholic now, but I don't think it made any difference in my life when I was still at home."

"He didn't, like, disown you when he found out you were gay?"

Ian shrugged one shoulder. "No. I'd done what he wanted, I became a firefighter; he just asked me not to be out. And he asked me to be sure."

"Like...?"

"Like, keep dating women. I thought it was more about wanting me to look straight for his buddies and the department. Wasn't that big a department. There were a couple other gay guys I knew of, but nobody was really out. I was the only one who kept it a total secret."

"So not even the other gay guys...?"

Ian shook his head before Sam finished the question.

"And you kept dating women," Sam said, pressing harder on Ian's heart.

Ian nodded. "Or at least I made it look like it."

Sam squeezed him even tighter, until Ian grunted. "Careful, kiddo," he said softly. "Those are my internal organs in there."

Sam laughed and brushed his lips back and forth across Ian's skin, burying his nose in his hair. *Mmm*, he loved that smell. Sam's hips snugged themselves up to Ian's butt without really asking permission, but he didn't object.

"The thing is, even though I thought he was an asshole, and his opinions weren't worth stressing out over...somehow it sunk in. Not the part where no one would ever love me—he's obsessed with me having someone to take care of me, whatever that means—but the part where I'd never have a relationship."

Sam lifted himself up so he could press his cheek on Ian's ear, arms and leg wrapped around him. Trying to smother him with reassurance without actually cutting off any major arteries or airways. "You are in a relationship, and someone loves you." And was getting hard for him. Was that inappropriate?

Ian dislodged him, rolling onto his back and looking up at him. Sam kept his body loosely caging Ian's, trying not to make his dick's demands too obvious. "That's what my problem was Thursday," he said so quietly his voice grated. "I got out of there, you know? I started seeing a therapist after the accident as part of my rehab, but it turned into dealing with all of this stuff. I got out of that job and stopped doing what he wanted me to, and I started coming out. I left the state and I even got my, you know—" Ian's eyes flicked away a second "—emotional stuff sort of worked out, and then he called and it got fucked up all over in my head. I was so sure, Sam." He grabbed the back of Sam's neck, pulling him slightly closer, so all Sam could focus on were Ian's eyes. "And then for a while after he called, I didn't know if this was real or I was fooling myself. Like, I lost faith or something. Am I making any sense?"

Sam nodded earnestly. Mostly he was making sense enough to follow, but Sam had one question. "You didn't know if *we* were real? Us?"

Ian swallowed and nodded. "Yeah."

"Do you know now?" Sam held his breath. He *thought* he knew the answer, but there was still that sliver of doubt.

"Yeah. We're real." Ian pressed harder on the back of Sam's neck, stretching up to kiss him. "I love you."

"I love you, too."

chapter 49

Sam kept kissing him forever, over and over, riding Ian's thigh and grinding one of his legs between Ian's. Ian arched up and pushed into Sam to encourage him, knowing what was going to happen. His heart thudded with it, and the muscles in his ass bunched up tight with want. "Maybe we shouldn't do this, I mean, your head . . ." He trailed off and Sam kissed him again.

"We don't have to do anything you don't want to do," Sam whispered, then came back for more. But they were going to. It wasn't as if he'd never bottomed before, but doing it for Sam—that was completely different. Terrifying because of how much it meant.

When Sam pulled off his T-shirt and boxers, Ian had to run hands over his chest, his tan skin against Sam's paleness. Sam loomed over him on extended arms, letting Ian pet him. He thumbed Sam's nipples and watched him shiver. Then Sam looked into his eyes and Ian dropped his hands, because Sam wanted him *now*.

Sam pulled off the sweats and briefs Ian had slept in, and Ian's dick bounced up into Sam's hand like it had been dying for the contact. He smiled, straddled Ian's thighs, and used his thumb and fingers to drive Ian nuts until he was squirming, pushing his hips up for more. Sam let go of him to hover over his lips again.

"I'm going to fuck you," he whispered, looking into Ian's eyes, waiting for a response.

"I know," Ian whispered back.

"That's okay?"

He swallowed and reached up to palm the back of Sam's head. "I want it."

Even if he hadn't wanted to, Sam's smile and then his kiss would have changed his mind. But he ached to feel Sam inside him. When he heard the soft *click* of the lube bottle, he took a deep breath and pulled his legs up, hands behind his knees, opening himself up for Sam.

Sam's fingers were magic. They did all kinds of amazing things that made Ian writhe and groan and arch up from the bed. Then they stopped, sliding out, and Sam was looming over him again, propped on one shaking arm. "Are you ready?"

"Yes, God, just do it." He yanked Sam down for a wild, wide-open kiss. "Please," he added, panting.

Sam smiled at him, and Ian dug his fingers painfully hard into the backs of his knees, yanking his legs farther up when he felt Sam's cock against his hole. He watched Sam's face as Sam watched himself push into Ian.

I love that face.

Then he had Sam inside him and he stopped thinking much at all.

Sam was slow and careful, but Ian wanted it so much that it only took a couple of minutes before Sam's balls were pressed against Ian's tailbone, and Ian's legs were hooked on his arms. They were both shaking, and Ian felt his heart throbbing in the muscles holding Sam's shaft so tightly inside him.

Finally he arched into it and let Sam have him, encouraged it with his body and the noises Sam drew out of him. Sam's gray-blue eyes watched Ian's the whole time. When Ian lost it and came, he was sure it was his first religious experience. *If this is enlightenment, I want more.* Fortunately, Sam had plenty to give and it spread through him, and through Sam too, he thought.

Afterward, Sam kissed his eyes closed, then down his face, placing small kisses all over his lips, then told Ian, "I love you."

Ian couldn't speak. He hugged Sam tighter and hoped that was enough to get his message across.

Sam combed fingers through his hair. "I know," Sam whispered, smiling at him.

EPILOGUE

Ian took a drink of his beer, leaning against the counter while Sam chopped vegetables. He surveyed the array of ingredients sitting out. "What are you making, chicken stew?"

"Coq au vin," Sam said absently, seemingly concentrating on cutting his carrots into perfectly cubed icons of vegetable-hood.

So, chicken stew.

Ian stifled a sigh. It wasn't that he didn't want Sam to learn how to cook, it was that he didn't give a damn. He didn't care if Sam became a gourmet chef, and he'd hoped when he came home tonight, Sam would be doing something Ian could tear his attention away from, like reading or writing or watching TV.

Tearing Sam's attention away from cooking was rough going. Ian suspected it was because Sam sucked at it, and he wasn't getting better with practice. The worse he got at cooking, the harder he tried. That part Ian did care about, because he kept having to pretend to like increasingly bad food.

"Why don't you make it tomorrow, and tonight I'll take you out for coq au vin instead?" he suggested.

"Coq au vin two nights in a row? Besides, I already chopped the onions," Sam said, leaning closer to his chopping board, tilting his head to one side then the other, poking at a triangular chunk of carrot with his knife, then frowning at it. "I'm not stopping now. I cried over the onions."

"Everyone cries when they chop onions."

"It wasn't that kind of crying. I cut myself." Sam held up a hand, showing off a bandaged finger.

This time Ian let the sigh out. He tried again. "What did you do today?"

"I went with Nik to see Miller in rehab." Sam stood up straight, turning to the sink and pulling celery out of the colander he had it sitting in.

Hell, that was all such a mess. Ian took another swig of his beer. "How's Miller doing? He better?"

Sam poked at the end of a stalk of celery with a knife, sort of digging at it. "He might be able to go home soon. Well, to Nik and Jurgen's, I mean." For a few seconds, Sam actually made direct eye contact with him. Then he went back to his celery. "Until he can be on his own and go back to his place." He managed to get whatever he was digging for, pulling on one of those strings in the stalk.

God this was becoming a worse and worse time to talk about serious stuff. Well, serious stuff between them. Miller getting ostracized by his family after being beaten half to death for being gay was pretty freaking serious. "His parents still won't talk to him?"

"No," Sam said. His second string broke, and he frowned at the celery. "Can we not talk about it right now? I'm trying to concentrate."

On pulling the veins out of celery?

Well, hell. If Sam was only half paying attention, maybe Ian could get some information out of him. He took a fortifying gulp from his beer, then picked at the bottle's label and asked, "How long do you have to date someone before you can ask him to move in with you?"

Sam dropped the knife on the counter. Ian looked up to see him frozen and paling.

That got his attention.

Sam swallowed and turned back to his celery, slowly picking up his knife and staring at it. "How would I know?" he asked.

Ian shrugged. "Well, you lived with Marley, right? So, when did he ask you? Or, I guess you could have asked him," he added in a mutter. He *hated* that idea.

Sam slowly started shoveling oddly shaped bits of carrot into a bowl. "Um, he never really asked me. There wasn't any asking at all. I just realized one day he was living there."

"Yeah? So when did that happen?"

"Um, the second time we hooked up, maybe?" Sam suddenly dropped his handful of vegetables on the cutting board and turned to Ian, wiping his hands on his jeans. Over and over. "Why do you want to know?" He sounded nervous. It was cute.

It helped settle some of Ian's own nerves, as a bonus. He carefully set his beer bottle on the counter and stepped up to Sam, smoothing back his shaggy hair. "I was wondering if we'd been seeing each other long enough for me to ask you. I mean, to move in here with me."

Sam opened his mouth, but it just hung there. Ian gave him a few seconds, but nothing came out.

Hell.

He fisted Sam's hair, trying to be gentle and not demanding. "If you count the first time we hooked up at Nik and Jurgen's, we've been seeing each other about three months. Almost two and a half if you count from that time on that little linoleum square at your place. That seems like long enough to me," Ian finished uncertainly. Why wasn't Sam saying anything?

"You've been keeping track?" Sam whispered.

"Of course I have." Fuck, hadn't Sam been? Ian had just assumed he was.

"What's today?" Sam asked quickly.

Fuck. No pain no gain. "Eight weeks ago today I waited by your door for you to come home from work, and then I . . ."

"You said you wanted to see me," Sam finished for him, his hands slipping around Ian's waist.

Thank fuck, Sam knew what today was. "Yeah."

"I love you," Sam said, yanking Ian close and kissing him. Ian tried to let him have control, because this was Sam's kiss, but he already had that hand in Sam's hair, and he had the hardest time not losing it when he felt Sam's lips against his.

"Is that a yes?" Ian asked when Sam let him go.

"If I move in with you, can I stop learning how to cook?"

"You don't know how happy that would make me."

"Then yes, I'll move in with you. Um, most of the stuff I own is already here."

"Good. That was easy." Ian grabbed the backs of Sam's thighs and lifted until Sam got the message and wrapped his legs around Ian's hips. "So you're all moved in?"

Sam grinned at him, wrapping his arms around his neck. "Almost."

Ian turned and set him on a clear spot on the counter. "And you already have a key."

Sam nodded, and Ian kissed him. "Are we—" Ian interrupted him with another kiss, then started nuzzling his whiskers up and down Sam's neck so he could ask whatever he'd been going to.

Sam seemed to have lost his focus, though. Ian loved making him mindless like that. He bit Sam's ear. "Are we what?"

Sam startled. "Oh. Uh, are we going to make love in the kitchen?" He tilted his head, exposing more of his neck.

"Kiddo," Ian said against it, "we're going to make love in every room in the house."

Sam sucked in a breath. "Tonight?" he squeaked.

Ian thought about it while sucking on the base of Sam's throat. "Probably only two tonight. We'll do the rest later."

Sam cupped the back of his head. "Oh, yeah," he sighed. "We have time."

Ian pulled back, holding Sam's face in between his hands. Sam's pupils were huge, and he was breathing faster. Ian gave him a fast kiss before telling him, "Plenty of time. We have the rest of our lives."

Sam's eyes widened. "We do?"

Ian swallowed. "If you want to spend that long with me."

Sam's hands threaded into Ian's hair, pulling him closer until their lips were touching. "Oh. Then yeah, we have the rest of our lives."

"And no more of that Too Stupid to Live stuff," Ian whispered against his mouth.

He felt Sam smile against his lips. "Being TSTL isn't so bad. I forgot one thing about it."

Ian kissed him quickly, tired of waiting, but wanting to know. "Yeah? What's that?"

Sam kissed him back. "The TSTL character always gets their man and their happily ever after." He pulled back to grin at Ian.

One of those weird balls of emotion welled up inside him, the kind Sam was always finding and teasing out of him. He had to breathe deep before he could speak. "As long as I get my happily ever after with you, that works for me."

Sam wrapped his arms around Ian's neck, pulling him close again. "Always. You're my perfect hero. Nothing but happy endings for us."

Ian grabbed Sam's chin and held him still for another quick kiss. "You're my perfect hero, too." Then he palmed Sam's ass and yanked him closer, close enough that he could feel the kid's hard dick through their clothes. "And we're about to have our next happy ending all over this counter."

ACKNOWLEDGMENTS

Thank you to Justin, Tom, and Shawn, (even though you aren't allowed to read the book) for technical help. Maybe someone will tell you I thanked you. Thanks to the Chicks and Dicks: Taylor V. Donovan, L.C. Chase, Edmond Manning, Thornton Sterling, and Alec Edge for support. Thank you most especially to mc, for the cheerleading and assistance.

also by **ANNE TENINO**

Task Force Iota series:
18% Gray (TFI #1)
Turning Tricks (TFI #2)
Happy Birthday to Me (TFI #2.5)

Whitetail Rock
The Fix (Whitetail Rock #2)

Theta Alpha Gamma series:
Frat Boy and Toppy (TAG #1)
Love, Hypothetically (TAG #2)

about the **AUTHOR**

Raised on a steady media diet of Monty Python, classical music, and the visual arts, Anne Tenino rocked the mental health world when she was the first patient diagnosed with Compulsive Romantic Disorder. Since that day, with her trusty psychiatrist by her side, Anne has taken on conquering the M/M world through therapeutic writing. Finding out who those guys having sex in her head are and what to do with them has been extremely liberating.

Anne's husband finds it liberating as well, although in a somewhat different way. He has accepted her need for "research," and looks forward to the benefits said research affords him. He thinks it's kind of cool she manages to write, as well. Her two daughters are mildly confused by Anne's need to twist Ken dolls into odd positions. They were raised to be open-minded children, however, and other than occasionally stealing Ken1's strap-on, they let Mom do her thing without interference.

Anne's thing is writing gay romance and erotica.

Wondering what Anne does in her spare time? Mostly she lies on the couch, eats bonbons, and shirks housework.

Check out what Anne's up to now by visiting her site, www.annetenino.com.

Enjoy this book?
Find more great romantic comedy
at RiptidePublishing.com!

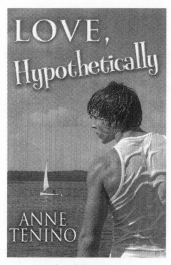

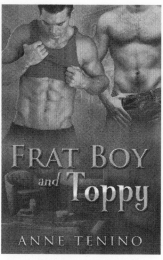

www.riptidepublishing.com/titles/
love-hypothetically

www.riptidepublishing.com/titles/
frat-boy-and-toppy

Earn Bonus Bucks!

Earn 1 Bonus Buck for each dollar you spend. Find out how at
RiptidePublishing.com/news/bonus-bucks.

Win Free Ebooks for a Year!

Pre-order coming soon titles directly through our site and you'll
receive one entry into a drawing to win free books for a year! Get
the details at RiptidePublishing.com/contests.